WHEN FIRST WE MET
THE SPENCER ISLAND SERIES

STELLA MACLEAN

Cataloguing and Publication information is available from The Canadian
ISBN Service System, Library and Archives Canada.

Title: When First We Met/Stella MacLean

Identifiers:
ISBN: Print: 978-1-7381405-5-8
Ebook: 978-1-7381405-4-1

Formatting Services: Sweet' N Spicy Designs
Cover Design: Sweet' N Spicy Designs

PROLOGUE

*H*i there. It's me, Helen Mason again. I know you may wonder why I'm being such a busy-body by taking on the job of introducing these stories about people from Spencer Island. And you'd be right. But you see, I can't help myself. I love Spencer Island and I firmly believe that the very best people in the world live here. And besides, it's home to me. It's where I belong; where I've always belonged.

The next story is about Nicole Simpson and Justin Hadley. Justin cares deeply about the welfare of people and has worked as a volunteer in Haiti, where he felt so needed. After his mother's passing, he came to Spencer Island to gain perspective on his life, never thinking for a moment that he'd meet someone really special.

Nicole has enjoyed her life with all its certainty in Spencer Island and has a large circle of friends. Having moved from Seattle, she's settled on her small farm, along with her two horses. Nicole loves her life so much she can't imagine ever living anywhere else.

Nicole loves the tried and true, the certainty of her world.

Meanwhile, Justin has always lived life to the fullest, giving himself to whatever endeavor that has come his way. He lives in the moment.

I can really relate to Nicole's way of looking at things, as I feel the same. I can't imagine my life being any different than it is now. But then there's Justin, a lovely young man who simply stole my heart the first time I met him. This is one of my favorite stories because the attraction between Nicole and Justin is so strong.

How could they not get together? Yet, life doesn't always unfold exactly the way we'd like...

CHAPTER ONE

*J*ustin Hadley wanted to yell out in pain... If he didn't faint first. Dr. Dixon had been meticulously putting stitches into his forearm and was now cleaning up the blood from around the wound. Justin didn't want to admit how much it hurt. Wimping out would hardly endear him to the people of Spencer Island, a small, tight-knit community on the coast of Maine.

"There." The doctor stripped off his gloves and dropped them on the table next to the stretcher where Justin sat, "All you need is a dressing and a tetanus shot, and then I'd like you to have some routine blood work done. The nurse will give you instructions on where to go for that."

It had been a rough day, made worse when he'd let his attention slip and cut his arm on the saw he'd been using to fix a client's back steps. "A what?" Justin asked. Feeling anxious, he glanced from Dr. Dixon to the nurse.

"Tina will explain everything," Dr. Dixon said, his glance swerving to the digital clock on the wall. "I have to go. The receptionist will give you an appointment to see me back here in two days. I'll check your arm, see how it's doing. Using an electric saw can be dangerous. You were lucky."

"I was." Justin didn't want to know any more than he had to. Medical things weren't his strong suit. He'd discovered that about himself when he was ten and fell out of a tree, breaking his leg, requiring surgery, bandages and, of course, needles. He figured he wouldn't have to deal with that stuff anymore until he went to volunteer in Haiti for two years as carpenter. There, he saw men working with him experience serious injuries, and it had made him even more careful. "Thanks, doc," Justin said, alarmed at how weak his voice-sounded.

The nurse applied a dressing then picked up a syringe from the tray.

"Is that needle for me?"

"Yes. It's a tetanus shot"

"Where are you going to put it?" he asked, holding his injured arm close to his chest.

"Can you roll up the sleeve on your other arm?"

"Sure, I guess so," Justin said, complying with her request. He looked away as she gave the shot.

"Okay, here's your requisition. The phlebotomy clinic is just down the hall to your right. She passed him the slip of paper, a smile dimpling her cheeks.

Justin stood. His legs were still holding him upright. He took a deep breath.

"Remember to keep your arm up as much as possible and keep your bandage clean until the doctor sees you again,"

"Thank you." Justin made his way out of the room, the requisition in his good hand, his pride intact. He reached the entrance to the phlebotomy clinic and approached the desk. There was no one there. He was about to sit down and wait when he heard voices from a room just beyond the desk.

He approached the door. Just as he did he heard a child's anxious voice telling someone he didn't want a needle. A child after his own heart, he thought, risking a glance into the room. A woman knelt in front of the boy, huddled on his mother's lap. A woman dressed in pink scrubs touched the little boy's arm, her voice so soothing he wanted to keep standing there and be soothed a little himself.

The woman was speaking softly to the child. Slowly the little boy held out his arm and let her put the needle in. Justin blinked to block the sight as he continued to listen to her soothing voice. When he opened his eyes again, she was staring at him. Her face was alight with interest and awareness.

In that instant he felt a connection he'd never ever experienced. Did he know her? Did she know him? It was as if they'd met before, but he was pretty sure they hadn't. He would have remembered this woman. She was totally unforgettable.

He stood there feeling a bit like an idiot. Yet he couldn't seem to move, to break the connection. He wanted to go to her, take her hands and simply be with her. How nuts was that? He'd never felt that way before about any woman. Even though there'd been many opportunities to hook up, this was different. Could it be the tetanus shot that was making him feel this way?

"Are you here to have your blood taken?" she asked, returning her attention to the child and his mother.

Suddenly the room around him seemed less welcoming. "I am."

"If you'd like to take a seat in the waiting area in front of the desk—." Her gaze returned to him, one eyebrow raised in question "I'll be there as soon as I finish here."

"Sure," he said, aware of how the single pearl on the end

of a gold chain she wore nestled into the V of her throat. Imagining what her skin would feel like under his fingers made his blood run hot.

Feeling awkward and a little strange, he went back and sat down. He struggled to divert his thoughts away from her, focusing instead on a flu shot poster on the wall.

A few minutes later, the woman came out with the mother and her son. Justin watched as she walked with them to the entrance, still speaking soothing tones, He couldn't help but notice how her top fit her body, how the loose fit of the pants couldn't completely hide the smooth thighs beneath the fabric.

She didn't glance at him as she went to her desk, and he felt... deprived, left out of some special secret. He followed her, resting his good arm on the raised counter.

She sat down at the computer and tapped a couple of keys. She turned her full attention to him, her eyes focused on his. Suddenly he couldn't remember what he was doing here. Think!

"Do you have a requisition you'd like to give me?" she asked, a tiny smile tilting one corner of her lips, the corner where she had a small beauty spot he noted despite his state of confusion.

What was happening? He felt so...so something. Was this how love felt? So hot? So weird? He'd never felt this way before, but that didn't mean it was love. He hadn't been in a relationship for a long while, hadn't felt anything for anyone since his return from Haiti—until this moment. That had to be what was going on here. He needed to get back into the dating game, back to his old life of enjoying every opportunity to meet a woman. And this was the perfect moment. "Yes." He rushed the word. "Right here." He passed the requisition to her, nearly hitting her in the face in his eagerness to comply with her request.

She looked it over, keyed in the information and placed the requisition on the top of a pile already on her desk. Behind her a printer groaned to life, disgorging a narrow strip of paper. She tore it off and stood up. "Please follow me," she said with a backward glance over her shoulder, her smile making him feel like a fifth grader.

Justin followed her, all the while his mind going over the possibilities. She wasn't wearing a wedding band, and her name tag said her first name was Nicole. He sat down in the chair she pointed to, resting arm on the armrest while he watched her efficient movements. So efficient, in fact, that she was suddenly standing beside him with a bunch of tubes and a needle.

"Hold out your right arm, please," she said, pulling a tourniquet from her pocket as she laid the other supplies on a steel tray next to his chair.

The scent of her hair, the gentleness of her touch distracted him so much he nearly missed what she'd said. Hastily, he straightened out his arm. She swabbed the bend in the elbow. She pressed her fingers into the space she swabbed, holding her needle angled toward his arm. "Make a fist."

His stomach rolled. He gasped.

She stopped, the needle poised over his arm, "Are you all right?"

He sucked in a chest full of air. When was he going to outgrow this childish fear of needles? *It's now or never unless you want this gorgeous woman to know you're a complete wimp.* "Yes. Of course." He made a fist.

She bent her head in concentration. Her presence filled his senses. He wanted to touch the strand of brown hair running along her cheek...

"Just little pinprick." The needle entered is arm.

He watched in nervous fascination as she put each of the

tubes into the sleeve attached to the needle, watching in horror as the blood flowed in.

"Open your fist," she said as she continued to withdraw his blood.

Hell! What had the doc ordered? He gritted his teeth to keep from asking what all the blood was for. He didn't want to know. All he wanted right now was to be done with it.

"There. You can release your grip on the arm of the chair. Wouldn't want you destroying hospital property, would we?" she asked, a quirky grin on her face as she pulled the needle out of his arm and put pressure on the spot. "Keep your arm up for ten minutes. Do you want me to put tape on it?"

He couldn't seem to take his eyes off her—her hair, the skin at her neck, her scent, all flowery... warm... He met her questioning look.

"Are you sure you're okay?" she asked,

"Me? Yeah, sure," he said.

"Well, then, do you want me to put tape over the gauze dressing on your arm?" she asked, a look of bemusement on her beautiful face.

"No. Yeah. Maybe you'd better, I have to get back to work."

Nicole saw the expression on his face as she'd drawn his blood. Justin Hadley was nervous. A grown man who was afraid of needles. Nicole Simpson had met a few of them before, but none as handsome as this one. His smile surrounded her like a gentle breeze, making her hesitate before taking the blood samples from the tray beside him. His address was one of the few apartment buildings in Spencer Island, on Salem Street. Most people planning to stay in Spencer Island bought a house, as houses were easily available with so many people moving away to other parts of the country to find jobs.

Spencer Island didn't have many young, single, gorgeous men, "Where do you work?"

She'd never seen him before, and she knew most of the locals because sooner or later they ended up in here getting blood drawn.

He eased back into the chair and met her inquiring gaze. "I'm a carpenter. 1 work for myself, I hurt my arm running a saw, Just a nick, though."

His eyes were fascinating, and very, very blue; his smile intrigued her. He didn't wear a wedding ring, but that was no guarantee that he was unattached. She'd made that mistake once before and had paid the price in what she called embarrassment tokens, her measure of yet another unsuccessful attempt at meeting a man.

"How long have you been in Spencer Island?", she asked as she took his blood samples to the counter behind her, placing each in their appropriate slots on the tray.

"Not long. In fact, I'm just getting my business under way. I've met some pretty wonderful people here."

She turned around to find his gaze openly moving over her. She'd grown accustomed to that look and ignored it. Men were shoppers, and window-shopping was their entry point in getting to know the merchandise. One of her ex-boyfriends had told her that.

"1...I'd better get back to work," he said, getting to his feet. "Thanks for being so gentle. I'm not good at getting my blood taken." He stood up, hugging his injured arm to his chest. She had to admit he was truly handsome and, in her experience, almost certainly unavailable.

Yet his gaze held hers in a way that made her feel totally connected, as if she was the only thought on his mind. In her experience, most men didn't spend a lot of time looking at her face in favor of some other part of her anatomy. "Being gentle is part of my job."

"I confess. I'm afraid of needles. I usually sit for a while before I get up. To cover my embarrassment, I make conversation with the tech taking my blood."

"Is that what you were doing with me?"

"No! No. I wanted to talk with you. I mean really talk."

"About what?"

"About maybe you and I going out somewhere. Nothing serious. Just coffee. 1 don't know many people in Spencer Island, and you could introduce me around," he said, his smile totally disarming.

"To somebody more interesting, you mean?" Well, at least he didn't pretend he wanted to date her.

He rubbed his face with his free hand. "I didn't mean that the way it came out. I... I'd like you and I to get to know each other, maybe be friends."

She couldn't help but smile at his discomfort. It was so endearing. "Are you this smooth with all the women you meet?"

"Didn't know I was being smooth. Thought was just being honest."

The last man pretending to be honest had her into paying his bill for fixing his car. Not one penny of which she'd gotten back.

He hugged his injured arm to his chest as he stared down into her face, his smile exciting, tempting her to trust him.

"Okay, I'll take your silence as a 'no'," he said as he moved toward the door. "Thank you."

The way his jeans hugged his butt made her rethink her position. Spencer Island was hardly crawling with eligible men. Her nightlife consisted of going to the pub with friends once a week and playing volleyball with the local women every Wednesday night. Besides, what harm could there be in having coffee with this man whose blue eyes were so engaging? "Sure. Coffee would be great."

"Where?"

"The Big Mug on Market Street?" She glanced at her watch. "Meet me around four?"

He grinned. "Today?"

"Yes"

"I know the place, I did a reno there a couple of weeks ago. See you at four. Your name tag says Nicole. What's your last name?" he asked, his voice eager, his eyes on her.

She wanted to laugh at the way he seemed almost inept around her. Most men were busy trying to put the moves on her. But Justin was...sweet. She touched her name tag. "Simpson. Nicole Simpson."

"Great! Good name!"

Justin drove to his worksite, a deck he was putting on the back of a house outside town, where he had his accident. He hoped that having to protect his arm wouldn't slow him down. He had a list of clients waiting for his services. Thankfully, it was his left arm that was injured and not his right, but even so, it might make working difficult.

He reached Ned Tompkins's yard and got back to work. As he hammered the nails into the deck his thoughts were solely on Nicole and what an idiot he'd made of himself. He'd practically bolted from the room. It wasn't really a date, he reminded himself, but still it was as close as he'd come to one since he moved to Spencer Island two months ago. He'd gone to the local pub downtown a couple of times, but the only women there were either with men or clustered in groups, whispering and giggling among themselves.

Blame it on Haiti, but what he was looking for in a woman had changed after living there. He wasn't interested in frivolous women, in dates consisting of expensive dinners and empty conversation or worse-—online dating. He wanted to really connect with a woman who loved her work and who believed she made a difference in people's lives. Because of Haiti, he wanted to make a difference no matter where he ended up living. Maybe he wouldn't stay in Spencer Island. Maybe he'd go back to Haiti for another two years. Whatever lay ahead for him, he wanted to be open to it. Life was about living in the here and now.

He had no idea what Nicole wanted out of life, but he sure would like to get to know her better. He checked to make sure he had his cell phone on him. He'd have to keep track of the time as he didn't want to be late for his coffee break with her.

He continued to work on the deck, skipping lunch in order to get the first parts completed. Ned Tompkins had had the concrete posts poured to support the deck, and all that was left was to build the wooden structure over the posts. Ned wasn't home, meaning there were no interruptions, allowing Justin to settle into an enjoyable rhythm. The feel of wood in his hands, the smell of it, the sun's heat on his shoulders reminded him of Haiti.

But he was done with Haiti, at least for now. He had to be. He'd been completely stressed out by his life there; the memories were painful. It was a life he'd once loved, and might love again once he had time to gain perspective on his experience in that country. He never walked past a child on the sidewalk in Spencer Island that didn't remind him of the two children whose lives he'd seen destroyed by the collapse of their home in Haiti.

He adjusted his tool belt and laid another board over the base structure of the deck. It wasn't until he realized that the sun wasn't on his shoulders that he checked the time...

. . .

Nicole sat in The Big Mug, glancing at her watch, answering questions from people she knew about what she was doing sitting there alone, did she want company and why wasn't she going home after her long day. She didn't know that a woman sitting by herself in a coffee shop could be such a point of interest.

She'd moved to Spencer Island two years ago after inheriting money from her father, money that guaranteed her escape from her mother and her life in Seattle; only to find herself in a community that took a great deal of pleasure in knowing each other's business. Still, she loved Spencer Island, the friends she made, her job and the time she spent with the local children both at the hospital and giving horseback riding lessons. She glanced around the coffee shop again. Maybe if she had her laptop with her, or a newspaper, she would feel less exposed...

Unfortunately, all she had for company was a rapidly cooling cup of coffee and rising sense of embarrassment at the way she'd fallen for yet another man's tall tale.

Yet Justin Hadley seemed sincere. He'd behaved as if he really wanted to have coffee with her. But had she read more into his behavior than was really there? Was her dateless life getting the better of her? She'd chosen a tiny booth at the back of the coffee shop where they could talk. He'd said he wanted to talk. She shook her head at her gullibility. She'd fallen for his charm and sexiness; his smooth talk—clearly the only talk he planned to offer her.

She glanced at her watch for the hundredth time—4:29 pm.

With a sigh she finished her coffee; gathered her coat, her bag and got out of the booth. Waving her thanks to the clerk, she headed for the side door leading to the parking lot. She pushed hard, only to have the door pop open nearly landing her on her backside. Great! Another embarrassing moment in her afternoon.

"I'm sorry!" Justin said, grabbing for her with his uninjured hand, pulling her against his broad chest, ending her rapid trip toward the concrete walkway outside the door.

He steadied her. "Are you okay?"

She heard the sincerity in his voice and steeled herself against it. Action, not words, was what she needed. "I'm fine." She adjusted her bag on her shoulder and stepped away from him. "And you're late," she said, instantly regretting the words that made her sound like a possessive woman.

"I'm really sorry. I lost track of time."

He looked so crestfallen she couldn't resist offering him a conciliatory smile, "Never mind. I have to get home. I have horses to feed, dinner to prepare."

He let the door slide closed, leaving them standing outside in the parking lot. "Can I make it up to you?"

His words made her realize how much she'd been looking forward to having coffee with him. All her brave thoughts about not minding being alone, of having accepted her single lifestyle, felt like a lie in the presence of this man.

She had tomorrow off, and she wasn't doing very much other than cleaning her tack room, doing laundry. If Justin Hadley wanted to make it up to her, he could take her to dinner. It was her policy on a first date that she always met the man somewhere away from her home, just in case he was a raving lunatic looking to avenge his angst against his mother on some unsuspecting female. A little over the top, she realized, but still...

She looked him straight in the eye. "Okay. Why don't we meet at O'Toole's in the Wayfarer Inn, say around seven tomorrow evening?"

"That sounds great. Does O'Toole's have a dress code?"

"Clean and neat as far as I know."

He turned, his body close to hers, his movement suggesting a closeness that didn't exist between them. "Can I walk you to your car?"

She moved out of his space, clutching her bag nearer her body. "No, that's okay. I'll see you tomorrow at seven."

"Don't be late," he said, a teasing tone in his voice.

CHAPTER TWO

*T*he next day, Nicole got up early, energized by a good sleep and the prospect of a day off. She'd taken her mare, Suzie, out for a long ride down into the fields next to her farm. The people who owned the property were summer residents but had given her permission to ride their wooded trails. She was sweating almost as hard as her horse when she walked Suzie back into the barn and removed the saddle.

On the ride her thoughts had been firmly on Justin, not a good sign at all. Given her track record in finding a man, she shouldn't get her hopes up. Coffee with him, after all, had not gone as planned. She'd been left feeling like an afterthought, suggesting to her that he'd not been as excited about seeing her as she'd been about seeing him. Would dinner be fraught with the same mismatch of expectations?

Every man she'd ever been attracted to had turned out to be a dud on one front or another. Her biggest disasters had been her online dating attempts. It convinced her that there had to be a lot of men out there who were more in touch with Photoshop than any woman who came into their lives.

Since she'd moved to Spencer Island, she hadn't dated anyone because she didn't feel like getting to know someone only to be disappointed. Why was it that so many of her friends had found Mr. Right while she couldn't find even one Mr. Maybe?

She finished caring for Suzie, let her into the paddock with Zeus and headed back toward the house. From across the yard she heard Ned Tompkins calling to her. She glanced over to see that he was standing next to a pile of lumber, and his deck was beginning to take shape. She looked again. Was that Justin Hadley?

"Nicole! Come on over and meet my new carpenter," Ned said.

She smelled like sweat and dirt and horse. She couldn't go over there without a shower. "Hi, Ned." She pointed to her house. "I'm in a bit of a hurry. I'll drop by on my way from town," she said, scurrying along the path from the barn.

"No. I need to talk to you. It's important," he yelled as he helped the carpenter with a long piece of wood. Wiping his hands on his pants, he said, "I want you to meet someone," he insisted as he beckoned to her. "Come on over."

"Oh, all right," she said, intending to stay downwind, so that her unwashed body wouldn't offend anyone—namely, Justin. Reluctantly, she crossed the open stretch of field between the houses: Justin stopped what he was doing and turned to face her. He was even more gorgeous in the morning light. How could that be?

Ned made the introductions, but she wasn't listening. She was staring up into those gorgeous blue eyes and the mess-me-up-a-little dirty blond hair.

"Small world," he offered, his hand extended in greeting.

"Yeah," she said, but it sounded more like a sigh.

"You know each other?" Ned asked, moving closer, his eyes darting from one to the other.

"We met at the hospital," Justin replied, looking deep into her eyes. What was it about this man that had her heart tripping in her chest?

Ned cleared his throat. "Okay, well, can you stay for a few minutes, Nicole? I need to speak to you."

If her world was perfectly in sync with her wishes, she'd stay right here and learn to be a carpenter. She'd spend long hours working up a sweat with this man. She tried not to look at the muscles curving over his shoulders and chest under his black T-shirt.

But her world wasn't perfect. She smelled like an armpit. She had to run errands in town, maybe pick up a new top for tonight. Something sexy.

She dragged her gaze from Justin and focused on Ned. "Sorry, Ned, but I have an appointment. Can we talk later?"

"I guess so. It's certainly not going to go away anytime soon...yeah...later."

Justin leaned toward her. She backed up, hoping not to shroud him in her horsey smell.

"I'll see you at seven," he said, low enough that Ned couldn't hear, for which she was very thankful. Nothing against Ned. It was just that she'd like to have a little privacy, and obviously so did Justin. Nice.

Just paced back and forth in front of the Wayfarer Inn. He'd dug out his best dress pants from among the stuff he'd brought from his mother's house in Bangor, ironed his only dress shirt and borrowed a tie from the guy in the apartment next to him, all in preparation for tonight.

He was about to make another lap around the front flower beds when he saw her coming across the parking lot. She hadn't seen him yet. Her stride was long, her silky brown hair clung to her cheeks and the sea green dress she was wearing skimmed her body in all the right places. When she looked his way, he smiled and waved.

Tonight was going to be special. He could feel it. He sucked in a deep breath and squared his shoulders. "I've been waiting for you," he said, then realized that he sounded like an overeager teenager.

Nicole glanced at her watch, "Am I late?"

"No, I'm early," he said as she came near.

She smiled at him, her eyes meeting his. "That's nice."

"What is?" he asked, unable to take his eyes from hers.

"You. Being early...for a change," she said, chuckling,

"I'm to be reminded of my one sin, am I?"

"Not if tonight goes okay. If all ends well, I will never mention the missed coffee date ever again."

"Deal," he said, placing his arm on the small of her back as he led her to the entrance of the inn. Walking beside her, letting her flowery perfume play along his senses, made him feel alive. The waiter showed them to a table by the window with a view of the side garden near the trestle he'd built for their climbing roses. He held her chair for her as she sat down.

"May I take your drink orders?" the waiter asked.

"Chardonnay for me," Nicole said, raising her eyebrows at him.

"Me, too," he offered. "1 can't remember the last time I had any alcohol," he said as the waiter left.

"You don't drink? You don't have to have a glass of wine just because I do."

"No. I drink. I simply haven't since I got back from Haiti"

"You lived in Haiti?"

He toyed with the lip of his water glass, his gut tightening He wished now he hadn't mentioned Haiti. Yet he'd done it out of a need to be completely honest with the woman who had held his attention since he'd met her. "Yes, for two years,"

"Did you like it?"

He'd spent the early weeks after he'd gotten back trying not to think about Haiti. He'd finally given up trying. Haiti changed his life. "I'm not sure. I don't know how to describe it."

"I'm listening if you want to try."

He met her attentive gaze and was tempted. Yet he wasn't quite ready to share those memories he'd held close to his heart, memories both happy and tragic. "Haiti is a special place. I was working for an NGO whose purpose was to build affordable housing. But now I'm back, ready to enjoy life, to make each moment count."

"I admire you for what you've done," she said, a smile lighting her eyes, her beautiful brown eyes. Eyes that seemed to encourage him to continue.

As much as he wanted to say more, he didn't want to ruin their evening by getting into a heavy topic like the devastation in Haiti. Their wine arrived. He picked up his glass. "To this evening."

"To this evening" she responded, putting her glass to her lips. He couldn't help noticing that her fingers were long, her nails painted in a subtle shade of pink.

They both ordered a steak. He was pleased to discover a woman who liked steak. Most of the women he'd dated didn't eat steak because it was too fattening, or too something. To him it was the perfect food. To each his own, he mused as he watched her sip her wine.

"You like to ride horses," he said.

"I do. When I came here, I was lucky enough to find a small farm property with a barn. I found two horses I love, and I'm planning to offer riding lessons. On a very small scale, of course, since I work full-time. What about you? What brought you to Spencer Island?"

"My mother passed away a couple of months ago. I inherited her house in Bangor, sold it and couldn't decide what to do after. Then one day it came to me."

Her eyes popped open, the corner of her lips tipped up in a smile. "What came to you?"

"The answer to where I'd move once all the paperwork around my mom's passing was finished. Mom summered in Spencer Island, out on Cranberry Point, when she was a kid. She loved it. Coming here was an easy decision. I just put some of my things in storage, the rest I put in the back of my truck and hit the road." He felt her interested gaze on him and wanted to share more with her, "It just felt right to come here, where my mom had been so happy." He played with the tines of his fork. "She hadn't been very happy the last couple of years."

"I'm sorry." she said quickly.

"I am, too. She developed cancer..." He was sorry he'd brought up this heavy topic. It had been a very difficult time for him. His mother's death and what he'd experienced in Haiti had left him desolate and uncertain for the first time in his life.

"Why did you choose to be a carpenter?"

"It's more like carpentry chose me. My dad liked to build things. When he passed away a few years ago, he left me all his tools. I found myself wanting to learn everything I could about working with wood. I found a program at the tech school in Bangor and decided to try my hand at it."

She smiled at him over her glass. He felt ridiculously pleased and happy. The best he'd felt since he'd gotten home from Haiti. As they ate they talked about many things, and he found himself thinking that it would be nice to do this every day. He loved the way she listened to him, made intelligent comments about his work, offered her ideas and generally made him feel that she understood why he'd chosen carpentry.

For the first time since he'd returned home, he wanted to share his feelings about his work in the past two years. What it meant to him. Yet, he couldn't seem to bring himself to face the memories on such a lovely evening.

When the waiter brought the dessert menu, they both chose the chocolate cake. "You and I have a lot in common," he said, enjoying the evening more than he'd imagined.

"Especially when it comes to food," she said.

"A great place to start, don't you think?" he asked, delighted that her gaze never left his face. "Why don't you tell me about your job? You're good at it, that much I know from my experience."

"I love it most of all because of the contact with people, and especially children."

They shared a love of children, as well. He wondered why a woman as attractive and interesting as Nicole wasn't already married or engaged. "Yeah, you put that little boy at ease."

"I aim to please," she said, color rising in her cheeks. He liked a woman who blushed when complimented.

Nicole hadn't spent such a pleasant evening with anyone in a long time. Justin was interesting to talk to, sexy, sweet, everything she wanted in a man. For him to be this perfect meant he had to have a huge flaw buried somewhere. No man was this easy to talk to, this much fun to be around and not have a female attached to him. Women loved men like Justin.

She needed time to think about this, to seek Angie Snyder's advice on what had to be going on. If her feelings around him were any indication, she'd just found the man of her dreams, and the search hadn't been easy. She'd dated a lot of men with potential, but somehow the relationship always hit a snag: Either she lost interest, or she learned something about them that turned her off completely.

Of course, she didn't have to overcome a huge secret like Angie did, or deal with a teenage son, but still she needed to talk to someone about this. Good advice was essential before she got in too deep with what seemed like just the right man. "Will you excuse me?" she asked as the desserts arrived.

"I'll order coffee while you're gone." he said. "What would you like?"

"Cream. No sugar."

"Hey. That's weird. Me, too," he said, a smile on his face, the one that made her want to smile back at him until her face cracked along the smile lines.

Definitely time to take a break from this enticing man.

Once in the ladies' room, she glanced at herself in the mirror. Her cheeks were positively rosy. Her eyes were shining. She looked like a very happy woman. Yet it felt strange, mostly because it had happened so easily, as if they were meant to be together.

She dialed Angie's number and was relieved when her friend picked up the phone. "Angie, it's me, Nicole."

"How's your date? Don't tell me. You're home already because it turned out to be a bad night."

"No! Not that at all. He seems perfect...too perfect."

"Is there such a thing?"

She propped one hip against the restroom counter. "See. That's it. There is no such thing as a perfect man."

"I don't know about that. I've got one sitting across the table from me."

Her friend had gotten engaged to Ted Langley two weeks ago and was so happy it almost hurt to watch her. "You're biased."

"I am. Tell me more," Angie said.

"Like I said, he's perfect. And I'm afraid."

"Of what?"

"Of what has to be going on beneath his gorgeous exterior. With my luck, he's been through a horrible divorce and is looking for a shoulder to cry on."

"Maybe..."

A woman came into the restroom and approached the sink next to Nicole. "Can you meet me for coffee tomorrow morning?", she asked, making for the door.

"Sure. I'll come in a little early and have coffee with you. Can't wait to hear all about him."

"I'll tell you when I see you." She hung up quickly, applied more lipstick, checked that her dress was fitting right over her breasts. As she adjusted her bra, she felt a sharp pinprick of pain on the side of her right breast. She loosened the bra a little and the pain eased. She opened the door and went back down the corridor toward the dining room. As she approached the door, she looked over at Justin to see that he was watching her as if she was the only woman on the planet. How sweet was that?

How much she needed to talk this over with Angie. There was something definitely amiss. Instant happiness hadn't happened to her ever before.

"I got him to hold our coffee until you got back," he said as she sat down.

"That's really nice," she said and meant it. "I love my coffee hot."

"I do, too"

She sat there feeling like a princess. It had a lot to do with the way Justin looked at her, as if she was special, even beautiful. Where had this man been hiding all her life while she kissed frogs and fought off groping hands?

The waiter placed a cup of coffee beside her untouched

dessert. She took a forkful of cake and sighed at the luscious chocolate flavor.

"Good or what?" Justin asked.

"What?"

"The cake. It's delicious, isn't it?"

"Absolutely." She took another forkful and tried not to groan with delight.

Justin walked her to her car and waited while she unlocked the door. "Thanks for tonight. I had a good time."

She glanced up into his eyes, her expression one of interest. "I did, too."

He wanted to reach for her, pull her into his arms and kiss the breath from her. But he wasn't very good at this dating thing. He definitely didn't want to blow his chances of seeing her again by doing something she didn't like. "You know, a braver man than me would kiss you."

"A braver man?" she asked, tilting her head back, exposing her long neck.

He wanted to touch her neck, feel her skin under his fingers. He settled for touching her shoulder. "I... I..." He leaned down to her as his fingers caressed her shoulder.

She edged closer, her sighing breath his undoing. He kissed her lips, gently and slowly. She tasted like chocolate and coffee. He wanted to follow her home, carry her to her bedroom and make love to her all night long, He wanted her in a way that shook him to his core. But he vowed he'd take it slow. If he had anything to say about it, they'd be spending the rest of their lives together.

Whoa! You're not ready for this.

He eased away from her, opening her door as he did so. "Maybe I'll see you at Ned's."

"Maybe you will," she said breathlessly.

He watched her get in, start her car, wave to him as she drove away. Or nearly. She drove over the corner of one of the flower beds as she left the parking lot. He grinned. "I won't tell a soul," he said, smiling to himself.

He drove to his apartment, feeling the best he'd felt since he'd come back home. He'd needed to go out with a beautiful woman the way a fish needed water. He'd missed that in Haiti. He'd been too exhausted after each day to wish for anything more than a chance to sleep without dreaming of the desperate lives of the people in Haiti.

Justin drove the three blocks to his apartment, his mind on the evening and how much he'd enjoyed it. He especially enjoyed watching Nicole drive over the flower bed. It could only mean one thing. She was feeling as excited as he was over their time together. Or maybe she was a really bad driver... Yet het car didn't seem to have any visible dents, no missing fenders.

He eased his truck into the parking space near the rear entrance of the building, got out and went up to his apartment. When he unlocked the door, the whole space seemed different, more inviting somehow. Or maybe it was simply his good mood. As he dropped his keys on the counter and pulled off his tie, he wondered what Nicole would say if he invited her here for dinner some night. He glanced around his living room, at the jukebox he'd salvaged early in his working career and the framed photos of his sister, Melody, and his parents. With so many clients to do work for, those photos were about the only decorating he'd done since moving in. But all that would change if Nicole became part of his life.

He had a lot he wanted to share with her. Ideas on how they could spend their time together.

He hoped she'd has a good a time as he'd had. He yanked off his shirt, pulled off his pants and climbed under the covers. It took two to make a relationship, and at no point did she say anything about her life or whether she was interested in him. He'd jumped to the conclusion that she was interested in him based on the fact that she'd driven over a flower bed.

Way to go, Hadley.

CHAPTER THREE

*T*he next morning Nicole awoke feeling great. Is that what a wonderful date with a gorgeous man did to a woman? Of course, there was that not cool moment when she'd driven over the flower bed. He'd been watching her mortifying misstep from his vantage point in the parking area: there'd be no way she could deny it. Would he bring it up to her when they saw each other again? Would they see each other again?

In the meantime, she needed to get to work and to coffee with Angie. She raced through her morning routine, including feeding the horses. When she arrived at work, the cafeteria was just opening up, and Angie was waiting for her.

"How was your date?" Angie asked as the early morning light streaked the sky outside the wall of windows, high-lighting the water clinging to the waxy leaves of a rhododen-drum pressed against the glass.

"It was perfect. Absolutely perfect. I don't get it."

"That it was perfect, or that it happened to you?"

"Both, I guess."

"Why don't you simply let things be? If he's that

charming and nice, he'll be in touch. If not, you won't get hurt," Angie said as they joined the coffee shop lineup.

"You think it's as simple as that?" Nicole asked, pouring coffees for both of them.

"I know it is. Don't chase him. I'm pretty sure he's going to be in touch really soon. The question will be whether or not you're ready for a relationship."

"Angie! I've been ready all my life. I just keep coming up with the wrong man. That's the kind of man I attract, which means that Justin will probably be just like the others." They paid for their coffees and moved toward a table near the back of the cafeteria.

"I don't think so, call it a hunch, but I believe you're in for a surprise."

"You're in love, meaning your judgment can't be relied upon," she teased.

"Possibly. But in my opinion, it's your turn for happiness, and this might be the man," Angie said, glancing around the space.

"Are you a fortune-teller in your spare time?"

"No. I simply believe that when two people are meant to be together, there's nothing that will stop them." Angie's smile warmed the entire room. "I happen to know that to be a fact."

Nicole pointed at the diamond sparkling on Angie's finger. "It's easy for you to be optimistic."

"Just trust your instincts. In the meantime, tell me more about this Justin person."

Nicole had no trouble spending the next half hour on Justin and their date. Angie laughed when she told her about him being late for coffee. Angie smiled knowingly when Nicole told her about him waiting for her at the inn. As they headed down the hall to work, Nicole realized it was the first time in her life that she had talked for so long about a man she'd only just met.

Later that day as she returned to her house. Driving along the narrow track road that led past Ned Tompkins's house, she did a quick check for Justin. He wasn't there, and she was disappointed. When she got to her driveway and turned in, Ned was waiting for her. Why was Ned in her yard? She pulled to a stop and got out. "Is there something wrong? Did Zeus get out again?" He'd gotten out a week ago, and she had to search the neighboring fields looking for him.

Ned approached her, his eyes bright. "This is probably not mine to ask, you understand." His eyes focused on hers. "What's your connection to Bill Cassidy?"

She'd come to Spencer Island, where her mother had grown up, looking for anyone who might know about her mother's past. She was very interested in whom her mother had dated growing up in Spencer Island, whom she'd been friends with. She hadn't been able to learn very much about her mother, only that her parents had both passed away.

Spencer Island was her only lead in finding who might have been her birth father. She'd first met Bill Cassidy when he'd found her searching her mother's graduation class photo at the local high school. Bill Cassidy had walked up to her wanting to know if he could help her. When she asked about Ellen Donnelly, he was curt with her. Feeling intimidated by his presence, she'd left the school. "He's the coach at the high school. He coaches the volleyball team 1 play on each Wednesday night." She had no intention of telling Ned about her earlier encounter with Mr. Cassidy. "Why do you ask?"

"Is that all?"

"What do you mean?"

"My sister is Lisa Sherwood. You know her?"

"You know she and I are on the same volleyball team."

Ned rubbed his chin and scuffed his feet on the dirt of the

driveway. "Some of the team feels that you and Bill are a little too chummy."

"What are you trying to say?" she asked, upset that people would talk about her that way.

"He's a man twice your age. That's all. You don't want people talking that way about you, do you?"

She clenched her fists and searched for a calmness she didn't feel. "What if I didn't care what people talked about?"

"Are you saying there's something going on between the two of you?" Ned's expression was one of fascination.

Nicole would like to tell her nosy neighbor to get lost. But she didn't need any gossip going around about her. And even worse, Bill probably had a wife who wouldn't be happy to have baseless rumors circulating about her husband. Most of all, Nicole didn't want Bill Cassidy to hear gossip connecting him to her. "He's my volleyball coach. He almost certainly has a wife. For the record, there is no relationship between Mr. Cassidy and me, other than the obvious one."

"Bill Cassidy doesn't have a wife. He doesn't have a girl-friend that anyone knows about." Ned continued to watch her in that odd way of his. "I wouldn't have asked about him, only he was over at your house one day," he said quietly.

"I'd told him about my horses. He probably came to see them when he was visiting someone further down the road. He's a great coach. That's all. He's kind to everyone, including me."

"I've known Bill Cassidy all his life, and he's never been interested in horses."

"People change," she said. Thinking about it now, it did seem very peculiar,

"If you say so," he mumbled, looking a little embarrassed.

Ned had been good neighbor in the two years she'd been here. But his sister, Lisa, was in a whole other league when it came to minding other people's business. If she were a betting woman, she'd bet that Lisa had pressed Ned to ask questions about her relationship with Bill.

She watched as Ned headed across the field, disappearing into his house a few minutes later. Nicole breathed a sigh of relief. She shouldn't have gotten angry with Ned. Although he was nosy, he was a good neighbor. When she moved in, he'd helped her fix the fencing, clean out the stalls. When she told him she'd pay him, be refused, saying that he was happy to have someone living on the road.

This was the first time he'd behaved so strangely. Maybe he was genuinely concerned about her reputation. She went into the house and turned on the TV for company as she organized her dinner before heading out to feed the horses.

She loved the routine of her day, especially looking after her horses. Gemma Dixon, one of Nicole's other friends at work, had stopped her today to ask about giving her step-daughter, Morgan Dixon, riding lessons. She was looking forward to the opportunity.

She had a volleyball game this evening and was looking forward to it. She loved the game, something she shared with her mother, Ellen. When she was a teenager, she and her mother used to practice around a net her father had put up in the backyard of the Craftsman house they lived in during her father's time in Canada. Her favorite place of all the places they'd lived.

When she got to the gym, everyone was there, ready to play. The game was fast and exciting, during which she scored four times, a record for her. Coach Cassidy had been generous with his praise, reminding her of Ned's inappropriate comments.

She was determined not to let Ned and his dreadful sister influence how she behaved around the coach and agreed to join the team for a drink to celebrate the win. She showered and dressed, ready for a fun evening.

She hadn't thought of the sore spot on her right breast since she'd been out on the court, and she didn't plan to think about it now. Tomorrow would be time enough. She had a routine physical in the morning, and she'd talk to Dr. Dixon about it then.

Once at the pub, they pulled a couple of tables together.

"That was a great game," Tina Sullivan, a nurse from the hospital, said as she settled in next to Nicole.

"It was. Thanks to our coach," Nicole said, feeling generous toward the man who had been pretty tough on all of them these past months. "To you," she said, holding up her beer to the man sitting across the table from her.

"Hey! This isn't about me. It's about you ladies. You deserved to win tonight," He raised his beer and clicked her bottle. "To all of you." But he seemed to be saying the words to her. Or was it her imagination? Had Ned's insinuations changed how she saw her coach? She hoped not. She'd learned more about playing volleyball since joining this team than she'd ever learned during all her high school years.

She sipped her beer, acutely aware that Coach Cassidy was watching her. Did any of her teammates notice? Or had this extra attention always been there, and she was the last to see it? She'd always played as hard as any of her team members because of his good coaching and because she loved the game. And of course, the coach had spent hours encouraging, teaching and sometimes cajoling them to try harder, to do better. It was only natural that he'd be paying attention to each of them.

Yet she couldn't completely block out Ned's words, and it made her feel sad and angry at the same time. She didn't know much about Bill Cassidy aside from the fact that he was the coach at the high school and the kids he coached all seemed to like him. The only negative thing she'd ever heard about him was from Angie. It seemed that her son, Troy, hadn't made the basketball team, and Angie believed he should have. Angie was very proud of her son and believed in him. It only made sense that she would want Troy to succeed in whatever he did. Lots of kids don't make teams. It was hardly a negative where the coach was concerned.

One thing was certain: neither she nor Coach Cassidy deserved to be gossiped about in the way Lisa Sherwood had done to her brother. She glanced across the table to see Lisa staring at her. She gave the woman a determined smile. It wasn't fair to her or Bill Cassidy, this feeling that somehow there was something going on between them,

Yet each time she looked in the coach's direction, he was glancing her way. She was beginning to feel vaguely creeped out. Whatever was going on, she didn't need any more trouble. Disheartened, she decided to leave when her beer was finished. As she got up, so did Coach Cassidy, and he followed her toward the door.

"I need to talk to you when you have a minute," he said, over the din of the bar.

"Can it wait?" she asked without stopping. When he didn't answer, she turned around to face him.

He rubbed his face, looked her up and down. "Something...I need to discuss something with you," he said his voice low and anxious.

Why was he suddenly upset? Coach Cassidy was always cool and in control. Whatever it was, she couldn't handle it right now. Not until she knew what the funny mark on her breast was. "I'm sorry, but I have to go."

"See you next Wednesday," he called to her as she strode purposefully toward the door leading to the parking lot.

She didn't know if she'd be at practice next week or not. She didn't need anyone talking the way Ned had earlier. She didn't need any more stuff to worry about. She had enough on her mind.

CHAPTER FOUR

*D*r. Dixon focused on her right breast, the spot Nicole described. He did a physical exam, probing the area. It didn't hurt anymore, which was a huge relief. Maybe the spot had hurt because she'd been wearing a new push-up bra. She was really embarrassed that she had to show him her breast. Yeah, she knew it was a physical exam that was very important, and Dr. Dixon was very professional, yet she still felt kind of strange...

"When did you last have a mammogram?"

She glanced quickly at him. "I can't remember."

He went to the computer and tapped a few keys. "Not since you moved here, correct?"

She tried to match his professional tone, afraid that he would say something to her about not having the test done all these years. "Correct."

She'd thought the spot on the right side of her breast was a pimple. In fact, she had been certain. Did he think she had something else?

"I want you to go this afternoon to the X-ray department

and have a mammogram done. I'll be in touch with you as soon as I see the results of the test."

"I don't understand. It's just a pimple, isn't it?"

"I'm not sure."

She didn't hear another word he said after that. He did her pap test and finished the rest of the physical examination. All the while she had only one thought on her mind. Her mother had had breast cancer years ago. As her daughter, she'd been advised to have regular mammograms but had ignored the advice. Had it been in defiance of her mother's harping about it? Or had it simply been that she didn't believe it could happen to her?

When the doctor finished the exam, he left her with a requisition for a mammogram and one for routine blood work. She put her clothes on, not touching her right breast that suddenly seemed to feel bigger, even painful. This couldn't be happening. She had a good life here in Spencer Island.

Don't get ahead of yourself. Get the mammogram done.

She got to the hospital and, in response to the sympathetic look from the technician, she said it was simply part of her physical. She winced when the machine compressed the tissue on the right side. She cried when she finally got home to her house.

Drying her tears, she went for a long ride on Zeus. The horse seemed to sense that she was fearful because normally he was very high-spirited. Today he was gentle and calm, giving her one of the best rides of her life. She returned to her house in time to hear the phone ringing. Caller ID displayed Justin Hadley's name. When she answered, his cheerful voice warmed her heart, leaving her scrambling for something to say.

"Is everything okay?" he asked.

"Yes. I'm fine," she said, her thoughts on her doctor's appointment.

"You don't sound fine. I'm taking my bill to Ned Tompkins for payment. I'm on my way there now. Mind if I stop by? I want to ask a favor of you."

She didn't want to see him. She didn't want to see anyone. Yet the plea in his voice, the mystery of what the favor was gave her something to think about other than her doctor's serious tones when he asked her questions during her exam. "Okay. Drop by, but only for a few minutes. I've work to do."

She went to the yard when he pulled into the driveway. She didn't want him inside her home, not when she had lots to think about. Besides, he'd be here for only a few minutes.

He smiled as he got out of his truck. "Thank you for a great evening. We haven't had a chance to talk since then, but I wanted you to know how I felt."

"I enjoyed it, too." She couldn't help but notice the way his cotton shirt hugged his body. His gorgeous body. The heat of her cheeks made her look away from his intense gaze. "So, what was the favor you needed?"

He tucked his cell phone into his pocket and pulled out a piece of paper. "I've purchased two tickets to the annual fund-raiser for the fire station. It's a dinner and dance. Would you go with me?"

She glanced at the sheet of paper he'd handed her, reading the details hurriedly. "Next week?"

"Yeah. I know it's short notice," He offered a disarming smile.

She'd never gone to a fund-raiser. She hadn't danced in years, other than in front of her mirrored closet doors. Yet she didn't feel like going and socializing when she was worried about the results of her mammogram. If circumstances were different... She glanced at him to see that his eyes were on her, waiting for her response. "I'm really sorry, but I can't go."

His smile faded. He looked away then back at her, revealing a look of surprise. Had he never been turned down before? He squinted at her. "Can I ask why not?"

Why was he looking so...so forlorn? She wasn't the only available woman in Spencer Island, "It's not that I don't enjoy your company. I do.""

"I enjoy your company, or I wouldn't have asked you. What's the problem?"

Most men she'd ever refused to date had always been either surly or at least disappointed. But Justin stood there, smelling of freshly washed shirts and spicy cologne. His hopeful expression made her want to change her mind, go with him and have a fun evening. "Please try to understand I'm really not—"

"If you don't wait to go with me, just say so." He sighed. "Sorry. I didn't mean to sound annoyed," he said, his eyes dark.

She felt awful. First, she really wanted to go, but how could she manage to stay upbeat and in the party mood knowing that there might be a cancer growing inside her? "What if I'm not very good company?"

His eyebrows clamped together, "What's worrying you? Is it something I did?" he asked.

"No. Not at all, I've got a lot on my mind, that's all."

"Whatever is worrying you is not my business, unless you want to tell me," Taking her shoulders gently in his powerful hands, he gazed down into her eyes, "I'm a good listener, if you need to talk. Or if not, it's still okay. But look at it this way. If you decided to go, you'd get to stumble around the dance floor with me."

"Stumble? I doubt that very much. I'll bet you're a good dancer."

"Then why don't you go with me and find out?"

Would an evening out hurt her? It might even make her feel less anxious. Even better, it could turn out to be enjoyable. Their dinner date had turned out better than she'd expected. If she didn't go, she'd spend the evening trying to keep her worry at bay by watching reruns of some made-for-TV thriller series. "When you put it that way, how can I refuse?"

"Great! I'll talk to you later about going to the fund-raiser." He turned to go, stopped and turned back to face her. "And by the way, I had a really great time having dinner with you."

"Me, too." She watched him pull down her driveway, feeling so much better than when he arrived. Maybe the dating tide was turning in her favor. She smiled and headed to the horse barn.

The next afternoon Justin had finished presenting his estimate to a new client earlier than expected. Realizing that he was only minutes from Nicole's house, he decided he wanted to see her. Turning off the highway and heading down her road, he realized he didn't have a clue why he was doing this.

He supposed what he really wanted was to see if she'd talk to him about what was bothering her. There was definitely something going on, and he was pretty sure it had happened after they'd been out to dinner. People would probably think he was nosy. Yet he had to know what had made her look sad and worried.

When he reached her house, he was pleased to see her out in the paddock hammering something on one of the posts, He jumped out of his truck and strode toward her. "I was just in the neighborhood."

There was a smile on her face as he approached, "Cut it out. You were not."

In all his life he had never seen a woman who could make jeans and a gray-checked shirt look sexy. Yet she seemed totally unaware of her effect on him. "What are you doing here? This is dead-end street. That means you're not on your way somewhere. Did you just suddenly decide to pay a visit?"

"I came to see if I could help you." He glanced past her at the work she was doing on the posts, "And this is right up my alley, if you need me."

She cocked her hands on her hips. "Unsolicited repairs are free?"

"I'll put it under 'helping a friend'."

She glanced from the fence rail to him. "If you insist."

"Let's have a look," he said, moving closer to the fence post where she'd been working. He could see right away that the post had rotted out just above the ground, making it a wasted effort to try to reattach the fence boards. "Have you got any more of these posts?"

"Yes, I believe there are some out behind the barn. I'll show you."

She started to walk ahead of him, offering him a view of her behind and the way her jeans fit that made his blood run hot. "Spectacular," he said under his breath.

"Did you say something?" she asked over her shoulder.

"Nothing, I mutter when I walk," he said, trying for humor when all he wanted to do was cup her bottom in his hands.

"Can't imagine what sort of noise you'd make if you had to run. Yell, maybe?" she said, tossing the words over her shoulder. "Here they are." She pointed to the pile of wooden posts against the back wall of the barn.

"Perfect." He picked one up and started toward the

paddock. "I'll get my tools out of the truck. I'll need a shovel if you've got one."

"Coming right up."

She was waiting for him with a large shovel and a hoe while he got what he needed from his tool locker. It was damned difficult to concentrate on fixing her fence with her standing there. Yet he managed it somehow, finishing everything up and putting things back.

He was about to head for his truck when two horses came galloping toward him, moving faster the closer they got. "Whoa!" he yelled and jumped back.

"They won't hurt you," she said, laughing as the two horses came to a stop in front of her and nudged her hands. "They're looking for treats. I've got some in my pocket."

He could have sworn there wasn't room to put anything inside those jeans other than her body, but sure enough she pulled two carrot chunks out of the left-hand pocket and fed them to the horses, "Have you always liked horses?" he asked, waiting for his pulse to stop playing around his chest.

"I used to ride when I was a kid: My dad would often ride with me. I've always loved horses."

"Bunnies or small dogs are more my style... Don't have either at the moment. Not allowed in the apartment building where I live."

"Will you get a pet when you buy a house?"

"Don't know if I'm buying a house."

She gave him an assessing glance. "Does that mean you're not staying here?"

"Not sure."

He realized once the words were out of his mouth that she wasn't pleased. She seemed to pull back. Her eyes searched the horizon. Silence stretched between them like an elastic band being pulled to the breaking point.

Finally, she spoke. "How did you decide to come here? I mean, there must have been job opportunities in Bangor."

"I came home. Sold my mom's house and came here." He shrugged. "Simple as that."

"Isn't that a little impulsive?"

He shook his head. "It's just the way I am. I decided to go to Haiti in a matter of days."

"Aren't you afraid that an impulsive decision could lead to problems once you've had time to consider what you've done?"

"No. I don't. I've always gone with my gut. For me, the right choice is the one I make the first time around. If I over-think a situation, I begin to doubt myself and end up making the wrong decision."

"You mean you always make the easiest choice?"

"Depends on how you look at it."

"And how do you look at it?" she said, her tone casual but the emotion clear behind it clear. She didn't approve of gut decisions.

"Something meant to be...like when we met."

She gave him a wry smile, "That wasn't meant to be. That was Dr. Dixon's order."

"Depends on how you look at it," he repeated.

"It was no accident that Dr. Dixon ordered blood work."

"But you have to admit that it was an accident that brought me in to see the doctor."

"Okay. We can agree on that much at least." She walked beside him to his truck, turning to face him with her hands tucked into the pockets of those tight jeans of hers that made his pulse do seriously strange things. "You've been very kind. Thank you."

"You're welcome."

"No man has been that kind to me, except my father. I

loved him very much." She rubbed. her palms on the sides of her jeans, squinting up at the sky.

He stopped, surprised by her remark. This woman's experience with men couldn't have been all that great if fixing her fence had been such a big deal to her. "Your dad must have pretty special. My father was the best. I miss him all the time. Mom, too, but it's different with Dad."

"My mother's still alive. I don't know about that."

He couldn't keep his mind from running over the possible reasons why a woman as beautiful as Nicole Simpson had commented on how a kindness was not a normal occurrence in her life. "Lucky you."

"Not necessarily, I haven't seen my mom in two years. Not since we had..." She rubbed her hands on her jeans. "You don't need to hear all this."

He reached the door of his truck aware that what he really wanted to do was to stay and learn more about this woman. He settled for taking her hand in his. "I do need to hear, if we're going to be friends."

"Friends?"

"Did you have more in mind?" he asked, keeping his tone light.

She shaded her eyes with her hand as she glanced over at the paddock. "I don't have much of anything in mind," she said, her voice soft, but her words offering a rebuke,

"You don't seem to have much faith in people. Is there a reason?"

She returned her gaze to him, her expression unreadable. "What would you do if your mother had lied to you all your life?"

"Whoa! Don't know. My mom and I were always close. Can't imagine how that would feel."

She turned to face him, a lost look in her eyes. "There are

moments I wish I could call my mom, but too much time has passed, too many missed opportunities."

He didn't know what to say to her to ease the naked loneliness capturing her face. He wasn't good at any of this sort of thing, of facing sadness or sorrow—part of why his experience in Haiti had been so difficult.

"Tell you what. Why don't we talk about what time I should pick you up? We both need a little cheering up, and the fire station fund-raiser sounds like fun."

"You're very convincing. I have to feed the horses after work, then get ready. Any time after that." She smiled at him and he loved it.

They agreed on a time, and he couldn't help wishing that she'd wear the dress she'd worn when they went out to dinner the other night. He left her place, his spirits high, anticipation making him glad he'd decided to stay in Spencer Island, at least for now.

The next evening the community center was packed with people by the time they got there. Delighted to hear that Nicole had a date for the fund-raiser, Angie and Gemma had agreed to hold a table where the three couples could sit together. Nicole glanced around the room, immediately spotting Matt Dixon. "There they are," she said, leaning into Justin, allowing her words to be heard over the noise of the crowd milling about.

"I'll follow you," he said, placing his hand in the small of her back, his fingers heated points against her cool skin. She wore the dress she'd worn to dinner, a last-minute decision, the result of getting home late because of a patient whose veins were difficult to find. The look in Justin's eyes when he arrived to pick her up told her she'd made a good choice.

She had been looking forward to tonight since she woke up this morning; such a relief not to be thinking about her doctor's appointment tomorrow. Although it would feel really strange to be socializing with Dr. Dixon tonight, when he had news that would either put her mind at ease or change her life. Her stomach fluttered at the thought.

They approached the group at the table, the expression on each of their faces one of open curiosity. She forced all thoughts of tomorrow from her mind. She introduced Justin. Just as they went to sit down, a woman came up to Justin and thanked him for fixing her mother's front steps. Nicole couldn't help but notice that the woman didn't give anyone else at the table one moment of attention. Not even Dr. Dixon, the man everyone admired for coming home to practice medicine and marry his high school sweetheart.

Angie leaned over to Nicole. "Is she flirting with him?" she asked.

"Yep." Nicole sighed. "Hope the whole evening doesn't end up this way."

"I doubt it. I saw the look in Justin's eyes as he escorted you over here to the table. The man's hooked on you."

"How do you know?"

"1 just know. Open your eyes, Nicole, and see what's right in front of you," Angie whispered.

What if Justin was hooked on her? Was it possible? Could someone care for her so quickly, so easily?

She really liked him, but like was a long way from love. Yet as she sat beside him, his shoulder brushing hers as he talked to the woman, she wanted Angie's words to be true.

Nicole's breath caught as Justin turned his attention back to her. She met his easy smile, saw the awareness in his eyes. A wonderful feeling of intimacy warmed her, making her a little anxious about what would happen next. She realized she didn't want any man hooked on her right now, not until she knew the outcome of her test. "Everyone at the table seems to have something to drink. Can I get you something?" he asked, leaning into her space, making her neck tingle.

"I'll have a glass of white wine."

"Me, too," he said close to her ear before going to the bar.

"Who would've thought that the six of us would be here this evening?" Gemma asked, her hand resting on the table, displaying her wedding ring. It had been only a few weeks since Matt and Gemma's wedding and people were still talking about it.

Adding to the excitement, Angie and Ted were now engaged to be married. Nicole felt like Alice in wedding land. But she couldn't help being happy for both her friends, even though at times she had to admit to being a little bit envious. Gemma and Matt were deep in conversation as were Ted and Angie, leaving Nicole with time to look around at all the people at the fund-raiser. Moving here has been the biggest risk she'd ever taken, and it had paid off. She happy here, content with her life, her job and her horses. She'd been happy to settle for all of that until she'd met Justin.

She was searching the crowd for him when he came toward her, two glasses in his hands. As he reached their table, the band began to play. Justin put the glasses down and took her hand. "This is our song."

"Our song?" she asked as she rose, "We don't have a song."

He pulled her into his arms. "We do now. A nice waltz, I'm pleased to report. What is it, by the way?"

"You don't know?"

He held her close, the powerful muscles in his, arms cradling her, "I haven't clue, But I must say it's perfect for what I want to do."

"And that is?"

"Hold you while we sway to the music." He smiled down at her. "I think it only fair to warn you that I've never had dance lessons. I make it up as I go."

"Fair enough. If you make moves I can't follow, I'll stand on your feet and you can carry me around."

His laugh was open and genuine. "Hang on, princess," he said, swinging her around as he moved through the other couples on the dance floor, his body locked to hers in such a way that she couldn't move. The truth was she didn't want to move, to let go of him, or even to make conversation with him. Not right now. Now was the time to simply have fun with this handsome man who was drawing looks from virtually every woman in the room.

Later she danced with Ted and again with Justin and then with one of her regular patients at the phlebotomy clinic. Matt danced with Gemma and Angie. He hadn't chosen to dance with her, and she couldn't help wondering why he hadn't. Were the results of her mammogram bad?

When the party ended, they all walked out together. Nicole had never been part of a group of couples and felt really pleased that tonight she was.

"See you at work tomorrow," Angie said.

"It was nice to meet all of you," Justin said, his arm snugly around Nicole.

Tonight had been perfect, fun and exciting, and it helped her to forget about tomorrow. But if she got a bad report, she would have to rethink any relationship hopes she had where Justin was concerned. She could not focus on a relationship if she had to face the kind of changes being diagnosed with breast cancer would mean to her life.

If she got bad news tomorrow, she was alone, without family here in Spencer Island and would have to rely on her friends for support.

She wanted to call her mom and talk all of this over. Her mother had had breast cancer when Nicole was twelve. She'd never really talked to her about what it had been like. In fact, she hadn't talked to her mom ever since she'd learned that her father, Marcus Simpson, wasn't her birth father. A lie she could not forgive her mother for. She loved her dad, and he'd loved her very much.

"Would a penny cover it?" he asked.

"Pardon?"

"Your thoughts. You haven't said a word since you got into the cab of my truck."

She glanced over at him, his open smile, his dark eyes-focused on hers. "Sorry. I didn't mean to be rude."

"Not a problem," he said, but she recognized the tone of a man who felt he'd been ignored.

As Justin pulled into her driveway, Nicole gathered her purse and her shawl preparing to leave and go into the house. Justin shut off the engine. Nicole reached for the door.

"What's the hurry?" he asked, his voice low and sensual.

"I have to work tomorrow," she said, opening the door and flooding the interior of the truck with soft light.

"We both do," he said, squinting in the sudden brightness. "That doesn't mean we can't enjoy the rest of the evening."

"You mean we go into my house and do what?" she asked. She didn't want to sound harsh, but she did need to be alone right now. Justin would probably not understand that, which meant he'd make his polite good-night, and she wouldn't hear from him again.

"As I told you before, I'm a good listener if you—"

"I really have to go in. Please understand."

He shrugged. "I get it. I read the signs wrong. You're not interested in continuing further."

"That's not true! I'm sorry if you think that."

"Then tell me what to think. Tell me what's going on."

"I can't. Not right now." She found herself searching his face for some indication that he understood.

"You want me to believe that you're interested in me, but not tonight. Maybe tomorrow. Maybe next week. Or next month. Whenever."

She heard the rising tone of his voice, and her tummy touched her toes. She couldn't share her worry with a stranger, and he didn't seem to aware that she needed privacy. Obviously, he was disappointed that she hadn't invited him into her house. She'd read this script before. Another time. Another place. Another man. "I want to go in and go to bed. I have a lot riding on tomorrow, and I need to be ready to face it. If you cannot accept that, then—."

He leaned across the console, placed his large hand firmly behind her head, drew her face to his and kissed her. A simple kiss that claimed her. She reached up to touch his face, to feel the faint stubble on his cheeks, the pulse along his chin line. He gently blocked her hand with his. Very gently he ended the kiss, nearly driving her wild with need.

"I believe I've made my point. Have a good night. Dream of me if you'd like" he said, a light teasing tone back in his voice. He touched his forehead to hers, and suddenly she wished he could come in. She wished she wasn't so anxious about her health, her life, about everything. A sharp pang of regret tightened her throat, making words impossible. He was being kind, very much the man she'd imagined she'd meet one day.

"We'll continue this at a later date," he whispered, planting another kiss on the end of her nose,

As her heart pounded and her thoughts scrambled, she clambered out the door of the truck toward her house. She'd wanted to stay right there with him, to let him kiss her until they had no choice but to move to her bedroom. She wanted it but she couldn't have it. Not tonight, and maybe not for a very long time.

He was everything she wanted and everything she couldn't afford emotionally. Not when her life would revolve around what the doctor had to say.

Yanking off her clothes, she climbed under her duvet and curled up into a ball. She'd never felt so alone in her life.

CHAPTER FIVE

*N*icole went into work, her mind on her doctor's appointment scheduled for eleven o'clock at Dr. Dixon's office. She had hoped that his office might call to say the mammogram was negative, but they hadn't. To her that meant only one thing. She drew in a deep breath to ward off the tears.

She hadn't eaten a bite, nor had she slept until around four o'clock, when she finally fell exhausted into a deep sleep, during which she dreamed that someone was calling to her. She'd awoken sweaty and disoriented, believing that someone was in the house looking for her. A long shower helped clear her head of the dream, a shower during which she didn't touch her breast.

When she reached the phlebotomy clinic, she turned on her computer at her workstation in preparation for the day ahead. Angie came by her desk, leaning her arm on the counter, a sympathetic smile on her face. "Want to talk about it?"

"I'm scared, Angie. I don't know what I'll do if this is cancer. If I have to go to Portland or Bangor for treatment,

STELLA MACLEAN

leave my job for days on end, find someone to look after my horses while I'm sick..." She tried to breathe over her fear, to draw air in past the knot in her throat.

"Gemma and I are here for you."

"I know you are, and I appreciate it. It's just that I've never felt this alone before."

"Why don't you let me call your mom?"

"No! She'd make this all about her. I don't have the energy for that."

"What can I do?"

Nicole came around the desk and hugged her friend, "Just knowing you're here and willing to help makes all the difference."

"Who's covering for you after eleven?"

"Janet Mills."

Nicole managed to make it through her morning patients, including a particularly exuberant four-year-old. When Janet arrived, she gathered up her purse and headed out.

When she got to Dr. Dixon's office, his waiting room was empty. Nicole was very thankful for the reprieve. Waiting in a room full of people, trying to remain upbeat when people started a conversation with her, would have been difficult.

Ethel Stairs, Dr. Dixon's receptionist, tipped her reading glasses down her nose and looked across her desk at Nicole. "Good morning, Nicole. It's nice to see you. You haven't been in the office for months, have you?"

"No, I haven't."

"And I have the correct insurance information on you, I believe," Ethel said and read the information to Nicole for confirmation. Ethel patted the file before placing it on the corner of her desk. "If you'll take a seat, Dr. Dixon will see you in a few minutes."

Nicole concentrated on the seascape painting across the

room, which offered a serene vista of the ocean, a calm she didn't feel at all.

A door opened, and Dr. Dixon walked out, took her chart from the receptionist and led the way into his examination room. Closing the door gently, he smiled at Nicole as she climbed up onto the exam table. "The spot that was bothering you would seem to be nothing other than irritated tissue."

Nicole sighed, feeling a huge weight lifting off her shoulders. "Yeah, it started to bother me right after I bought a new bra." She smiled in relief. "I'm putting that bra in the trash. To think I frightened myself silly over a bad fitting bra."

Dr. Dixon didn't smile back. "But you can be thankful that it prompted you to look into the problem. I'm afraid that although that spot isn't a problem, the mammogram did find another area we need to biopsy." He looked at her chart open in his hands and back at her. "We'll need to do it right away."

She hugged her arms against her chest to quell the anxiety racing through her. "When?"

"Tomorrow morning. I've scheduled a procedure room at the hospital for eight to do an incisional biopsy. You will need to be off work for a day or two."

Who would care for her horses? Nicole felt the tears flood her eyes. "I'll rearrange my schedule," she said as sadness and worry engulfed her.

"This will be a simple procedure. All you need to do is be at the hospital about fifteen minutes before your appointment. I'll meet you there," he said, his voice calm, his eyes kind.

"Then what?"

"The biopsy tissue will be sent to Portland, to the pathology lab there, and we'll have the results in a matter of days. In the meantime, I would encourage you not to focus on this too much. I know that's nearly impossible to do under the circumstances. But look at it this way, if it's nothing, then it's over and you can go on with your life. If there is something there, the success rate in treating breast cancer has greatly improved in the past few years. There are support services and groups, as well." He smiled encouragingly. "You have a lot of good friends who will help you if you should need them."

She could hardly hear what he was saying. It couldn't be cancer. She couldn't face it. She needed time to absorb this, to get her head around the idea that this biopsy would be a turning point in her life regardless of the outcome. Suddenly she wanted her mother. She needed her desperately.

Tears surged down her checks. She needed to take Zeus out for a long run, to feel the wind in her hair, to know that at least one part of her life hadn't changed. She would have to ask Ned to care for her horses. She wiped the tears and drove carefully toward home, focusing all her attention on the next few hours, in which she would try her best not to give in to the panic she felt.

Justin hadn't heard from Nicole today. He'd been a little put off by the fact that she hadn't invited him in after the dance, but he accepted that she needed her space. There would be lots of time for them to get to know one another better. He planned to see her today if he could.

When he arrived at her desk, she wasn't there. Instead, an older woman greeted him. "Do you have a requisition for blood work?" she asked.

"No, I'm looking for Nicole Simpson."

"She's taken a day off. Personal time, I believe," the woman said, making it clear by the prim set of her lips she planned to say nothing more on the subject of Nicole Simpson.

Was she ill? Had she not been feeling well that night after the dance? Angie and Gemma both worked in the clinics, and he made his way there as quickly as possible. He saw Angie at the desk, her eyes on the computer screen in front of her. When he walked up, she stopped and glanced up at him. "Hi, Justin. How are you?"

"I'm good, thanks. I'm looking for Nicole."

"She's not working today."

"I know that. I was wondering why she's taken, a day off in the middle of the week."

"You'll have to ask her." Angie's smile was kind, but like the woman at Nicole's desk, she wasn't forthcoming.

"Thank you." He headed out to his truck, started it up and drove out of town toward Nicole's house. She probably wouldn't want to talk to him, but he had to know that she was all right. When he pulled in her driveway, he saw her. He jumped out of his truck and went to her. "They told me you were off today. I came to see if everything's all right."

"Why shouldn't it be?" she asked, patting the huge horse before turning to him.

The horse gave a snort and galloped off toward the other side of the enclosure. Justin felt his shoulders relax when the horse took off. He wasn't comfortable around horses.

He waited, hoping she'd tell him something. He suddenly felt silly and inappropriate for rushing out here without calling first. "I needed to see you."

She smiled at him, but her eyes were wary. "That's very kind of you. But I don't need anyone here right now, if you don't mind."

He stared at her, at the nervous way she rubbed her palms over the sides of her worn jeans, the way she wouldn't look at him. There was something going on with her.

"Look, I didn't mean to barge in like this. I went to the hospital, and they told me you were home. I was worried. I

57

really enjoyed the dinner and dance the other night. I was hoping we might do something tomorrow. If you're up to it, that is."

It was his turn to rub his palms over the sides of his jeans as he waited for her to say something. She didn't utter a sound as her eyes searched the open field where the horse stood quietly now.

"Look, I can see it was a mistake coming here. Why don't I call you later, maybe? See if you're all right...or you call me...or whatever?"

Nicole couldn't resist the look of anguish in his eyes. When she saw his truck pull up in her yard, she'd been prepared to send him away. She didn't need company right now, but she had to admit it was rather nice to have him show up. "No, please. I had a good time the other night, as well. I was out for a ride to clear my thoughts."

The relief in his eyes drew her to him. He was genuinely anxious about her. And he really did want to see her. "If you don't mind waiting, I need to have a shower and get cleaned up."

His face broke out in a broad grin. "Yeah. I can wait." He offered his arm. "Let me escort you. I'll wait wherever you tell me to wait."

She couldn't help but smile. "I think the living room would be good."

"Or I can make a pot of coffee?" He looked down at her as they walked toward her back door.

"Let me get cleaned up first. Maybe we can have coffee later."

She left him sitting in the living room. She hurried through a shower, being careful not to touch her breast. Tomorrow would come soon enough. She put on clean jeans and a T-shirt before heading downstairs. When she reached the bottom step, she could see him peering at her bookshelves filled with books and horse magazines.

"Those were my father's. He was a chemical engineer, worked for an oil company that took him all over the world."

He studied her over the book he held open "So, you've traveled to a lot of places with your family I assume."

"When I was in ninth grade, Mom and Dad talked about putting me in a boarding school to offer me a more stable existence. I was so upset I wrote a long essay on the reasons why I should continue to travel with them, broaden my horizons, get to learn about the world outside the United States. But I think it was my final argument that won."

"And what was that?"

"I'd run away if they tried to send me to a boarding school. It was the last conversation I had with my father before he left for a business trip to Chile. He didn't come back. The plane he was in crashed."

His expression was one of open concern as he put the book down, pulled her into his arms and held her in a way she hadn't been held before by a man. It felt like coming home to a safe place. She nearly cried out.

"I'm sorry," he whispered into her hair, making her feel cared for and protected.

"Why don't we sit down, and you can tell me all about your life. You mentioned Haiti," she said, struggling to recover from the wonderful feelings sliding through her at the way he'd held her.

He followed her to the sofa. "I thought we were going to talk about you," he said.

"We will." She smoothed her hair from her face, her fingers trembling.

"Would you like me to make coffee?"

"No. I'm fine."

He looked at her for a few moments, as if he wanted to say something, then changed his mind.

"Well, let's see. I went to Haiti, part of a two-year contract. I'd been asked by a friend to join his team of carpenters going in repair work after the earthquake, and to build new ones where we could."

He twined his fingers together and stared at them before going on. "It was easily one of the most difficult times of my life. And in many ways, it was the most surreal, reward, heartbreaking experience I've ever had. I can't explain it. Many people in Haiti need so much, yet the ones I met have spirit and enthusiasm you don't often find back here at home. We take our lives for granted. We're preoccupied with having everything we want. We worry about the future. Maybe it's because their future is so uncertain that they have learned to live in the present."

She watched how he flexed his fingers, especially those on his injured arm. He was struggling not to break down, and she could relate to that. She'd wanted to have a good cry ever since her visit to Dr. Dixon's office. "I admire you for being able to do what you did. Many couldn't."

She found herself really liking him. And in telling her about Haiti, he'd helped her control her worry. Having him here had been a huge benefit, unexpected and wonderful.

"I should have done more." His jaw worked, he lowered his head and stared at his hands. "Sometimes I wish I hadn't left."

"You must have needed to come home for some reason. Was your mother in poor health?"

"I'd gone to Haiti after she passed to get a better perspective. My sister wanted me to move to Texas to be near her. I couldn't imagine myself in Texas," He glanced at her, his expression one of sadness. "Then I remembered my mother's stories about her summers in Spencer Island, and that sort of made the decision for me."

"You make decisions so easily," she mused. "I find it difficult to make a decision, especially one that could change my life. But I'm glad you decided to come here. And everyone is singing your praises, even Ned Tompkins. Pleasing Ned isn't easy," she said, teasing him just a little bit.

"I do make decisions quickly. But they have mostly worked out...except maybe my year at a summer camp in northern Maine." He chuckled. "Let's not go there for now." He leaned back and looked at her. "But I didn't come to talk about me. I came here to talk about you. To see if you were all right."

"I am."

"That's it?"

As close as she felt to him right now, she couldn't tell him about her health issue. She had to believe it was simply a scare and would all be over in a matter of days. Besides, the men she'd known wouldn't be around for long if there was a problem requiring them to do anything. She suspected that Justin wasn't like that, but she wasn't willing to take a chance when her life was so uncertain.

Justin couldn't believe his good fortune. His impetuousness had paid off. "Why don't I take you out for something to eat, and we can talk some more?"

"I could make something here, if you like. I have dinner planned and there's enough for two," she said, getting up and heading across the room to the door leading to the kitchen.

She got out some pots and pans, took several pieces of haddock from the refrigerator, removed the wrapping and rinsed the fish in the sink. He watched her easy movements. "You cook a lot, I take it," he said.

"I do. Mostly out of necessity. I'm a little way from town, away from the restaurants and fast-food places. That means I keep food on hand. I hope you like fish. I could make you a grilled cheese sandwich if you want," she said, giving him a quick smile.

"No. Fish is great. Can I peel potatoes, cook rice, make a salad?"

"Yes. Rice and a salad would be perfect while you tell me more about Haiti."

He couldn't tell her the real reason why he'd come home. He hadn't told anyone other than a psychologist he'd seen for a short time after he got back. Until he knew Nicole better, he wouldn't allow himself to confide in her. He didn't want her to see him as a weak, indecisive man, someone who had allowed his experience in Haiti to determine how he felt about life here in Spencer Island. He had a good life here, the respect of the locals and was sharing the kitchen with a woman who intrigued him. Yet he couldn't ease the feelings of guilt, the sense that he'd abandoned people who relied on him, especially his team leader, Grant Williams.

He took the bag of lettuce, the cucumber, celery and tomatoes she gave him and found a knife on the rack next to the stove. "The people I met in Haiti were the friendliest on the planet: interesting, committed. The friends I made while living in that country will always be a part of my life."

"Wherever my parents and I lived, we always enjoyed learning about the local culture. It's amazing how much we can learn from others, about how they live and work."

"That's true." Yet it was more than that for him. He'd been a part of the community. And that acceptance had resulted in him feeling needed and appreciated in ways he'd never experienced before.

They worked alongside each other in silence for a few minutes, he washing vegetables and she working on the rest of the meal. He couldn't help but notice how easily she battered the fish and put the frying pan on the stove in preparation for cooking the haddock.

"I'd better got going. I don't want you to have the fish ready before the rice is cooked," he said.

"I'll wait for you," she said. Her glance swept over him, her lips pursed.

"Is there a problem?" he asked.

"You need an apron." Pulling one from a hook on the side of the fridge, she wrapped it around his waist.

The way she moved to tie the knot, as if they'd been doing this for years, touched something in him. "Thank you," he said.

Nicole hadn't felt these feelings before. This sense of connection to someone, the feeling that he would understand should she decide to share her worries. Yet she wasn't about to do that, especially when she had this deep-down feeling that she might have found a man who had serious potential. She couldn't risk getting involved with him, only to have him walk out on her if she had to face treatment.

She didn't want to spoil her first real chance in years to have a relationship that might turn into something a lot more. No. Sharing too much this early on about something that might turn out to be nothing at all was hardly the way to hold on to a man who had the potential to be just what she was looking for.

She put her best place mats on the table, and all the while she kept glancing at him, at the way he so skillfully put the salad together. Clearly he had experience in the kitchen.

He taught her looking at him and smiled. "Rice?"

"In the long cupboard next to the fridge," she said.

Too late she realized she'd crammed that cupboard with

boxes of cereal and parts of her grocery order she hadn't found a place for yet. "Whoops!" She watched as cereal boxes tumbled out, landing at his feet. She rushed to scoop them up. "Sorry about that," she said, gathering up the boxes.

"I'm not sorry," he said, his voice a slow drawl that played along her spine, a thrill passing through her. She clutched the boxes in her hands as their eyes met. The deepest, bluest eyes she'd ever seen. There was just hint of stubble on his jaw. She wanted to run her fingers through his sun-bleached hair.

This man was simply too good to be true. There had to be a story here. Where were all the women in his life? No red-blooded woman could resist those eyes. Not a chance.

She pointed to the top cupboard. "The rice would be just over your right shoulder," she said, her voice sounding breathless in her ears. She put the cereal boxes on the counter and found the rice steamer in the bottom drawer next to the dishwasher, acutely aware that her rear end was sticking up in the air as she fished around the depths of the drawer.

Feeling self-conscious, she went to set the table, arranging a bowl of pink peonies she'd cut earlier. By the time she was finished fixing and fretting, her pulse was racing.

"The rice is nearly finished."

Darn! She'd forgotten to start the fish. "The fish will only take a few minutes," she said, hurrying back to the kitchen.

He'd already turned on the burner. "Butter?" he asked.

Wordlessly, she pointed to the white butter dish resting near the back of the counter. The man filled her tiny kitchen with his presence, his easy way, his sexy body. "Now, all we need is music," he said, maneuvering the frying pan over the hot burner to the sound of sizzling butter.

"What do you like?" she asked.

"When it comes to music, I'm old-fashioned. I was raised on '60s music, thanks to my mother's love of it."

"I like it, too."

He watched her slid the fish into the frying pan. "Did you get that from your mother, as well?"

"Not really. It's just great music."

"Couldn't agree more." He turned those blue eyes on her again and she felt her mouth go dry. "Plates?"

"Oh, yeah." She went to the cupboard and took out two plates. "I'll take the salad to the table," she said, feeling like a teenager suffering through her first crush.

They ate their dinner together, laughed lots to the accompaniment of their favorite music. "I haven't had this much fun since came to Spencer Island," he said, holding his coffee cup in his hand, his attention on her.

"Me neither."

He put his cup down and reached across the table, taking her hand in his. "Thank you."

"For what?"

"For inviting me to dinner. I should have called first, but was worried about you. Anyway, it's all turned out for the best, at least for me."

"For me, too," she said, suddenly remembering that she'd come home worried about her health, about what an illness might mean in her life, and ended up having a wonderful evening with a very sexy man.

"Let's get this cleaned up," he said, breaking the moment.

They carried the dishes to the kitchen, scraping them and putting them in the dishwasher. "I'll wash the frying pan," he offered.

"I like to let it soak in soapy water for a while to get any fish odor out before I wash it." She met his assessing glance. Was he waiting for something? Did he expect and invitation to stay the night?

"Look, I know I'm prying when I ask this, but are you really okay?"

"Why do you ask?" she hedged.

"Because you're different than the day we met. You're anxious, and I wondered if I'd done something to upset you."

"No. Not at all. You've actually made my day much better than it was."

"I'm glad, because you made my day for me. Seriously. I haven't had such a good time in a long while."

She hesitated, trying to decide… "I have a health issue I'm dealing with at the moment. Tomorrow, actually."

"And?"

"And I'm worried."

He leaned closer, his scent enveloping her. "Can I help?"

His expression was sweet and caring. How could she resist? "I'm going in for a biopsy tomorrow on a lump in my breast."

He pulled back, his eyebrows raised in surprise. "I'm sure it'll be fine. Lots of people have biopsies done and it's not cancer."

"How do you know?" she asked, annoyed by his dismissal of her concern. Even more annoyed with herself for confiding in him. Had she told him to have him show he cared? Did she want him to take over for her a little, offer her support, maybe take her to the clinic appointment, even though Angie had volunteered to drive her? Was she that desperate?

"Look, I know you're worried. Anyone would be. But you can't change the outcome by worrying. I found that out when my mom was diagnosed. You have to live for now, for what today holds. Life is for living every moment." He tipped her chin up, forcing her to meet his gaze. "I want to be here for you. This will be over, and you'll go on with your life. Don't invite trouble."

"Easy for you to say," she muttered, wrenching her gaze from his. "You don't understand."

"I do. I was there for my mother. I do understand. I just don't believe that worrying solves anything."

"Have you ever been in my position, waiting to know the outcome of a biopsy that has you terrified?" she demanded, her voice rising at each word she uttered.

"No. I haven't. I understand you're upset and need time to figure this all out."

"Meaning?"

"Think positive. Don't worry so much," he said soothingly, running his fingers along her cheek, which would have made her want him even more if he hadn't made her so annoyed by his attitude.

She couldn't cope with her feelings for him and her fear of the biopsy tomorrow all at the same time. She had never felt this confused and mixed-up and scared in her entire life. "It's been a long day, and I have to be at the hospital early tomorrow for my procedure. I'd like you to go."

His fingers stilled. A slight frown formed between his electrifying eyes. "Got it," he said.

She heard disappointment in his voice. But what had he expected? That they'd have sex? That her worry wouldn't affect the evening? And to think she'd been enjoying her time with him only a few minutes earlier.

She followed him out to the door, admonishing herself for wishing he'd pull her into his arms. Justin was all about Justin, about not getting close enough to support her in the way she needed.

When he got to the door, he turned. "Thank you. I had a great evening."

Did he really have a great evening, even after she'd told him about her biopsy? "You're welcome. Thanks for helping with dinner." She stood perfectly still, waiting for him to leave, wanting him to say something that would make her feel better, wanting him to offer his support.

"Next time we'll do it at my place," he said, giving her a look that said he wanted to say more, but couldn't.

Before she could respond, he opened the door, walked out to his truck and drove away. She couldn't believe it. He hadn't said one word that would make her feel better about what she faced tomorrow.

Was she right? Was he running away from her because of her health scare?

CHAPTER SIX

*B*ill Cassidy stared across his living room at the private detective he'd hired weeks ago. Ted Langley, a police officer who now worked for community policing, had recommended Peter Leighton as a good person to investigate Bill's suspicions around Nicole Simpson.

Shortly after she moved to Spencer Island, he'd met Nicole in the high school, looking at the group photos of the graduates that hung in the hall. Curious, he'd asked her what she was doing. She hedged for a few moments before asking him if he knew which year Ellen Donnelly had graduated and if her photo was here.

He'd been surprised at her question. He hadn't thought that anyone was interested in Ellen, certainly not anyone he knew in Spencer Island. And yet this young woman had taken the time to come to the school to find her. When he'd asked her why, she didn't answer. Having had a difficult day with a couple of his best basketball players and a championship game looming, he'd been very short with her. Rude, in fact. She hadn't brought the topic up to him again, even

though she'd been a regular member of the women's volleyball team he'd coached for the past year.

From the first practice when Nicole arrived on the volleyball
court, there had been something familiar about her. Because
of her skill and her willingness to learn more about the
game, they'd formed a close bond. He'd been giving her a
little extra instruction on her play around the net when he
spotted a birthmark that looked just like Ellen Donnelly's
birthmark. Yet because of his antagonism over Ellen, he'd let
it go. Lots of people probably had similar birthmarks. And
besides, Nicole Simpson hadn't said anything about why she
was interested in Ellen. But as the months rolled on and he
continued to coach every Wednesday night, he'd become
determined to satisfy his curiosity about her, which meant
that he needed to find a way to go about his inquiry without
letting anyone know.

He and Ellen had been in love in high school and had
planned to marry. Or so he believed. Until the day he'd come
home from college in Bangor to find she'd left Spencer Island
without saying a word to him. He'd tried to locate her, but all
her parents would say was that she'd left to live in Boston
with relatives. When he'd learned that wasn't true, he'd been
so angry he'd let the whole thing drop. If Ellen didn't want to
see him again, he would accept that.

Call it an aging man's need to connect with some element
of his past, but he couldn't help wondering if Nicole was
related to Ellen. Was Ellen her aunt? Was that why she'd
moved to Spencer Island? None of Ellen's family lived here
anymore, but maybe Nicole simply wanted to live by the
ocean. But the birthmark was just like Ellen's, and he hadn't
been able to quiet the suspicion that maybe Nicole was
Ellen's daughter. Wouldn't that be an amazing coincidence?

Yet his idea seemed far-fetched. He hadn't dared to share it with anyone. That's why he'd hired Peter Leighton to investigate for him.

Ellen Donnelly had been someone he couldn't forget, and if this was her daughter... "So, what do you have to tell me?" he asked.

Peter opened his file and handed Bill a photo of Nicole Simpson, taken a few years ago. "I got this photo off her high school site in Seattle. Nicole is the daughter of Ellen and Marcus Simpson. Her father was a chemical engineer for one of the big oil companies and has worked all over the world. Nicole has lived on virtually every continent, ending up in Seattle her last year in high school. She was in the top ten of her class, excelled at sports and was very popular. She trained to be a phlebotomist at the hospital and worked there for a few years. One day about two years ago, she left and moved to Spencer Island. The friends of hers that I interviewed said that she decided very suddenly to leave Seattle. Two of her high school friends are still in touch with her, and one suggested that Nicole had had a falling-out with her mother over something. They didn't know what."

"And her mother? Could you find anything on her?"

"Well, that's the interesting part. As best as I could determine, Ellen Donnelly Simpson left Spencer Island—"

Bill's sudden intake of breath was audible over the detective's voice. Peter Leighton looked up from his report, surprise evident on his face.

"I'm sorry. I didn't mean to interrupt. Go on."

"Ellen Donnelly left Spencer Island. I had a hard time locating where she went after that. There was no record of her in Boston, so I searched for Marcus Simpson. I discovered a marriage record in Virginia Beach. Marcus Simpson married Ellen Donnelly October 15, 1986. There is a birth record also of their daughter, Nicole Mae Simpson, born

December 10, 1987. Marcus is on the birth record as the father."

Bill did a quick calculation. Marcus was certainly not Nicole's father. Ellen hadn't left Spencer Island until September, just after he started his last year of college. Nicole had to be his daughter. Anger burned through him at Ellen's callous behavior. He had a right to know that he'd fathered a daughter. He had a right to be her father, to be aware that she existed and the chance to know her.

Instead, the woman he loved had gone off and married a man she hardly knew. Had Ellen done it simply to give her child a name? Or had she loved Marcus Simpson? Bill didn't believe in love at first sight, but maybe it happened. Who was he to know? He'd only ever loved Ellen, and that hadn't gone well at all. Now, he had proof that she hadn't loved him nearly as much as she'd pretended. Her lack of caring had left him out of his daughter's life completely.

He'd waited for twenty-nine years to hear from Ellen, but now be didn't care if he ever heard from her. A woman who would hurt another person like she had didn't deserve anyone's love of respect.

But Nicole was a different story. He wanted to get to know her; to tell her about her past...that she was his daughter. But how would she react to the news? Bill sighed. Nicole had to have known that her mother grew up here when she moved here. Had that been her motivation for coming here? And if so, how had she not known about him? Surely someone would have mentioned something to her,

"That's the basic facts of my investigation," Peter Leighton said.

The basic facts that told him the raw truth about the woman he'd loved. He balled his fingers into fists. "That's very helpful. I'd like to settle what I owe you."

The investigator passed an invoice to him. Bill wrote out

the check, his attention wavering as his thoughts raced. He had a daughter who was twenty-nine years-old, a phlebotomist, owned a small horse farm and played volleyball. That was all he knew about her. He intended to find out more: what her interests were and what mattered to her in life. Had she found someone to love? There had not been anyone waiting for her after their weekly practices or any of the games as far as he could remember.

"Thank you for your business." Peter Leighton said, breaking into Bill's thoughts.

"Thank you. You did a good job, and I appreciate it."

After the investigator left, Bill sat for a long time, remembering how much he'd once loved Nicole's mother. How that love had been a driving force in his life. But reading this report showed him that she sure as hell wasn't the woman he'd loved. That woman would never have kept his daughter from him. One thing was certain. After finding out about his daughter, he would not let this rest until he knew the whole truth. If Nicole was his daughter, he wanted to be part of her life. He ran his fingers over the file and then suddenly opened it to the page with the contact information for Ellen Simpson.

CHAPTER SEVEN

The next morning, Nicole was up early. Angie had insisted on picking her up and taking her to the hospital for her biopsy appointment. Nicole was ready when she pulled into the driveway. "Good morning," she said as she climbed in beside Angie.

"How did you sleep?" Angie asked, turning the car around and going down the driveway.

"I didn't. When I did I had this really strange dream about my mother calling to me from across a wide room, but I couldn't make out what she was saying."

"Ah, honey, you're missing your mom."

Without warning, Nicole's eyes stung with tears. She glanced out the window while she let the wave of loneliness pass. "I've never faced any type of surgery without my mom there for me." She took a deep breath, focusing her attention on the road ahead. "But I'm not a child anymore. I can go through a simple procedure like a biopsy without her being there."

"But this kind of biopsy?" Angie asked, her voice gentle as she eased up to a stop sign.

Nicole swallowed against her fear. "I know it's crazy, but I swear I could feel something this morning when I showered." Nicole smoothed her hair from her face and wiped the tears perched on her cheeks.

"You're going to be fine. You know that, don't you?"

Nicole loved that Angie was so upbeat, but Angie didn't know of her mother's history with breast cancer. Nicole had never felt the need to talk about her mother very much, much less about her breast cancer.

"Have you heard from Justin?" Angie asked as they drove into the parking lot at the hospital.

"He dropped by yesterday."

"And?"

"He stayed for dinner."

"Wow. You never have a guy stay for dinner. Is there something you're not telling me?"

"He arrived unexpectedly. I was feeling pretty awful about my doctor's appointment. He seemed really nice, very upbeat. I needed that."

"And?"

"Turned out he was way too upbeat for me. I decided to tell him about my procedure today. He acted like it was no big deal."

"A good-time-only kind of guy."

"Who knows?"

"I'm sorry he behaved that way."

"Me, too." Nicole frowned. "I think he's hiding something."

"What?"

"I'm not sure. It's just that he's so self-contained. Whenever you ask him anything he doesn't want to answer, he turns the conversation back on you. If there's anything unpleasant or unhappy, he makes light of it. If you ask me, he has some hidden flaw that makes him seem...removed from the normal problems of life."

"Let's not worry about him right now," Angie said, as she turned off the engine.

They went into the building together to the outpatient check-in. "This is where I leave you," Angie said. "Good luck. I'll pick you up when they discharge you."

"I really appreciate this. Thank you."

Angie hugged her. "Anytime."

Nicole was shown to a cubicle where she was instructed on what she needed to do. She was told the doctor was on time. Although Nicole had worried about the procedure, the biopsy barely hurt at all.

Gemma and Angie arrived together when it was time for her to leave. "So?" Gemma asked.

"Your husband is such a kind doctor, and he made me feel confident that everything would be okay."

"I'll tell him that," Gemma said with pride as she very gently hugged Nicole. "Now all you have to do is enjoy the ride home."

Nicole wished if were that simple. She was really worried, given her mother's history. For the second time that morning she wished she could call her. But calling her mom meant being willing to talk about their argument. That her mother told her that her dad wasn't her biological father was bad enough. She simply couldn't forgive her mother for not telling her the truth before, and for not saying who her biological father was, no matter how much she needed to know. Yet, she needed her mother right now, but getting in touch with her was more than she could handle at the moment.

As she looked from Angie to Gemma, she realized that although she'd come here searching for her mother's family, she did have a family of friends. Two women who were more like sisters. "You two are the best friends I could ever ask for"

They laughed as they linked arms and walked to the clinic entrance.

Angie drove her home, with the promise to come back and feed the horses for her. Nicole was sure she'd be okay to do it, but it was a lovely gesture. As she entered her house, her thoughts returned to her mother and father.

When Nicole decided to move from Seattle, she'd looked at the lot of properties on the internet but really focused her search on Spencer Island, where her mother grew up. Whoever her father was, he might have's connection to the place.

If he wasn't somewhere in or around Spencer Island, where was he? Why hadn't he come looking for her years ago?

She changed her clothes, donned sweats and a plaid shirt she'd kept of her father's and settled in to read on the sofa. She touched the small dressing over the incision and once again thought of her mother. Taking a breath, she reached for the phone to call her. As her fingers rested on the keypad, she couldn't decide what to do. Calling her mother meant listening to her plea that Nicole come to Seattle, that they needed to be together. Her mother would insist that cancer care was better in Seattle.

Yet it might be really helpful to hear more about the circumstances around her mother's cancer. All Nicole could remember was that she'd found a lump and they'd removed it.

Her thoughts on her past and her parents' behavior, she didn't hear the back door open, only the sudden knocking.

"Anybody home?" a now familiar voice asked.

She glanced up from her book. "Justin, what are you doing here?"

He stepped inside the door, closing it behind him, "I came by to see if you're okay."

He was the last person she expected to see today. "I'm fine. Angie drove me in and brought me back home."

"1 know. I stopped by and asked her about you."

"You did?" Despite his kindness, she was reminded of last night and his dismissive attitude toward her situation.

"I also brought a couple of sandwiches from the deli downtown if you're hungry," he said, his smile gentle as he held up the deli container.

She looked up into his handsome face, the reassurance in his eyes, and was suddenly so relieved that he was with her. "I'm famished."

"Good. I have a Greek salad and pastrami on rye or ham with Swiss cheese?"

"Ham," she said, reaching with her left arm to get two plates out of the cupboard. "Cola or water?"

"Water is fine." He placed the sandwiches on the plates and took them to the table.

They ate in companionable silence for a few minutes, "I have an ulterior motive for showing up here," Justin said between bites.

"I'm listening"

"I wondered if you might like to go out with me tomorrow night."

"Another date?"

"I thought we might take in a movie in Bangor, a little cheer-you-up adventure. Might even show you the house where I grew up."

Nicole listened to Justin's voice, a deeply sensual voice that made her feel excited and happy. After he'd left the other night, she wasn't sure she'd hear from him again. She'd consoled herself with the idea that not seeing him was probably just as well, given her health concerns and his earlier attitude. "A movie in Bangor? Sounds nice."

"You haven't asked what's playing," he said, humor showing through his words.

"You have one in mind, I assume," she countered.

"Do you like old movies? Tom Hanks in You've Got Mail?"

"I love that movie. And Tom Hanks and Meg Ryan are so good together."

"Then we're off to the movies tomorrow. I haven't been to a movie since I got back from Haiti. I've missed going to the theatre, loading up on popcorn and a soft drink and settling in with nothing to do but stare straight ahead at a screen,"

"You're not the kind who falls asleep in the middle of a movie, are you?" she asked.

"Not so far, but wait and see," he said, pointing his finger at her playfully.

He left shortly after, having cleaned up the kitchen for her. As she watched him, she had to admit that although he had appeared to take her health concerns lightly the other night, he'd gone out of his way to take her mind off her worries. She hadn't expected him to be so kind. Maybe she'd been a little unfair in her assessment of him.

The next day Justin had a client outside town, not far from where his mother had spent her summers on Cranberry Point. The road wound around the cliffs leading up from the ocean. The breeze was warm and filled with the scent of pine and saltwater.

The home he was going to belonged to Shelly Webster, a woman known around Spencer Island as willing to give her money to good causes. He drove up the long, tree-lined corridor to a large brick mansion covered with Engelman ivy reaching its leafy tentacles into the rough edges of the brick. He'd agreed to build a gazebo for her. When he stopped in front of the house, Shelly appeared from the backyard. Justin hopped out of his truck and came around to greet her.

"I'm so glad you're here. I've been quite a long time making up my mind on what wanted. But your lovely diagrams made the decision for me. The lumber you ordered arrived earlier and I had them place it where the gazebo is to go."

She turned and walked along the path to the back garden chatting about the luncheon she attended that morning, her diamonds sparkling in the sunlight, her perfectly coiffured hair and expensive suit stating emphatically that money was no object.

Justin couldn't help but contrast Shelly's life with those of the women in Haiti he'd become friends with. The perfumed air of the garden floated around them as they walked along the path, past copper sundials and statuary that complemented the ambitious landscaping plan.

"Isn't it beautiful?" she asked, her smile warm. "I had a landscaping company in Portsmouth do the design and installation."

Her words made him wonder why she hired him. He didn't have credentials other than the recommendation of a few locals, none in her financial league. "It's extraordinary," he said, searching his memory for a garden in Haiti even close to this one. The president's palace may have had such gardens, but if so he hadn't seen them.

Justin was pretty sure that the yearly upkeep of this place would go quite a way toward funding another orphanage in Haiti. "I'm wondering why you hired me to do this work when you have people you've dealt with before who would be guaranteed to do a good job."

"Good question." She turned to him. "I've decided to buy

local wherever I can, and you were highly recommended by Greg Mollins at the grocery store. You built a deck for him."

"I did." He watched her, wondering if he should approach her about the fund-raiser for Haiti he was hoping to organize here in Spencer Island. The one for the fire station had gone so well, he wanted to give it a try. "I spent time in Haiti, helping out with reconstruction. Hope to go back there someday."

"That's interesting."

"I plan to do a fund-raiser here, but I need local support. Would you be interested?"

She glanced at him, her expression guarded. "I thought Haiti had all the money it needed. Gracious, I remember the money pouring in from everywhere after the earthquake. Surely that's enough." She fingered the diamond pendant at her throat.

He tamped down his annoyance, realizing that the media coverage suggested that there was a lot of money going into Haiti. "No. The devastation is incredible. It's almost unbelievable."

"What's involved?" Shelly asked.

"Well, I'd like to run a silent auction and a live auction like they did for the fire station. A dinner and dance would certainly attract people in the area."

She eyed him.

He waited.

"Leave it with me: I'll see what I can do. In the meantime, I want you to build me a beautiful gazebo. If you do, I'll do everything I can to make your fundraiser a success. Deal?"

"Deal," he said, surprised. Grant Williams would be pleased to know that there would be more money for the plans he had for another orphanage,

"If you like, we can meet to discuss it while you're building the gazebo. Does that work for you?"

"It sure does," he said, adjusting his tool belt as he inspected the lumber. Getting her support had been much easier than he'd expected, making him pleased he'd acted so quickly.

That afternoon Nicole had just finished styling her hair and applying lipstick when Justin's truck roared up the driveway. She smoothed her blue flowered top with the drawstring neck and the short blue skirt over her body one last time. She slipped on her navy-blue sandals, grabbed her cream jacket and purse, locked the back door and went outside. He jumped out of his truck, a wide grin on his face.

"Well, aren't we eager to get to the movie...or maybe to see my handsome face," he teased, reaching into the back of the truck and pulling out a large bag of carrots. "I was doing a little work for a lady who likes to garden. I told her about your horses." He hefted a bag of fresh carrots over to the back step and put them down.

"No! Not there. Come with me," she said, leading the way to the barn. "We can't leave treats like that out where other creatures can find them." She opened the barn door and pointed to a huge metal container near the horse stalls.

He placed the bag in the can, dusted off his hands before turning to her. "So now you owe me."

"Owe you what?" she asked, enjoying the flirty tone in his voice.

"A thank you."

She smiled. "Thank you. And the next time you bring my horses something, I'll give you a free riding lesson."

"As much as I like new experiences, that's not on the list. Horses and I don't mix."

"You mean you're afraid of horses as calm and caring as Zeus and Suzie?"

"Thanks for the compliment...I think. It is my duty to inform you that big doesn't always mean fearless."

She couldn't help but laugh at him.

"You look so much better when you laugh," he said, taking her chin in his hands and kissing her lightly on the lips. ""You look a little like Claudette Colbert in The Egg and I."

"Who's she?"

"A legendary actress from the 1940s."

"You're that old?"

"Very funny," he chided her, but there was laughter in his voice. He took her hand, the callouses on his fingers scratching her palm. "I love old movies. Those were the real days of movie greatness."

"That's why we're seeing an older movie tonight?" she asked, trying not to squirm under his direct gaze and the pressure of his fingers on hers.

"I'm going to a movie with a very attractive woman, and devouring popcorn. That's probably enough for one night."

"Actually, we might already be late, Bangor is about an hour away. Want to take my car?"

"No offense, but your car is the perfect moose landing strip. You know, low to the ground, easy to fall onto the front and through the windshield?"

Nicole shuddered. "You're kidding me."

"No. There are moose on that highway, and they are big awkward animals who don't find it easy to get out of the way of a vehicle. We're much safer in my truck, It's higher off the ground, more engine and chassis to protect us should we hit one—"

"Enough! You made your point."

"By the way, who's paying? I eat a lot of popcorn," he said, a big grin on his face when she turned around.

"I'm paying?"

"Why not? This is, after all, an equal opportunity date. I drive. You pay."

"We'll see about that," she said.

They drove to the theater, laughing and talking all the way. This was shaping up to be a great date. He was fun, cute and sexy and had a body that any red-blooded woman would want to explore.

"Who would have thought that I'd be going out with a man who loves old-time movies?" she commented as she climbed out of the truck.

"Hey! Go easy on the old stuff. People might get the wrong impression about me," he said, coming around the truck and offering her his arm.

"Meaning?" she asked, linking arms with him.

"That because I like old stuff I must be dull."

She stopped. "You? Dull? Don't think so. But I do have one small request."

"Name it."

She pointed at his pocket. "Turn off your cell phone."

"Don't we do that inside the theater?"

"Yes, some of us do."

"You're in the habit of going to the movies with text-aholics?"

"One text message, and the date is canceled. That's my policy,"

"Got it," he said, turning off his phone.

"We'd better hurry," she said,

"Not until I tell you one of *my* policies."

"That would be?"

"I never go into a movie theater with a beautiful woman unless I'm holding her hand." He slid his hand into hers, his skin warming, inviting and oddly protective. "Oh, yes, and my other thing. Rule, actually." His eyes brimmed with laughter.

"And that would be?" she countered, loving his attention, his easy banter,

"You have a standing invitation to come to my apartment any day you like and watch any or all of my old-time movies."

"Very kind of you, I'm sure." she said, wondering what his apartment looked like, whether it was festooned with take-out boxes and dirty laundry, or whether he was as neat about his home as he was about his appearance.

The movie had already started, but neither of them seemed to care. Justin paid for the tickets, making her smile. The movie was wonderful. But all of it paled against the excitement Nicole felt sitting so close to Justin. She couldn't stop watching him, the way his hands held the bag of popcorn, how his lips curled around the straw. Everyday things took on a life of their own as she watched him.

His eyes met hers in the darkened theater. "Are you sure you don't want something to eat? I can go out and get you something."

"We're having dinner later, aren't we?"

"Yep. I've already picked out the spot." He placed his popcorn and drink on the floor beside his seat. Leaning back, he put his arm around her. She snuggled against him.

"Then I'll wait to see where we're going. Don't want to ruin my appetite," As she sat so close to him, she found it difficult to concentrate on the movie or the characters.

Justin drove carefully along the narrow road leading down to the beach at Murphy's Cove. He didn't want to make Nicole's ride uncomfortable. He had no idea whether or not she'd experienced any pain or discomfort since he'd picked her up at her house. The moon bathed the inside of the truck cab with soft white light, illuminating Nicole's heart-shaped face. "I had a good time this evening."

"So did I," she said, leaning back in the seat, a smile on her face. He loved it when she smiled. He loved it even more when he was the one who made her smile.

He executed the final turn along the road that opened out onto a long stretch of beach shimmering in the moonlight. He heard her sudden intake of breath and turned to look at her.

"What do you think?" he asked, wanting this moment, her eyes on him, to last forever.

"It's unbelievable. How have I lived along this coast for two years and not been to this place?"

"Don't know. I do know you're in for a treat. Sharkey's Fish and Chips are the best in Maine."

He pulled the truck into the only parking spot left along the front of the weathered building nestled against the rock face that ringed the beach. They walked in together. He loved the feeling of strolling along beside one of the prettiest women in the place. The top she wore showcased the swell of her breasts. He couldn't take his eyes off the short blue skirt she wore and her high-heeled sandals. The one part of a woman's wardrobe he loved more than sexy underwear was high heels.

They took a booth looking out over the water, the moon cutting an elongated sliver of light into the dark ocean water. The waiter arrived, placed plastic menus in front of them. "What would you like to drink?"

"Nothing alcoholic for me, I'm driving. But you have whatever you like, especially since I'm paying," he said, picking up the menu as he waited for her response.

"How kind," she replied, her gaze sparkling in fun, "And I'll take your advice, mostly because I'm starving." She checked out the menu then closed it. "I'll have your fish and chips."

"Large or super large?

"Really?" she asked.

"They only come in two sizes." The waiter held his pen over his scrunched-up notepad.

"I'll have the large and an iced tea."

"Knew you were a city girl the minute you walked in here. We don't serve iced tea. Ginger beer—great drink—no alcohol."

"Better do as the man says," Justin offered, hiding his grin behind his menu.

"Sounds good."

"I'll have the same," Justin said.

In a matter of minutes their food arrived, the fish crispy and the chips homemade. "I found this place on the day I moved to Spencer Island. I decided that I wanted to walk on the beach and spotted their sign on the highway." He took a huge bite of fish and smiled in pleasure.

Nicole picked up a chip and popped it in her mouth. A surprised smile lit her eyes. Her sigh of delight made him feel really good. He'd made the right choice. "Like them?"

"Love them," she said, cutting off a piece of the fish and eating it quickly. "With fish this good, I may want them to adopt me."

"It could be arranged, but I imagine you'd have to know something about cooking fish, cleaning deep-fat fryers, mopping up the kitchen, hefting large bags of garbage into a Dumpster-—"

"I get your point. Maybe we could settle for eating here a couple of times a month," she said, smiling. Her mention of dates to come made him unreasonably happy.

He couldn't believe that they were out on a date at his favorite restaurant on a moonlit night. He'd waited all his life for a woman like Nicole. He couldn't describe his feelings where she was concerned, except that being with her felt like coming home. Tonight, Haiti seemed so far away, so removed from his life.

They ate and laughed and talked. He didn't want the evening to end. "Instead of dessert, I have something entirely different in mind."

"If it's a moonlight swim, I didn't bring my swimsuit," she warned.

She'd be one hot-looking lady in a swimsuit. "No. But come to think of it, that's a great idea,"

"My objection still stands."

"Okay, Let's wait and do that another evening, one of those future evenings you mentioned earlier. But there's still something we can do."

"I'm not into feeding fishes," she teased, wiping her lips with her paper napkin.

His gaze locked on hers. "Close, but not the right answer."

"I'm waiting," she said, holding his gaze.

"We can go for a walk in the moonlight, along the beach, listen to the water pound the shore..." He reached for her hand. The sounds in the restaurant dimmed.

"That sounds wonderful," she said, her voice so soft and light he wanted to pull her into his arms.

"I'll pay the bill and meet you out on the deck. There's stairs down to the beach from there." He wanted to high-five someone, holler at the moon. Instead, he paid the bill.

She was waiting for him on the deck. "Now about that beach."

"You'd better remove those shoes of yours. Not really beachwear."

"I see your point," she said, kicking them off and leaving them on the deck near the stairs.

They went down the stairs onto the sand, linked hands

and began their walk towards the shaft of moonlight playing on the water. "This is awesome," she said as they strolled together, moving slowly now, feeling the cool breeze off the water, "I don't think I've ever seen such a beautiful sight. The coastline near Seattle is pretty nice, but this place..."

Eager to show her more of the beach, he pulled her along. When he got near the spot where he knew there was a dip in the sand hiding them from the restaurant, he stopped. "This place is one of the reasons I couldn't live anywhere else but Maine." Unable to resist her nearness, he put his arm around her shoulder.

"I could stand here forever, just like this, just the two of us," he said, startled by the rush of emotion his words had created in him. He'd meant every one of them. That was the really scary part. He meant them.

"Exactly how many women have you brought here on a date?" she asked, looking up into his eyes.

"Truth?" he asked.

"Of course."

Her upturned face glowed in the moonlight. "None...until now."

"I'm flattered."

"You should be. I have plans to start picking women up off the street and bringing them here any day now," he said, keeping the mood light.

She chuckled, a wonderfully melodious sound, "You have an answer for everything."

"Ah, that's where you're wrong," he said, shifting his gaze to the shoreline, watching the dark water roil and roar over the stones along the edge. "If I had the answer to everything, I'd know what you were thinking."

"That's easy. I'm thinking I haven't had such an enjoyable evening in a long time."

"My pleasure," he said, pulling her close again. He tipped her chin up and kissed her, slowly at first, tasting. Waiting...

She slid her hands up over his chest, around his neck, her body capturing his. He held her and kissed her, his body hard against hers. He held her tighter, his need for her growing stronger.

Her breath came in short gasps. With her body pressed to his, she whispered, "Make love to me."

He began to unbutton her top.

She leaned into him, her breath coming quickly, hot against his neck. She looked up into his face, her eyes dark, her lips parted. "Is this what you want?" he whispered, drawing her closer.

"Yes."

Suddenly remembering her incision, Nicole pulled back. "I'm just a little anxious." She let her arms come to rest against his chest, easing his hands away from her. Pushing a man as warm and sexy as Justin away was the last thing she'd ever imagined doing.

"Don't be sorry. I didn't hurt you, did I," he asked, stepping back.

"No."

"I want to hold you." He caressed her arms, making them tingle. His hands cupped her shoulders as he pulled her closer, his lips touching hers in a gentle kiss that made her head swim.

She moved into his arms once more, her fingers working up his muscled chest. "I haven't been with a man for a very long time," she said, her body trembling with excitement.

He pulled her closer and picked her up in his arms. "One evening when I was down on this beach, I found a great spot just a little farther along." He smiled down into her face, his eyes dark.

He carried her down the beach to the spot and eased her down along his body until she was standing on the cool sand. "I've never known anyone like you," he said, his hands working their magic through her hair, massaging her skin as his lips found hers again. With one easy movement, he slid to the ground, pulling her with him as he deepened the kiss.

With a deep groan of pleasure, she wrapped her arms around his neck and returned his kiss, her lips parted, her tongue tangling with his.

"I want you," he said, his voice a rasp as his hands explored her body. She was excited, anxious and eager. She wanted him, too. More than anyone she'd ever been with. Suddenly she didn't care about anything other than this man.

Out of nowhere laughter rang out. Voices competed with each other under the light of the moon. "We have company," she moaned, her heart skipping several beats.

Justin pulled her close, nestled her next to him, his grip solid and reassuring, "It would seem we do." He waved at the two couples laughing their way up the beach to where they lay semi-sprawled in the sand. "Nice evening."

"It is. Looks like you two are making the best of it," one of the men said. As they reached where Nicole and Justin now sat, one of the men leaned toward them. "Well, hello, Nicole. Nice to see you somewhere other than at the blood lab."

Nicole stared up into the man's face, "Peter Sherwood."

"That it is." He continued to stare, and Nicole knew beyond a shadow of any doubt that the minute he got back to his house he would tell his mother, Lisa Sherwood, that he'd seen her here. The woman believed she had something going on with Bill Cassidy, and now she'd have more gossip to share.

As they moved away, Nicole eased out of Justin's embrace

and hugged her knees, watching the foursome meander along the beach toward the restaurant. "You'll be the subject of gossip before midnight."

"What?"

"That was Ned Tompkins's nephew, also known as Lisa Sherwood's son. She is always minding other people's business. Now, she'll be minding yours."

"Couldn't care less," he said, pulling her back toward him.

"I care."

"Why?" he asked, his hands beginning their slow slide along her body.

"I'm sorry, Justin, but we need to go."

"Are you all right?" he asked, pulling her hand into his as he helped her up.

"Those people..." She stopped. What could she say that wouldn't sound stupid?

"Don't let them get to you. It's our night out. What they do doesn't matter, does it?"

"It does to me," she said, stepping out of his reach.

Justin cocked his hands on his hips and stared at her. "We could go to your place or mine, if that would be okay. But either way I want you."

"For how long?"

"What?"

"I'm not in the mood for a fling. Coming down here to the beach was a mistake."

"You really think that all I care about where you're concerned is having sex with you?"

"I honestly don't know," she said, searching his face, seeing the way the moon highlighted his strong features.

"How many ways can I prove it to you? I care about you. No, I can't read the future, but I would like us to have one."

"Am I to assume this isn't casual sex?"

"Hold on. Let's not start labeling things just yet." He

grimaced. "When it comes to women, I never seem to be able to say it right."

"Say what right?"

"I want to be with you tonight. Let's just go with that. You and me and the moonlight."

"And I want you. But you make it sound so...I don't know...so impetuous."

"I am impetuous, especially when it comes to you." He reached out and took her hand. "But we're consenting adults. We want each other. Let's just go with that."

"And if I don't?"

He frowned. "Nicole, what's going on?"

"What's going on is that you make me feel like less of a woman than I already feel. Have you forgotten what's going on with me?"

Even in the subdued light on the beach the shock on his face was evident. He pulled her against his chest. "Oh. God. I'm sorry. I wasn't thinking. I would never make you feel that way. You're the most gorgeous, sexy woman I've ever met. I would never hurt you."

His fingers gently massaging her back was such a turn-on she wanted to wrap her body around his. "Maybe next time? Another moonlit evening?" she asked.

The silence between them was unnerving. Why didn't he say something?

"Let's call it a night," she said, escaping his embrace and striding up the beach.

CHAPTER EIGHT

*J*ustin had spent several sleepless hours on why he'd behaved the way he had during last night's date. They didn't seem to be on the same page, and he didn't know how to fix it. He couldn't share his experiences in Haiti with her. And she was in a difficult place over her surgery. And he'd acted like an idiot on both counts.

What he hadn't bargained for was how he felt when he dropped her off at her place. He was trapped between his feelings for her and his sense of loss over leaving Haiti, especially the two orphaned children he'd been powerless to help.

How could he explain what happened to him there when he didn't understand it himself? Yet if he loved Nicole, he should be able to talk to her about something that mattered a great deal to him.

And Haiti mattered to him in ways he never expected. He'd been working as a carpenter in Bangor when he met Grant Williams. He'd been sitting in a coffee shop on his laptop when Grant sat down across from him. They struck up'a conversation, discovered that they both worked in construction, only Grant's work involved helping others, something that appealed to Justin. When he'd gotten to Haiti and saw how much he was needed, it was as if he hadn't lived. He'd returned, believing that his life in Haiti was over. He wanted Haiti to be over because he felt torn between his life there and living a familiar, predicable life at home.

But the longer he was back in the United States, the more he realized how he needed to go back. As much as he enjoyed his life here in Spencer Island, he couldn't give up his dream of making a difference in a place like Haiti. He'd felt exhilarated, essential and so involved there. And he couldn't seem to stop feeling that he'd abandoned the people who needed him.

How could he feel this way and expect a woman like Nicole to understand?

As he finished his coffee and headed out of his apartment to his truck and his workday, he felt a deep sense of having messed up the one relationship that mattered to him. He didn't know what to do next, but he did have to get to his appointment at the clinic with Dr. Dixon.

Once across town, he drove along the road leading to the clinic that was attached to Bonar Medical Centre. The air was scrubbed clean of any last remnants of fog, the sky seemed bluer today and the trees greener. He loved the pines, the spruce and the maple trees that lined the road, spreading up over the hills that climbed toward the sky. Yeah, he'd picked the right place, he thought as he pulled into the parking lot.

Once inside, he was tempted to stop by and see Nicole. Yet, he was well aware that until he'd come to terms with his feelings, his worries and his indecision, he had no right to involve her. If Haiti was part of his future, she needed to know that. Asking someone to make that kind of commitment in a relationship was a huge risk that few people could accept.

A few minutes later he checked in at the clinic desk and was immediately escorted into the treatment room. He hadn't seen either Angie Snyder or Gemma Dixon when he arrived, which was probably just as well. Nicole had almost certainly told them about last night.

In a matter of minutes, Matt Dixon appeared. "Good morning, Justin. Your blood work came back. All the tests were within normal limits. No worries there. How's your arm?" he asked, motioning for him to sit up on the stretcher while he washed his hands before opening the suture removal tray.

"It seems to be fine. I put a fresh dressing on it each day, cleaned up the incision like the nurse told me to do. Not too much blood."

"I take it you're not crazy about the sight of blood."

"You could say that," Justin answered, remembering the day he'd been here getting stitches and how he'd felt. He wouldn't forget that day for two very good reasons.

Matt approached him with a disposable sheet and put it under his arm on the table. "This won't take long," he said, removing the bandage and checking the stitches.

"Did you enjoy the fund-raiser the other night?" Matt asked as he began removing the stitches.

Justin didn't feel a thing, but that didn't make him want to look where the doctor was working on his arm. "It took a little convincing to get Nicole to go, but once we got there, we both enjoyed it. I haven't danced in years. Good to know I still remember my right foot from my left. What about you?"

Dr. Dixon smiled in understanding. "We had a great time, too. Brought back a lot of memories for Gemma and me. When we were in high school, we used to go to the dances, where I would routinely tread on Gemma's toes. Not much has changed in the dancing department, but it was fun to try."

"I know what you mean," Justin said, liking Matt better each time they met.

Justin watched each movement Matt Dixon made. He was relieved there hadn't been any blood. He didn't want to wimp out in front of a man who was so at ease around such things.

"I understand from Gemma that you and Nicole have started dating."

They'd been talking about him? "Yeah."

"Glad to hear it. Nicole's a wonderful person." There was a smile on his face when he looked at Justin. "I'm not into matchmaking, but I have a wife who thinks that everyone on the planet is entitled to find the perfect person to share their life with," he said.

"I'm not very good at relationships," Justin admitted, sensing that he could talk to Matt, one man to another.

"Same here, I made a huge mess of my relationship with Gemma back when we graduated from high school. Took me years to put things right."

He was relieved to hear Matt admit that he'd had problems when it came to women. He wondered what else they might have in common. Having been busy getting his business started, Justin hadn't had time to meet any guy friends. He sighed in resignation. "I'm not sure that I can make a commitment right now, and so I don't want to lead Nicole to think that I can. But then, I don't want to come across as not interested, because I am. Seriously interested, I mean."

"Damned if you do and damned if you don't. I hear you. Women seem to find the whole relationship thing so easy." Matt put a fresh bandage on Justin's arm without causing him so much as a twinge of pain.

"You're right. I'd rather build a whole house than figure

out how to make a woman happy. I'm just not good at it, and it makes it pretty hard when I'd like to get it right so bad."

"You really like Nicole, don't you?"

"I do. She is gorgeous, so easy to talk to, a great sense of humor, and she—" Justin stopped. He sounded like a kid describing his first girlfriend.

Matt smiled. "I get it." He peeled off his surgical gloves and placed them on the tray. "But don't give up. I did the first time, and I lived to regret it."

"How did you manage to get it right the second time?"

"I just kept trying, I had hurt Gemma and didn't have much faith that we'd make it. But knowing she'd never really given up on us made anything seem possible."

"Nicole and I don't have any history that might help us."

"Not having a history can be a good thing. No leftover hurt, no past behavior to atone for."

"I can understand that."

"Justin, want to grab a beer sometime? I work a crazy schedule most days, but I'd enjoy getting out to the pub some night if you're interested. I bought a lovely old Victorian house on the edge of town that you might find interesting. The woodwork's outstanding."

At the man's words, Justin was suddenly aware of how much he'd like to have a male friend. He missed his team leader, Grant Williams, his closest friend and a man he admired for his devotion to his aid work. "A beer some night would be great. I don't work nearly the hours that you do, or carry that kind of responsibility, but a night out is just what I need."

"Then let's do it." Matt gave him his private cell phone number. "You can reach me on this."

"You're the one with the heavy schedule. Call me any evening and I'd be game to go." He passed his business card to Matt.

"Thanks, I will."

Justin left the clinic area, encouraged by Matt's admission and anxious to drop by to see Nicole for a few minutes. He wanted to explain how he felt, why he wasn't quite ready to be involved in a relationship. When her clinic area there was a lineup and he could hear a child screaming in the room behind the desk. Not a good time to pay her a visit. He'd call her later when she got off work.

In the meantime, he had another job to go to, this time down by the harbor. The old pool hall had been closed, but a group of teenagers had started using it as a hangout. The new owners had liability concerns and wanted the building closed up and the exterior areas cleaned. A large floodlight was to be installed near the old entrance to the building. He'd have to get an electrician for that part, but the rest he'd manage on his own. Climbing into his truck he checked his cell phone. No new messages.

Nicole's day had been filled with crying children, older people who didn't hear well and needed her to talk louder, and the phone never stopped ringing: all of it leaving her with a pounding headache when she finally got off work. Despite all the activity, she couldn't keep her thoughts off Justin and last night. After his strange behavior on the beach, when they got to her house, he'd made it clear he wanted to come in with her. She'd been totally confused,

She wasn't going to tolerate being treated like some pathetic, lovesick woman. She'd lived through one of those scenarios with a man she'd dated a couple of times back in Seattle. She'd believed he shared her feelings, only to discover that he told one of her friends she was needy. An unpleasant scene had ensued, during which she told the man she didn't want to see him again.

If sex was all Justin wanted, he was about ten years too late for that. She learned early in her search for a man that having sex was meaningless if it was done simply to pretend an intimacy that didn't exist. She remembered how she once believed that having sex was the beginning of making a commitment. How wrong she'd been. Lesson learned, she mused.

Life always seemed so complicated once there was a man in it. Justin Hadley was completely wrong for her, regardless of how charming he was, or how much she was attracted to him. They didn't share the same values. He was a man who lived life in the moment, one moment at a time. He didn't worry about tomorrow: lucky for him.

In contrast, she didn't take risks if she could avoid them. It made her uneasy to find herself faced with uncertainty. She needed to feel in control, prepared for whatever happened next, not flying by the seat of her pants like Justin did,

In her experience, the one way to limit risk was to plan ahead, to know where the pitfalls were in any situation. Her dad had taught her that. He'd lived and worked in several different countries where if you didn't have a plan, didn't know the country and its customs, things could become complicated and sometimes dangerous. Marcus Simpson was one of the smartest people she'd even known, and he'd taught her how to live her life. To prepare for the future and to learn from the past.

She fed Zeus and Suzie, then cleaned up the kitchen. She'd have a relaxing soak in the tub, read for a while and forget about Justin, about whether or not they had a future together. Her future held more urgent issues at the moment.

There had been a message on her phone from Dr. Dixon's office. He wanted to see her. She tried not to think about what might happen tomorrow. She wished she could call her mom, share her fears. All she had to do was pick up the phone. It would be three hours earlier in Seattle... But she didn't have the energy right now. Her mother would talk for a long time, try to convince her to return to Seattle. Try to tell her what to do about tomorrow.

She filled the tub, put in some of her favorite bath salts and lit the candles along the wall. She'd worry about calling her mother after tomorrow. Tonight, she needed to relax and hope that she could get to sleep.

After a restless night Nicole entered Matt's office the next morning, her palms were sweaty. She'd slept two hours total and was now facing a long day that could go either way. When the receptionist called her name, she went in and sat down.

Dr. Dixon walked in and closed the door behind him. She held her breath as she met his glance.

"You don't have cancer. The biopsy showed at benign cyst."

"No cancer," she echoed, her voice breaking. She'd been so afraid, so anxious about what cancer would mean to her, to her life, that she'd forgotten that the test could come back negative.

"No cancer," he confirmed. "However, with the history of breast cancer in your family, you need to have mammograms regularly. I need you to fill out a family history form so that we can determine your risk."

How could she fill out a family history when she didn't know who her biological father was? Her mother's history of breast cancer was a huge concern, but her mother had been okay since her first incident.

She thanked Dr. Dixon and left his office, heading over to the clinic to tell Angie and Gemma her good news. She parked her car and hurried into the clinic area. Angie looked up as she approached the desk. "How did it go?"

"I'm okay," she said as tears of relief filled her eyes.

Angie came around the desk and wrapped her in hug. "I knew it."

"I didn't. When Dr. Dixon walked into the room, I was sure he was going to give me bad news. What an awful feeling! To have him say the cyst was benign was such a relief."

Gemma rushed toward them from down the hall. "Nicole. Tell me," she demanded.

"No cancer," Angie said, releasing Nicole.

"That's great news. Why don't we go out tonight to celebrate? We haven't done that in ages. We could have supper at the pub."

"Sure. That sounds great, I'll have to go home first and look after my horses," Nicole said.

"Okay. Let's do it. I'll get supper ready for Troy and Ted and meet you at the pub." Angie stopped. "Oh, wait a minute, Troy has a group project he has to work on tonight."

"Not to worry, Morgan is in his group. Matt can drive them and pick them up. He's not on call tonight," Gemma said.

"Maybe you'd rather spend the evening with him," Nicole said, remembering the wedding and the wonderful ceremony.

"It's okay. He's off on the weekend, and we're planning a trip to Boston, He wants to take Morgan und me to a baseball game."

"That sounds like fun. Okay, you two, I'll see you at the pub around six. Would that work?" Nicole asked.

"Are you going to tell Justin your good news?"

Nicole chewed her lip, glanced from Angie to Gemma and back again. "I'm not sure about Justin. I mean, I told him about the biopsy, but he was so flippant about it. He made me feel like was worrying about nothing."

"Turned out he was right," Angie said.

"That's not the point. I needed him to take my concerns seriously. And when we were out to dinner last night, and he..." She looked at her hands. "He... One minute he seems excited to be with me, and the next he's acting like I'm in the way. And he's so distant at times, so hard to read. One minute he's fun, the next withdrawn. As if he'd rather be somewhere else. I wonder if going out with him was a mistake."

"Why? You've enjoyed being with him, haven't you?" Gemma asked.

"Yeah. But Justin's not into anything more than the present tense, if you know what I mean."

"Maybe he's afraid of commitment," Angie offered.

"I'm not asking him to commit to anything. I just want to have fun." That wasn't strictly true. She wanted more than that, and she was disappointed by his attitude. "I'm not sure what he wants."

"Do you suppose he's not sure, either? What would happen if you talked to him, explained how you felt?" Gemma asked. "It made a big difference to Matt and me. Still does."

"It's different for you. You and Matt are in love," Nicole said. "You trust him not to hurt your feelings."

"If you ask me, you and Justin are both afraid of commitment," Angie said.

"What do you mean?" Nicole said, a little surprised by Angie's suggestion.

"You're not a risk taker. Admitting that you're emotionally involved with a person is risky business," Angie said. "I should know. Remember how afraid 1 was that Ted couldn't possibly love someone like me? I had to be dragged kicking and screaming into believing that he even cared."

"But you seem to forget that I packed up and moved all the way across the country to Spencer Island, a place I'd never been before and where I knew no one. I'd call that pretty risky, wouldn't you?"

"That's not the kind of risk I'm talking about," Angie said, giving her a knowing smile. "I'm talking about risking your heart, your feelings."

"It may not be the same thing. But it doesn't make you right about whether I'm a risk taker is all I'm saying," Nicole argued.

"Okay. Enough, you two. I'll see you both at Rigby's," Gemma said, picking up a chart and heading down the hall toward the exam rooms.

Later, around six in the evening, they reached the pub and found a booth across from the bar. Country, music pulsed from the speakers. The smell of French fries soaked the air.

"I think the last time the three of us were here together was for your birthday, wasn't it, Nicole?" Gemma asked, scooting across the wooden bench to let Angie sit down next to her.

Nicole sat down across from them, feeling so lucky to have them as her best friends. "Was it that long ago?"

"I remember that night only too well. I joined a group huddled around the respiratory therapist-hot though he was-to discover he was not nearly as hot as he thought he was," Angie said, adjusting her sparkling diamond on her ring finger.

"Just think. If you'd stuck with me you would have met Ted a lot sooner than you did," Gemma said, her eyebrows dancing.

"As I remember that evening. You didn't stay around long enough to introduce anyone to anybody. You went off home, leaving me to find my own way," Angie said, pretending to pout.

"Don't kid with me. You can take care of yourself," Gemma said.

The waiter arrived, and Nicole recognized him immediately. "Marty Smith, I didn't know you worked here."

"I like to make a little extra to send Blake to day camp next summer. How are you doing? Thanks for all the help you've given Blake. He's reading a lot better. We really appreciate it. I was going to talk to you about riding lessons the next time you're at the house," Marty said.

"It would be so much fun to teach Blake how to ride." If Blake liked Suzie and Zeus, she'd give the parents a break on the cost of the lessons. She introduced Marty to Angie and Gemma.

Marty smiled in welcome. "I'm your waiter for tonight, ladies. I'll take your drink orders and leave the food menus with you."

"I'll have a Coors draft," Nicole said.

"Same for me," Angie chimed in.

"Ginger ale for me," Gemma said.

"Have you got an upset tummy?" Angie asked after Marty left the table.

Gemma's smile was shaky. "No. Well, yes, just a little."

"Is your blood sugar okay?"

Gemma picked up her food menu. "Yes, I checked it just before I left home," Gemma said.

They sipped on their drinks, gave their orders when Marty returned-seafood casserole with rice for Gemma, chicken quesadillas for Nicole and Angie—and settled in for a quiet chat while they waited for their food. "By the way, what does either of you know about Ned Tompkins?" Nicole asked.

"He was in my class in high school, He didn't play sports and he didn't take part in most school activities except the debating club. He was pretty good at that," Gemma said.

"He was here the night of Nicole's birthday party, right? Wasn't he dancing with you, Gemma?" Angie asked.

"You're right. Yeah, he was talking to me about how a reunion of our high school class would be a good idea now that Matt had moved home. I think he was hoping to see what I'd say on the subject of Matt. Half the town was waiting to see what would happen between Matt and me," Gemma said ruefully.

"The biggest romance to hit Spencer Island ever, and I was here for it. Part of the wedding party, as well," Angie said proudly.

"What else do you know about Ned?" Nicole asked, drawing quizzical glances from both of the other women.

Gemma stirred her ginger ale with her straw, forcing bubbles to rise up the glass. "Not much. Although he was an A student, he didn't go to college. He took a job at the supermarket. His parents died a few years ago and left him and his sister, Lisa Sherwood, financially well off. I've heard that

neither Ned nor Lisa need to work again if they don't want to."

"Did he ever have a girlfriend?" Nicole asked.

"He dated one of the girls in the year behind us, but her family moved away from here before she graduated. Why are you asking all these questions?" Gemma said.

"In all the time I've lived on my firm, he mostly kept to himself, helpful and all that. Lately he's been asking me questions..."

Angie sat up straight and looked directly at Nicole. "What kind of questions?"

"He wanted to know about my relationship with Coach Cassidy."

"What! Why would he think you had a relationship with the coach?"

Nicole hadn't planned to say anything to anybody about her conversation with Ned. Somehow, admitting to Ned's remarks made what he implied real. But now that she'd brought it up, she felt the need to keep going. "Ned told me that Lisa told him that Coach Cassidy was paying too much attention to me, and people were starting to talk, or words to that effect. I don't have any relationship with Coach Cassidy except on the volleyball court, but since Ned made the insinuation, I can't help but worry that others may think there's something going on. You now, once a rumor starts it's hard to stop."

"Don't you worry. No one will be saying anything about you and the coach around either of us," Angie said.

Gemma patted Nicole's hand. "Stop worrying. He's harmless."

Nicole watched her friends begin to eat as she played back their comments in her mind. Ned was a man with not much of a past and probably not much of a future. No one special in his life, no plans and probably little opportunity or willingness to break out of the rut he was living in.

She didn't want that to happen to her. She wanted someone to love, someone who would love her and care for her. Someone to have a baby with. She smiled ruefully two herself; she wanted it all.

The next day, after a fun evening with her friends, Nicole was content to be back at her desk; her health worries over and her life back to normal. Her day went really well, and she was ready to head home to her horses and take a long ride out over the fields behind her house. She pulled into her driveway only to see Ned Tompkins coming across the field from his place. A little annoyed, she got out of her car. "Hello, Ned."

"Hello," he said, coming toward her. "Busy day?"

"Yeah. What can I do for you?"

"It's more what I can do for you. I'm pretty handy around the property, and if you need my help with anything; you only have to ask."

"Ned, that's very kind of you. I really appreciate it. I'm sorry I was so sharp with you the last time we talked."

"That's okay. I don't mean to come across so nosy, but I can't help but worry about my neighbors. Until you moved here, my only neighbor was a summer resident. It can be pretty lonely here when no one lives along the road. You've been here nearly two years, and I should have been more of s neighbor than I've been."

"We can both try to be good neighbors, can't we?" she asked.

"Absolutely. When I saw my carpenter over here doing work for you, I realized that it wasn't very neighborly of me to not be offering to help you. I'm pretty good at handyman stuff."

"Any good at looking after horses?" she asked, half-joking, as she walked toward the barn and opened the door to the sound of stamping horse hooves.

"Not really, but I could learn, I suppose," he said, sounding a little anxious.

She opened the stalls and led both animals out into the paddock. "I left them in today because I plan to ride both of them this afternoon."

"Your horses sure can run. I've watched them galloping around your field." He followed her out of the barn. "You know where I am if you need me." With that, he crossed the field and went into his house.

Nicole saddled up and went for a ride on Suzie, feeling the best she'd felt in a long time. She had good friends, a man who wanted to be a good neighbor and great horses. But most of all, she didn't have cancer.

She hadn't heard from Justin, He hadn't called to see how her appointment went. She'd been hurt by his lack of interest. She couldn't deny that she found him fun, sexy and entertaining, but that wasn't all it took to have a lasting relationship.

Given that he hadn't been in touch with her since her appointment, she couldn't help but wonder if she'd been right the first time. Justin Hadley wasn't into anything that wasn't upbeat and positive.

After she finished riding, Nicole went into her tack room. She had been avoiding it for weeks because every part of the space needed a good cleaning. As she stepped inside, the first thing she noticed was that the hinge on the door didn't squeak, something that had been driving her nuts every time she entered the room. The second thing she noticed was that the room was absolutely spotless. Every piece of horse harness, leads, saddles, her helmets, the oils and cloths used to keep the equipment clean were neatly stashed on shelves or hooks. Even the window had been cleaned inside and out. She glanced up into the rafters of the small building housing her tack room, and there wasn't a cobweb in sight.

The only person who would have done this was Ned. Had that been why he'd popped over here? Did he want her to thank him for doing all this work? Or did he have something else in mind?

She went back out the door, glancing over at Ned's place searching for his truck. His bright blue truck was parked near the flower bed along the side of his house. She crossed the field to him. "Hi, Ned," she said.

The shovel leaped out of his hands. "I didn't see you there," he said, picking his shovel out of the dirt before turning to her.

"I didn't mean to startle you. I came over to thank you for everything."

"What do you mean?"

"The way you cleaned up my tack room. It hasn't been that nice since I moved into the place. And the plastic bins you put in to take care of the odd pieces of harness gear are wonderful. Wish I'd thought of doing that."

He gave her a blank stare. "I didn't clean your tack room."

"Then who did?"

"I haven't a clue."

"But you must have seen someone going down past your place." She glanced around the open fields toward the house at the end of the lane. "The Crandall family haven't been here in weeks, so I don't know who else would have been here."

"I didn't see anyone," Ned said stubbornly.

Nicole felt a shiver tingle down her shoulders. "I didn't, either, so we've got to find out what's going on."

"If I were you, I'd talk to the police," Ned said. "Was anything stolen?"

"Not that I'm aware of."

"Then contact the police. I'll go with you if you need me," he said, his expression sincere.

"Thank you, but you needn't bother. I'll go in on my way to work."

Ned squared his shoulders. "If you ask me, this is real serious. I'll keep a more careful eye on your property when I don't see your vehicle there."

. . .

Nicole didn't go to the police the next day. She'd gone into work still wondering who had been at her house. The thought that whoever it was might just as easily have been in her house unnerved her.

Yet, she wanted a chance to talk to Gemma about this. Getting someone in trouble for an honest mistake or misunderstanding didn't seem fair. She still wasn't convinced that Ned hadn't done it. He was the only one who would know whether she was home or anything about her daily pattern. Anyone else would have had to find a time when she wasn't there and when Ned was away, as well. Otherwise, whoever it was would run the risk of being found out by Ned.

Gemma always said that Ted Langley, her cousin and Angie's fiancé, would be able to answer any legal questions because he'd been a member of the Boston police force before being shot and injured. When Gemma dropped by Nicole's desk on her way in to the clinics, Nicole explained what had happened to her.

"You're kidding me," Gemma said, her eyes wide with disbelief.

"Cross my heart. I came home, went into my tack room and it was totally neat and cleaned, swept, everything organized and ready for me to enjoy. It hasn't been that clean since I bought the place."

"And your neighbor?"

"Denies any involvement."

Gemma tapped the counter in thought. "Well, I have no idea who would do this, but I'll call Ted and see what he can suggest. I'm sure he'll want you to go to the police."

"I realize that, but I just feel funny about it all."

"Why?"

"Because someone went to a lot of trouble and nothing was stolen. I have to say that I really appreciate what this person did for me."

"Do you have a secret admirer? Someone you haven't told us about?" Gemma asked, twitching one eyebrow and smiling.

"I don't have any admirers, secret or otherwise."

"What about Justin? He seems like a man who wants to do nice things for you."

"Except for his Happy Harry attitude."

"A trait many women would appreciate."

"I'm sure. And I'm equally sure that's why I haven't heard from him. He's busy being appreciated by some new woman in his life."

"You didn't answer my question. Is Justin a candidate?"

"I doubt it."

"But you'll ask him."

"I'll call him today and find out."

Nicole nodded in the direction of the corridor. "Speaking of your cousin. Is that not the man glued to Angie's side?"

Gemma turned to look down the corridor. "It is." She beckoned to them. "Come here you two. We need advice."

Ted and Angie walked together into the phlebotomy department, wearing matching smiles with not a care in the world. Ted wasn't using his cane this morning, and Nicole was pleased. Angie had told her that he'd been feeling better, had been sleeping better and as a result he'd been having less discomfort in his hip. That's what love can do for you, Nicole mused.

"What's up?" Ted asked.

Nicole explained her situation.

Ted rubbed his jaw in thought. "I'm going to speak to a few people and see what I can find out. You only have one other permanent resident on your road if I remember correctly?"

"And he says he didn't do it."

"Is there anyone else who might have?"

"Justin Hadley came over one day and offered to do any handyman chores I needed done."

"What about him?" Ted asked.

"I don't think he'd go near anything to do with horses. He's afraid of them."

"But he wouldn't need to go near the horses to clean your tack room, would he?" Ted asked.

"I suppose not. I'll talk to him when I get the chance. He had been doing work for Ned Tompkins and might have seen someone at my place," Nicole offered, relieved to have someone as competent as Ted Langley to take this on for her.

CHAPTER NINE

*B*ill Cassidy had had a long, frustrating day, and one filled with sadness and regret. He'd been trying to keep himself from going to Nicole Simpson's house and talking to her about the evidence he had that she was his daughter. Since the private investigator he'd hired had delivered his report, Bill hadn't slept. He wanted to talk to his daughter.

It had been Ted Langley who had recommended the private investigator to him, and it was Ted who had been the only one he'd confided in about needing one. He had chosen Ted because he was an ex-police officer, and someone he knew well.

He was just finishing up some paperwork when Ted Langley arrived at his office. He welcomed him in, noting that his friend had always appeared calm, taciturn and serious, a very typical police officer in Bill's mind. But today Ted looked so different, so happy.

Bill listened as Ted talked about a young teenage girl, Linda Holmes, who was having trouble at home, and who was skipping school and hanging out with the wrong crowd.

A very typical story among teenagers today, Bill thought as he listened and offered what help he could. He'd grown up with Linda's aunt Cindy, who had worked at the local pharmacy. Some days it felt as if he'd grown up around half of the population of Spencer Island.

Ted cleared his throat. "I haven't noticed any difference with Linda Holmes. She's always tried to get out of the physical education classes, and that hasn't changed. I see her once in a while hanging out with a couple of girls who share her attitude about going to class. Other than that, I'm afraid I can't be much help."

"I had a meeting with her teacher. We're planning a meeting with Linda's parents, and I'd like you to attend."

"Sure. Just let me know when."

Ted leaned back in the chair, his gaze fixed on Bill. "Linda Holmes isn't the only reason I'm here."

Bill frowned. "What else did you want to talk about?"

Ted rested his forearms on the arms of the wooden chair. "Bill, do you know anyone who might have been near Nicole Simpson's house or farm buildings?"

"What?" Bill asked, startled.

"She's asked me to look into it. I thought you might know something."

"Why me?" Bill asked.

"I'm asking anyone who has a connection to Nicole. Given that you coach her in volleyball, I wondered if you might have heard something."

Bill glanced at Ted and sighed in resignation, "Yeah, I went out there one day hoping to find her home. She wasn't, I was curious about where she lived. When I found her tack room in such a mess, I cleaned it for her."

The look on Ted's face was a mixture of disbelief and shock. "Why?"

Bill drew in a deep breath. "I don't want this to get around because I haven't talked to Nicole about it yet." The way Ted looked at him was a little intimidating. "Remember when I got the name of the private investigator from you back a couple of months ago?"

"Yes. Did he work out okay?"

"He did. The man carried out my request, and it turns out that Nicole Simpson is my daughter. He found a birth record in Virginia showing that Ellen had a baby girl, that she married Marcus Simpson, the man whose name was on the birth record as the father. According to the investigator, that can't be true. Nicole is my daughter."

"Nicole is your daughter?" Ted looked at him with complete surprise.

Bill rubbed his palms together. "That's why I needed a private investigator. I wouldn't have had to go to such lengths if Ellen Donnelly had told me about her."

"How can you be so sure?"

"Because her birth record showed that she was born almost exactly nine months after the last time Ellen and I were together. Peter Leighton flew to Seattle a few weeks ago and interviewed Ellen, and she told him the truth. Nicole is my daughter."

Ted leaned forward. "What a way to find out. I don't know what to say."

"Neither do I. I have no idea about how to talk to my daughter, how to tell her the truth or how she'll react. It will be one hell of a surprise to her, given that Marcus Simpson is the name on her birth certificate."

Ted leaned closer. "This seems like quite the coincidence, the two of you living in the same town all this time. You're sure Nicole doesn't know about you? She moved here. Maybe she wanted to be near you, and maybe she doesn't know how to approach you about it."

"I can't believe she wouldn't have said something by now.

She's on the volleyball team I coach, and she's lived here for two years. If she chose Spencer Island to get to know me, or for us to spend time together, why wait so long?"

"What you say makes sense. Have you talked to Ellen?"

"I'm planning to call Ellen before I approach Nicole." He gripped the edge of the desk as anger burned through him. "I don't know if I can ever forgive Ellen for keeping Nicole from me, depriving me of the single most important thing in my life. I love kids. That's why I became a physical education teacher in this school. Kids have been the focus of my life. But to answer your question, I need to have Ellen tell me the truth about my daughter."

"That's really too bad. Don't know how I'd feel if I were you right now. I've always wanted children," Ted said, meeting his glance. "I don't want to add to your difficulties, but you know you shouldn't be going out to Nicole's place without her permission. Such behavior could be seen as stalking."

He leaned back in the chair, appalled at the thought. Why hadn't he thought about how his innocent trip to Nicole's home would look to anyone but him? He scrubbed his fingers through his hair, embarrassed by what he'd done. "You're right. I wanted to be helpful. It won't happen again."

"One of us has to tell Nicole. She's worried and concerned, as you can imagine."

"I'll call her and apologize."

But it was a lucky break that Ted had brought this to his attention, or it might have turned out to be even more embarrassing if Nicole had gone to the police. He needed to talk to Nicole, get this all out in the open. "Thank you for telling me about this, I really appreciate it."

After Ted left, Bill went home. He found Ellen's phone number in the PI's report and called her. When she picked up the phone, he knew her voice instantly, "Ellen."

"Yes. Who's this?"

Did she not have caller ID? "It's Bill Cassidy."

There was a pause, then an audible gasp. "Bill!" Her phone clattered onto the floor. A few minutes later she came back on the line, "I'm sorry, I wasn't expecting to hear from you. It's been a long time. How are you?" she asked.

"How do you think I am? Why didn't you tell me I had a daughter, and that she has been living here in Spencer Island for the past two years?"

The silence on the other end of the line gave Bill a moment of satisfaction. Now it was her turn to feel a little of what he'd been feeling.

"I don't know what to say."

"You can start with why you walked out of my life without saying goodbye, without bothering to tell me I was going to be a dad."

"Bill, I'm sorry for everything I did back then. Everything I did to you, to us. But I couldn't face a lifetime in Spencer Island, and you wouldn't consider living anywhere else."

He wanted to deny her words but couldn't. It was true. "You could have talked to me."

"You always changed the subject."

"I'm not changing the subject now. I want to know why you didn't tell me about Nicole."

"There is no excuse or explanation that will make sense to you. I left, afraid you'd follow me and find out that I was expecting our baby. But you didn't. My mother knew where I'd gone. She told me you called a couple of times. When you didn't try to reach me, I assumed you didn't care enough to find me."

"That's not true! You walked out."

"And you made no attempt to find me."

"I was angry, hurt and embarrassed. You told people here that you were moving to Boston. How could you do that to me? To us? We were supposed to be getting married when I finished college."

"Did you ask me to marry you?"

"No. I wanted to have a job before I proposed."

"Did you really think that you having a job would have changed my answer to your proposal?"

He sucked in air, his chest hurting from her question. "Why didn't you say something about the baby?"

"Because you were wrapped up in your degree program, and I was stuck in Spencer Island without you, holding down a job I despised."

"You didn't tell me that."

He heard her sigh, and his heart seemed to stretch in his chest. "Ellen, I'm really sorry that we didn't talk more. I had this idea in my head about how our life would go, that whatever we wanted would be ours."

"No, Bill. It was what you wanted in life that mattered. When I left Spencer Island, I enrolled in an interior design program, something that gave me so much happiness. When I met Marcus, he listened to me. We fell in love. When I told him I was expecting a baby, that he wasn't the father, I took a terrible risk. But 1 couldn't lie to him. He wanted to be Nicole's dad, and he was in every possible way."

Her words cut straight through him. "If you and this Marcus Simpson person were so happy, why couldn't you tell me about Nicole?"

"Do you have children?" she asked.

"No. I never married," he confessed, feeling so vulnerable to the love he still had for this woman despite everything she'd done to him.

"Why?" she asked.

He hesitated. "That's really none of your business," he said, wishing the conversation hadn't gone in this direction.

Trying to get back on track he said, "Why didn't you tell Nicole about me?"

It was her turn to hesitate. "I didn't, and that was a terrible mistake. She found out after Marcus died, and she blamed me for keeping her from her biological father. She moved all the way across the country to get away from me. I was shocked when she bought a property outside Spencer Island. I should have told her about you, but I was still mourning the loss of my husband. I wasn't able to do what needed to be done in my own life, not to mention hers. I really hoped that I'd be able to talk to her, explain everything, but she hasn't spoken to me since she moved to the East Coast."

"So she doesn't know anything about me. Does she know you grew up in Spencer Island?"

"Yes, she does."

Bill gritted his teeth. "And you never mentioned me."

"No. All I told her was that Marcus wasn't her dad. I don't know if she ever tried to find you."

Now he understood why Nicole had been asking him about Ellen Donnelly that day at the high school. How he wished he could live that day over again. He might have known about his daughter a lot sooner. "How could you let this happen?"

"I... wanted my life to go on the way it had all those years with Marcus. I never expected Nicole to question anything. I understand why she's angry with me, but she won't allow me a chance to tell her about it, to explain a little. And even if she did speak to me again, it would be to find out her father's name. I miss her so much. I shouldn't have let her leave without telling her the whole truth. I want to tell her everything, but I don't have any idea how to go about it."

"Why didn't you come to Spencer Island to see her? It's been two years."

"Because I was afraid that she would refuse to see me, that I'd be reminded once again what I'd done to her, to you, my parents."

"Why didn't you come home when they died?" he said.

"We were living in Indonesia at the time. "There had been a typhoon, and all the phones were out. I didn't find out for a week, and when I did it was too late to come home to the funeral."

"You didn't see any reason to come home one last time in their memory?"

"They were living in the Fairview Assisted Living Condominiums. They'd made funeral arrangements before I left home."

"Were you always this selfish?"

"What?"

"You heard me."

"Bill, have you forgotten that my mother was forty-two when I was born? My dad was fifty-five. My mother had dementia for years. She and my dad lived in assisted living while may dad tried to care for Mom. I'll never believe that their accident was really an accident, I believe that my dad couldn't face losing any more of my mom. I think they went out for that drive intending never to come back," she said, a catch in her voice.

Bill remembered the accident very well. Matthew Donnelly still had a car, had been driving right up until his death. He had taken his wife, Sarah, out for a drive along the coast road leading to Cranberry Point, had lost control and the car plummeted into the ocean.

"Well, that's all in the past. We need to concentrate on the future. I am going to talk to Nicole, to tell her who I am."

"When are you going to do that?" Ellen asked.

"I'm calling her today and arranging to visit her farm."

"Bill, if you wouldn't mind, could you let me know once you've set a time with her?"

"Why?"

"Because I want to be available should she decide to call me. I promise to support you any way I can. It's the only chance I'll have to make it up to her and to you." He heard her quiet sob. Longing for the past they'd shared wound itself around his heart.

He took a deep breath, hardening his resolve toward the woman who took his love and tossed it over for another man. He didn't owe her anything after all these years and all the hurt she'd caused him. But he did want to do what was right where his daughter was concerned. "I'll be in touch."

"Thank you so much," she said just before the line went dead, leaving him with his feelings of loss over what might have been.

Bill ended up not making the phone call until the next afternoon after work. Talking to Ellen made him suddenly aware of how his meeting with his daughter might go. Getting in touch after all this time might prove difficult. It was possible that she knew he was her father, that he lived only a few miles from her. Maybe she had chosen not to get in touch with him. Yet, he had no choice but to get in touch with her. He had to know if she knew about him. He'd make the call and be as gentle and kind as he could, telling her everything she needed to know.

He counted the number of rings, waiting for Nicole to pick up. He couldn't leave a message. After Ted had alerted him to what appeared in her eyes to be suspicious behavior, he'd wondered if she might have found out from her neighbor about him being there. If she had, she almost certainly wouldn't respond well to a message.

"Hello?" Nicole said, her voice uncertain.

"Hi. It's Coach Cassidy. How are you?" he asked, feeling suddenly very ill-at-ease.

"I'm fine."

He could feel the sweat on his palms, the racing of his heart and didn't know if he could go through with it. Maybe he should have waited, talked to her mother a little bit about Nicole's life growing up to prepare him, to demonstrate his interest in her. "Look, I'll get straight to the point, I need to see you as soon as possible."

"Is something wrong?"

"No. Not at all. I Need to talk to you, to explain something," he said, realizing how awkward he must sound.

After a long pause, she said, "Why don't you come over now?"

His relief was almost as powerful as his fear. Yet there was no turning back now. He was committed to doing this. He'd made the call and he had to follow through. "I'll be there in a few minutes."

Placing the private investigator's report on the seat beside him, he drove carefully, his mind racing over all the possible ways he might begin the conversation. Should he simply come out and tell her? Should he talk about his past, about growing up in Spencer Island, about how he knew her mother? Should he ask her what she knew about her birth father? Ellen had no idea if Nicole had searched for him, but with little to go on, a search would have been difficult.

He was at her driveway before he knew it, his blood pounding in his ears. As he eased into her driveway she was waiting on the step. She was clearly anxious to hear what he had to say without allowing him into her home: a careful move on her part. A woman living alone had to be aware of her own safety.

Clutching the private investigator's report, he got out of

the car and walked toward her. He could see her mother's eyes when she searched his face for an explanation. "Is there somewhere we can sit down and talk? It doesn't have to be inside," he hastened to add.

"Over there by the tack room." She pointed to a wooden bench looking as if it had been propped along the wall.

"Sure."

He followed her, sitting down next to her. His daughter. His only child. "Nicole, I have something to tell you. This is really an unusual situation, to say the least." He looked at the pages he held in his hand, searching for the right words.

"Thirty years ago, your mother and I were in love. We planned to marry when I finished college. I came home on my spring break my third year, believing that we were going to be together forever. When I got home after working all summer in Portsmouth, she had left Spencer Island without saying a word."

"I knew Mom lived here. That's why I came here."

"Yes. She grew up here. We went to the same high school. She played volleyball as well."

"What? My mother would have told me about you."

"And you were born in Virginia Beach?"

Nicole's glance was suspicious. "How do you know that?"

He dodged the question, which wasn't what he wanted to do, but somehow telling her that he'd hired a PI didn't sound very good regardless of the reasons for doing so. "Remember the day at the high school when you were asking questions about Ellen Donnelly?"

"Of course, You were almost rude with me."

"That's because I couldn't figure out why you were asking about Ellen. And you didn't offer an explanation."

"I wanted to know what you knew about my mother."

If only he dared to reach out and touch his daughter, the child he'd never known. Instead, he drew in a deep breath, focusing on the words he needed to say. "I have information I'd like to share with you. Something I'm sure you'll want to know."

"Like what?" she asked, a challenging tone in her voice.

Impulsively, he blurted out the words. "I'm your father." He heard his voice as if from afar, as if someone else had said the words.

Nicole gasped and slid to the corner of the bench. "You can't be. You're not telling the truth. Why would you do that?"

"I'm telling you the truth. I'm your father," he repeated the words, aware that Nicole's glance held only contempt. He tried again. "We were going to be married when Ellen left Spencer Island without one word about being pregnant with you."

"Why should I believe you?"

He wanted to put his arm around his daughter, to console her. Seeing the suspicious look on her face made such behavior impossible. "Because I just learned what happened. When she left, she didn't tell me we were expecting a baby. She walked out on our life, on our plans and on our love for each other."

"This can't be right. My mother would have told me about you when she knew I was moving here. She would have told me about you," she repeated, as if trying to grasp the idea. The look in her eyes was too painful to bear. He reached for her hand.

She pulled away, out of his reach.

"Nicole, I'm really sorry you had to learn about me this way. If I'd had any opportunity to know about you, I would have been a part of your life a long time ago. I would never have let you grow up without me, without knowing how much I loved you. I've wanted children all my life?" he said, watching her expression."

"When did you find this out?"

"A few weeks ago."

"How?"

He stared at his hands.

"You can't be my father. Someone would have told me before now. You wanted children, that's all."

"I have the investigator's report right here that says you're my daughter. I talked to Ellen, and she told me the truth."

"You talked to Mom? She told you I'm your daughter?" Nicole demanded, her voice rising. "Give me that report." She grabbed it from his hands.

"Nicole, I sympathize with what you're going through. We've both been lied to, and now we have to figure out what to do next."

"No. I'm not going to listen to any more of this. You and your investigator got this all wrong. Besides, why should I believe you or Mom? The two of you can't seem to get your stories straight. Mom never mentioned you. You brushed me off when I asked you about her. Now suddenly I'm supposed to be excited that you're my dad? I don't think so." She stood, her body language making it clear she wanted him to leave.

He got up, scribbled his cell number on the front of the file and handed it to her. Without saying a word, he went to his car, got in and started the engine. He glanced one more time at his daughter to see tears streaming down her face: It was clear he wasn't welcome in her life, and no wonder. The shock of his revelation had to be very difficult. If Nicole should call Ellen, he hoped that for the sake of their daughter she'd be honest.

It was the only chance he had to play a role in his daughter's life a long time ago.

CHAPTER TEN

*N*icole was shaking so badly she could hardly make her legs carry her to the back door. When she finally closed the door behind Bill Cassidy, she slumped down on the bench in disbelief. How could he come here, out of the blue, and start talking about being her birth father? Clutching the report he'd given her, she went to the kitchen, sat down and began to read. The words were clear, concise and irrefutable. The investigator's report included a short interview with Ellen Simpson in which she stated that Nicole Simpson's biological father was Bill Cassidy.

She glanced around her living room, at the dark wood-work, the shiny wood floors, the stone fireplace, all the things she loved about this Craftsman house she'd first seen on the internet. She remembered that day so well. She'd been searching for hours on the internet, ready to give up, when she found her place, her home.

People had thought she was crazy to move so far away, over a house she'd seen only in pictures. What they didn't understand was that she'd known from the minute she saw the house she had to have it. Her inheritance had made such a purchase possible. To think that she moved here, to a place she'd come to love, to the place where her biological father lived and her mother had never once said anything about this man who claimed to be her dad.

Her fingers still shaking, she dialed her mother's number in Seattle. She didn't care what time it was out there because this couldn't wait. She listened to the phone ring three times, each ring making her angrier at her mother and her lies.

"Hello," her mother said, cautiously, "Is that you, Nicole?"

At the sound of her mother's voice, she was back to that day years before when she'd asked her mother to tell her who her father was and where he lived. She remembered it all so vividly: the tears that wouldn't stop when her mother refused to tell her, the ache in her stomach at the realization that her mother had kept the truth from her, let her live a lie created by the one person who should have told her the truth.

From that moment on, her trust in her mother had caused a break that nothing could heal. From that day until she arrived in Spencer Island, she could never bring herself to believe a word her mother said. "Yes, It's me." She forced the words out.

"I'm so glad you've called. I've missed you terribly. I'm sorry for how we left things. We need to talk."

"Mom, you have a whole lot to explain. How could you lie about my father? Why didn't you say that he lived in Spencer Island? How could you do this to me?"

"Nicole, I'm sorry, but can we do a video call?" her mother asked softly,

"What?" she shot back, her anger a hard fist in her chest.

"Please, I want to see you face-to-face while we talk about my past. Please," she repeated.

"Fine." She slammed the phone down, only to hear the chime from her computer indicating that someone was initiating a video call.

She went to her computer and accepted it. "That's better," her mother said. "Now we can talk."

Nicole stared at her mother. She couldn't help but notice that her mother had let her hair go gray, that her skin was sallow and wrinkled. Longing welled up in her, longing and loneliness and a feeling that she'd made some sort of mistake that couldn't be fixed.

She shoved all those feelings aside. She couldn't allow the sudden rush of emotion to change anything. "So. let's start with why you kept my biological father from me."

"Because I couldn't go back to Spencer Island. I'd left it a long time ago. Going back would mean little when my life was with Marcus. We loved each other." Her mother's expression was both eager and sad. "Marcus and I had good life, and you were the center of it. We only wanted what was best for you."

"You leave Dad out of this."

"I can't, honey. He was part of everything I did from the moment I met him. Your dad wanted you to be happy. When we met and fell in love, he insisted on having his name on your birth certificate. He wanted to be your father in every way that mattered!"

"Why should I believe you?"

"I understand how hurt you feel."

"How could you know what I'm feeling when I'm not sure myself," she said to her mother, feeling for the first time the depth of need to find someone who would love her.

"Oh, Nicole, how I've missed you. We need to talk about everything."

"Mom, this call isn't going to change anything."

"Maybe not, but before you decide, can I explain a little bit about my past?"

Nicole didn't want to hear her mother's excuses. Yet, she needed to know how it was that her mother could have kept her past a secret from her only child. "If you want," she said with little enthusiasm.

"There's a whole lot I haven't told you."

"No kidding!"

Her mother sighed, her gaze moving to a spot below the computer screen. "I grew up in Spencer Island. I never felt a part of the community because I was...different. I spent most of my time in my room. My parents were older when I was born, and they didn't know much about parenting. I felt completely stifled, and at the same time I couldn't seem to make friends with anyone. Most of my free-time was spent drawing and dreaming. I met your father, Bill Cassidy, in Grade 8. He was a jock. I never quite understood why he liked me so much. But that didn't stop me from dreaming about a life with him somewhere sway from Spencer Island, somewhere we would both be happy."

"He told me he loved you very much. Do you not know the difference between like and love, or didn't you care?" Nicole asked, ashamed of the harsh words but unwilling to apologize.

"I did care. When Bill went to college, I was excited. I was in twelfth grade, dreaming of the day he'd graduate and come back. Then we'd move somewhere exciting and where I could follow my dream of being an interior designer."

Her mother's face filled the screen, tears making her eyes shine. "It never happened. While I worked and waited for Bill in Spencer Island, he'd decided that he was moving back home. His dream was to graduate from college, marry me and spend the rest of his life in Spencer Island. He didn't ask me what I wanted, didn't seem to care how desperate I was to escape a place that held no meaning for me. I felt betrayed by him. I had wasted three years waiting for him while he hadn't bothered to tell me that he intended to live his life in Spencer Island. We spent his spring break together, and two months later I knew I was expecting you. I knew if I told him I'd be pressured into staying in Spencer Island, that my life, my dreams, would be over. Instead, I'd spend my life in a town that felt more like a prison every day."

She touched her fingers to the screen. "I didn't know what else to do. Those years while Bill was at college, I'd taken a secretarial course and knew I could get a job wherever I wanted to go. I chose Virginia, got a job and enrolled in a program on interior decoration and design. I met Marcus on a blind date arranged by the woman who owned the boarding house where I lived. We fell in love, but I knew I had to tell him the truth about being pregnant. When I told him, he was excited and happy. He didn't want out. He wanted you. He wanted me. We were married in a civil ceremony and spent our honeymoon, a long weekend was all the time we could get off, walking the beach and making plans. He... I love him. I miss him every day." Her mother's tears brought tears to Nicole's eyes. The one thing they shared, that they would always share, was their love for Marcus Simpson,

"Mom, I still don't understand why you didn't tell me about my dad."

"Because I was afraid that you would leave me and go to him. I felt ashamed of what I had done, walking out on him like that. I should have handled it differently, but I was panicked by the thought of being forced to remain in Spencer Island."

"Why? It's lovely here."

They stared at each other, neither saying anything.

"Nicole, I apologize for not telling you about Bill. I made a lot of mistakes, and you had to bear the brunt of them. Sometimes I imagine what I might or could have done differently, but each time I realize that there's no going back. I did what I did. Now I'm paying the price."

"Are you trying to make this my fault?" Nicole asked angrily.

"No! Never! I take full responsibility for everything I did. And for what it's worth, I should have told you a long time ago about your biological father. It would have been easy to do after Marcus died. I didn't and I'm so sorry."

"So where does that leave me?" Nicole asked.

"You mean about Bill?"

"Yes, about Bill."

"I'm hardly the one to be giving you advice after the way I've behaved. But if I were you, I'd get to know him, learn everything I could about him. The Bill Cassidy I knew and loved was a nice man, a decent, honest person."

So why didn't you talk to him, tell him how you felt about living in Spencer Island?"

"Because I knew there was little hope that he'd change his mind. I couldn't stay with him if it meant living in Spencer Island."

"You didn't really love him, or you would have been honest with him about your feelings."

Ellen sighed, rubbed her forehead and gazed into the screen. "Maybe you're right. Maybe I didn't love him enough to give up my dream. Maybe we both weren't being honest with each other, and our lack of honesty had an impact on you that we didn't really think about. I'm dreadfully sorry for what I did."

"Mom, Bill Cassidy had no choice in the matter. But you did. You made mistakes that hurt two people."

"You're right. But we can't change the past, can we?"

"No, we can't. All I know for certain is that I'm happy here. I don't know what to do, Mom."

"Nicole, please don't make a hasty decision like I did. It's not that I would have made a different decision, but life altering choices need to be shared with those we love. I should have talked to Bill about what was going on, but I didn't. I felt compelled to leave before he got home so that he couldn't talk me into changing my mind. But for you, it's not too late to have a relationship with him. Think about what you want out of life. You're happy there. So is Bill. Make that a starting place for both of you."

"I'll think about it."

"Nicole, I miss you. I'd love to see you sometime."

She saw the naked longing in her mother's eyes, and a huge lump rose in her throat. "Mom, I miss you, too. It's just that you hurt me so much."

Her mother's anxious smile faltered. "We were such a happy family. Somehow telling you about Bill didn't seem to matter."

"Mom, I don't know what to say. I've got enough on my plate right now. First I have to figure out what to do about Bill Cassidy."

"What can I do to help? I'm here, always, if you want to talk. I love you."

Looking into her mother's face, seeing how she'd aged in the two years since she'd seen her, feelings of loss, of missed time together filled her. "I love you, too, Mom."

Her mother's gaze was suddenly intense as she looked at Nicole. "I....I wonder. Are you all right?"

"Me? What do you mean?"

"I've always been able to know when something is bothering you. And something is now. Are you? Have you been ill?"

It had always been this way between her and her mother, that sixth sense that something was wrong. "Mom, I had a breast biopsy a couple of days ago."

Her mother's hands flew to her face. Tears spilled from her eyes "Not I'm so sorry. Was it...?"

"No. It was a benign cyst."

"Thank heaven."

There was long, protracted silence. Neither woman said anything while they stared at each other on screen. Telling her mother about the biopsy made her want to tell her mother other things; about her life, how she enjoyed her job, whether her mother still loved her work as an interior designer. That Nicole's house was a Craftsman house, a love of design they both shared. She wanted to talk about all of it, but the past they shared, the anger she'd felt for so long held her back.

The past still held the power to keep her away from her mother.

CHAPTER ELEVEN

*B*ill Cassidy drove around for a while before heading back to his house. When he finally pulled into the driveway and clicked open the garage door, exhaustion deadened his limbs. How had his life been reduced to this? To the anger and need for revenge against a woman he'd once loved with all his heart?

He'd promised Ellen that he would call her when he knew where and when he'd be meeting with Nicole. That hadn't worked out so well, mostly because he couldn't wait to talk to his only child, his only daughter.

Hell! How did life get so complicated? All he ever wanted was a family, and now that he'd found his family, nothing seemed to be going right. He might as well make the call he'd promised her and get it over with. What he had with Ellen was long over.

He dropped his keys on the counter to the pealing sound of the phone ringing in the hallway. Caller ID showed Ellen's number in Seattle. His first thought was to ignore the call. He wanted to do it on his time, on his terms.

Yet as the phone kept ringing, he thought that maybe it

might be easier now rather than later. Nicole's rebuff of him had focused his anger where Ellen was concerned, and it was time that a few things were straightened out between them. He picked up the phone. "Hello, Ellen."

"I talked to Nicole. I'm sorry that things didn't go very well when you talked to her. Truly sorry."

"You can understand her anger and disappointment."

"And it's my fault. I made every mistake imaginable where Nicole is concerned. I should have told her about you."

He knew Ellen was waiting for him to say something, but this was her call.

"This is awful. I wish I could make up for my mistakes. It's just that when Marcus died, my world fell apart. I had never felt such loss, such longing. Grief is a terrible thing. When Nicole demanded that I tell her about you, I couldn't face any more sadness." Ellen's sobs reached out to him across the phone line. "But I should've done better. I should've called you when I knew she was moving to Spencer Island. You might have been able to help her through this. Now, she is angry at both of us, and it's my fault."

The anguish in her voice made him wish that things were different between them, that he could find it in his heart to comfort her even if he couldn't forgive her. "Ellen, I don't know what to say, All I know for certain is that I want a relationship with my daughter. I deserve at least that."

"Anything. I'll do anything to make amends." She sniffled and cleared her throat. "Any ideas what we could do?"

"I'm going to try again with her, see if anything has changed,"

"If it helps any, Nicole has a very kind heart. She wouldn't intentionally hurt anyone."

"How would that help us?"

"Us?" she asked, her voice low, almost inmate, reminding him of how much he once loved this woman.

"Do you ever wonder what our life would have been like if you hadn't run off the way you did?

"Please, Bill, can we not go into this now? We have a more urgent problem at the moment."

"That problem started with what you did back then. But you're right. We have a more urgent problem—Nicole."

There was a long pause, during which he assumed she was preparing her argument in defense of her behavior. Instead, she said, "Bill, would you object if I came to Spencer Island? Nicole doesn't really want me there, but I need to be there to help you. I owe you at least that. And after Nicole's cancer scare, I want to see her."

"Her cancer scare?" he asked, his heart pounding with worry,

"Please don't tell Nicole that I told you. I'll tell you all I know if you'll let me come to see you."

He couldn't ignore the pleading tone in her voice. The plea in her voice was genuine. He could either accept her request or he could deny it and let the distance between them continue. He felt a warm feeling in his stomach that climbed his chest into his throat.

His love for Ellen had encompassed his life, defined him in so many unacknowledged ways. If he could simply let go of his anger he might be able to find happiness, get to know his daughter and have a decent relationship with Ellen.

"Ellen, why don't you come to Spencer Island? You could stay at my house."

"You mean it?"

"I do. And if you'll give me your flight details, I'll pick you up in Portsmouth."

Suddenly the line was filled with a gentle laughter, a joyful sound he remembered from their past. A sound that made him remember everything he'd lost and how much he wanted it back.

"What will we tell Nicole?" Ellen asked.

"Let's talk this all over first."

"Will you mention anything to her?"

"No. If you come here, it will be up to you to tell Nicole about your visit."

"It's going to be hard to do, but I'll find a way."

CHAPTER TWELVE

$\mathcal{N}$icole was down on her hands and knees furiously digging weeds out of a flower bed, her arms aching, her hands grasping the trowel. She hadn't slept last night after her conversation with her mother. Not only was it what they said but also how her mother looked—older and less confident. Not the successful, upbeat person she remembered.

Had their separation done that? Or was it simply her mother getting older? She'd left home and, hadn't been in touch. She'd been really angry back then about not being told who he was, but now that she knew... Would she feel differently where her mother was concerned? She and her mom had once been very close. Nicole missed that.

Guilt swirled around her at the thought that she had hurt her mother. She hadn't meant to. She simply couldn't deal with the lies. She had remained in Seattle for a year after she found out. She'd tried to find out the name of her birth father but she had little to go on and she finally gave up. She couldn't forgive her mother for stopping her from finding her father.

Stress and anxiety tightened her shoulders as her thoughts turned to her tack room. Who had cleaned it? Ned had denied any involvement, and she believed him, which meant that some unknown person had been on her property, inside her tack room when she wasn't there.

She'd led Ted Langley to believe she was okay about it, that she was okay staying in her house alone. Now she wasn't so sure. She'd bought this farm, believing she'd found her dream place. Now, if someone was on her property, cleaning her tack room, what would they do next?

She dug deeper and harder into the flower bed. She sat back on the ground, looking at all the work she'd accomplished. If nothing else, being outside in the fresh air, digging like someone possessed, she'd managed to finish the entire bed. She glanced around at the sound of a vehicle coming up her driveway.

Justin's truck spit gravel as he came toward her house. She scrambled up from the ground, dusting off as she walked toward him. He shut off the engine and opened the cab door.

"What brings you all the way out here?" she asked, suddenly remembering that he didn't know about her results.

Justin got out and came toward her. "I've been worried. I had hoped I'd hear from you about your biopsy."

"I thought you'd call me, want to know how I was doing," she countered, fighting the urge to step into his arms, feel his body close to hers.

"I did want to know. But I was waiting for you to tell me. Why didn't you call me?" he asked, his eyes dark, a hurt tone in his voice.

"Not everything is about you," she said, feeling hurt. She regretted her words, but she was weary of always being the one responsible for someone else's happiness. She'd seen the look on her mother's face and accepted that she'd been responsible for making her mother unhappy. She wasn't responsible for Justin's happiness.

"You're right. This isn't about me. It's about you."

"I've had a lot to deal with these past few days," she said, wanting to share her feelings with him but afraid that he'd make light of them like he did before the biopsy.

"Does that mean you're not going to tell me?"

Looking up into his eyes and the caring she saw there, she was aware of how much she'd wanted to share her news with him: "No. Not at all. The biopsy showed no cancer."

"Thank God!" He pulled her into his arms, holding her close to his chest, so close she could hear the frantic beating of his heart. "I was so worried." He held her away from him and looked directly into her eyes. "When my mom got word she had cancer, she didn't tell me. She told my sister. I never felt so left out in my life." He smiled in relief. "I couldn't help but wonder if history wasn't repeating itself."

Nicole closed her eyes to ward off the eager concern on his face. She hadn't expected him to be so relieved at her news. She'd misjudged him and she was sorry. "Because I didn't call and tell you the biopsy was negative, you assumed the worst."

"That's about it," he said, leading her toward her tack room, where they sat on the bench along the side of the building. "I'm relieved to know you're okay. I want to spend time with you."

She'd been hoping he'd say something like that to her. The past few days had tossed her life around in so many different ways, but it had also made her see that she needed to face her insecurities. "Me, too." His presence surrounded her, drawing her closer to him. It was a strange feeling, yet one she liked. "I'm sorry I didn't call you. It's just that so much has been happening."

Looking like a cowboy in his faded jeans and checked

shirt, he leaned closer. "Like what?" he asked, his attention riveted on her.

God! It felt good to have his attention focused on her. He made her feel as if everything that mattered to her also mattered to him. She nodded toward the building behind them. "Did you by any chance clean my tack room?"

"What? No, of course not. I wouldn't do it unless you asked me to. And never without telling you. Why?"

"Because someone did clean it from top to bottom. I had been meaning to do it for months. Then the other day when I came home it was clean."

"Did you call the police?"

"Ted is looking into it for me."

"He's the guy I met at the fire department fund-raiser?"

"Yeah. He was really great. He helped Angie. That's how they met."

He rubbed his face, then returned his intense gaze back to her. "Is that all that's bothering you?"

She couldn't seem stop looking at his blue shirt how it matched his blue eyes, the way his jeans hugged his thighs. "Isn't that enough?"

"Not enough to make you as anxious as you seem." His eyes held hers. "What's going on? What's upsetting you?" He touched her chin, turning her face up to his. "I didn't. come here to talk about your friends. I came to talk about you."

"I'm okay; really. I don't have cancer, and that's huge."

"Okay. While Ted is looking into it, would you like me to stay here with you? I wouldn't get in your way. You wouldn't be alone at night..."

She tried to imagine what it would be like sharing her home with him, having him so close. She flushed in pleasure. "That's a wonderful offer, but I'm sure I'll be okay. Even better when Ted finds out who did it. He says if he can't find the person, he'll call the police."

"Why not call them now?"

"I'd rather not. I'm sure there's an innocent explanation."

He raised one eyebrow. "If you change your mind about my offer..."

Her heart did a slow thudding movement against her ribs. "My birth father came to see me."

"Whoa! Nicole, you've had a lot of stuff going on in your life. Why don't you start at the beginning?"

Settling next to him, looking out over the paddock where the horses stood near the low hedge line, she told him everything about her mother, her father and her birth father. As she talked to him, she felt relief and a strange sense of happiness. Justin never took his eyes off her, never once made any attempt to stop her, to make a point or to make her feel that she was responsible for the events that unfolded after her father's death.

She smiled at him, a new feeling of appreciation for him surfaced as she talked. "That's about it, Coach Cassidy is my birth father. My mother grew up in Spencer Island. I haven't seen her since I left Seattle other than a video call the other night."

Justin hugged her close to him, kissed her forehead and took her hand in his, "You've led a complicated life since Marcus Simpson died."

"It didn't need to be that way if my mother had told the truth."

He sighed. "So often telling the truth is the most difficult thing to do. Do you think you can ever forgive her?"

"I don't know. A part of me wants to, but my mother has never been able to see life from anyone else's point of view but hers. If she had, she would have known how painful it was for me to learn that she lied to me, about my dad and about Bill Cassidy."

"Nicole, your dad was part of that lie. He had to be, or else he wouldn't have put his name on your birth certificate."

"He was doing it out of love for my mother."

"The fact remains that he put his name on the document and never told you," he said, his tone insistent.

Nicole flexed her tired fingers. "He didn't do it because he thought it was the best answer, he did it because of his love for her," she said.

"Did you consider that maybe your mother did it because of her love for you? That maybe she felt you'd be happier with your life as it was without the complication of finding out about a man who played no role in your life?"

She gritted her teeth. "He played no role because he wasn't given the chance."

"Are you sure? What do you know about Coach Cassidy?"

"Not much. He's a great coach. He's well liked"

"Why didn't he go looking for your mother after she left Spencer Island? Why didn't he hire a private investigator to find her long before he did? Why did he wait for almost thirty years before going in search of the woman he loved?"

She looked at him, surprised that she hadn't been able to see the situation in a more balanced way. "You're saying that I let my anger at my mother stop me from seeing the whole picture?"

"I'm saying that you need to take it slow, look at everything that happened. Give your mother and Bill a chance to explain themselves." He stared at the sky for a few minutes. "Do you want your birth father in your life?"

"Yes. At least, I'd like to get to know him."

"In my opinion an extra parent is not all bad. My mother was a huge influence in my life."

"She sounds really special."

"She was. She had a great sense of humor, right up until she passed away. When the will was read, her note to us

146

started with her statement that whatever she had to bequeath to my sister and me might be seen as a dead giveaway. It sounds a little quirky, but that was my mom. My sister and I were very lucky to have the parents we did. Dad was great. He was the one that inspired me to follow my heart, to take life as it came, not be wishing for something I didn't have. He lived his life that way."

"I had great parents, too. I really loved my dad. Mom and I were devastated when he died."

His look of concern encouraged her to continue, "He'd gone on a business trip. We were living in Alaska at the time, but Mom was already certain we'd be moving to Chile. My dad and I argued before he left. I didn't want to be sent to boarding school. I wanted to move with them, I never got a chance to say I was sorry."

He smiled, a sad, reflective smile, "It's so easy to look back and wish you could change something in your past."

"Isn't it strange how easy it is to let the moment pass?"

He shrugged. "Been there. Done that."

She sighed. "It wouldn't have mattered where my dad ended up working. My mom never once considered not going with him. They were never apart for very long."

"It sounds like a wonderful love story. It must have been so hard for your mother to lose him."

"It was. For me, too. Maybe that's why discovering the lie she told about Marcus being my birth father hurt so much."

"How did you find out?"

"I had to have surgery, and they tested me to find out my blood type. When I learned I had a different blood type from either of my parents, I insisted on the DNA test being done to determine whether or not they were my parents. It wasn't until the results came back that I learned that Marcus wasn't my birth father."

"That must have been very difficult for you."

"It was. Now that I know who my dad is, my mom wants to see me." She stared at her hands in frustration, "After all this time, all the hurt she inflicted by not telling me, she wants to come back into my life as if nothing happened."

"But she'd have to realize that coming back into your life wasn't possible without some sort of explanation. That you would both need time."

"You'd think she would."

"Do you want your mother in your life?"

"I honestly don't know." She sighed as she gazed into his mesmerizing blue eyes. "If I couldn't trust her to tell me the truth, how could I trust her back in my life?"

"How would you feel if she were ill? Would you still feel this way? I remember how I felt when my mom was diagnosed with cancer. I couldn't have stayed away no matter what."

"But your mom didn't lie to you, did she? I don't believe you can know how you'd behave in my situation."

His eyes moved over her face, his expression one of watchfulness. "Why not talk to Bill Cassidy? He loved your mother. He may be able to give you a different perspective on her."

"I really appreciate your concern," she said, soaking in the nearness of him.

"I'm concerned because I care about you. I genuinely care about you," he said.

"And I care about you. You've made such a difference in my life."

"I want to be here for you, for you to know that whatever you feel you need to do, I'm right here."

For the first time since she talked to Bill Cassidy, she felt more at ease, more able to deal with all of it. "Thank you," she said.

"Can I make dinner for you? Take you out for something to eat?"

She met his gaze and saw the sincerity there. More than anything, she wanted to go out with him. She'd never felt closer to him than she did right now. "I really appreciate the offer, but it's been a difficult week, to say the least. And you're right, I have to face my mother. Facing my mother means getting in touch with my father. I was kind of rude with him. After he told me his news I asked him to leave. I'm sure I hurt his feelings. I need to tell him I'm sorry."

He touched her cheek softly. "You do what you need to do."

His touch was so soothing. "Having you around is really nice."

He kissed her lightly on the check, making her skin tingle, "Stick with me. It'll get even better."

He took her hand, pulled her to her feet. "Call me and let me know what you've decided. If I can help..." He smiled as he took her face in his calloused hands and kissed her, a long intense kiss that had her head spinning.

Walking with him to his truck, she wanted to change her mind, have him stay with her. She sighed in resignation. She had things to do.

Once in the house she dug out the piece of paper with Bill Cassidy's phone number on it. He answered on the first ring. "I'd like to talk to you sometime," she said.

"Anytime you'd like. Anytime at all," he said, his breathing audible.

"What about this Saturday morning around ten at the Bobby's Bistro?"

"Sure. And, Nicole, thank you for agreeing to meet me."

. . .

When Saturday arrived, Nicole's tummy was doing a flip-flop that threatened to toss her hastily eaten breakfast. She'd been awake half the night thinking about what she wanted to say to her dad. The closer she got to ten o'clock the less certain she felt.

She entered the bistro, closing the solid wooden door behind her and shutting out all the sound from the street. It was so comforting in here with the scent of cinnamon hanging in the air and the aroma of fresh coffee. She spotted Bill Cassidy in a booth along the back wall.

"Hi, there," he said as she slid into the booth across from him.

"Hi. I hope I'm not late," she said, instantly anxious about whether she'd feel better about their meeting when it was over.

"Not at all," he said, and she could tell by the way he flexed his hands and kept looking at her, then looking away, that he was probably as anxious as she was. Odd as it seemed, his anxiety helped to quell hers.

She clasped her hands, trying to think of something to say, every thought having flown from her mind. The waitress arrived, took their orders for coffee, returned with two large mugs and two croissants with butter.

Bill didn't touch the coffee or the croissants. "It feels almost surreal to be sitting across from you like this."

She saw the anguish in his eyes and touched his hand. "I didn't know about you until the year before I moved here. Mom wouldn't tell me who you were. Do you know why?"

"No, I'm sorry I don't. When I came home from my summer job in Portsmouth, your mother was gone. She didn't say where, and she left me no forwarding address."

"But you and Mom were involved, sleeping together?"

"Yes. We were in love. We planned to marry."

"What changed her mind?"

"At the time I had no idea. When I spoke with her the other day, she said she couldn't marry me and settle down in Spencer Island. She said I didn't offer her a choice."

"That doesn't make sense. Why would she do this to me? To us?" Nicole asked in frustration.

"Does it matter anymore? We've found each other now, and we have a chance to share our lives."

"How did you figure out that I was your daughter?"

"When you asked about Ellen that day, I wondered why. Then when you joined the volleyball team and I saw the birthmark on your shoulder." He shrugged.

"My birthmark?" She touched her shoulder.

"Yeah. My sister had this weird mark on her shoulder. I didn't pay much attention. Then I looked types of birthmarks up on the internet, talked to my family doctor and became interested in the idea that you might be related to me."

"Why would you think I was related to you?"

"Your smile is your mother's. Your brown eyes...and a feeling that I knew you." He picked up his coffee cup and cradled it in his hands. I played a hunch, found a private detective, gave him all the information I had. He found your mother in about a week, little more. You saw the file he did up."

"It was that easy to find Mom and me?"

"Hard to believe, isn't it?"

"Then why didn't you search for me sooner?" she asked.

"No idea you existed, until the PI's report."

"What a coincidence. I come here to live. You see me, have this feeling you are connected to me."

"I will never doubt my feelings again." He leaned back in the booth and gave her an assessing smile. "You realize that you do look a lot like your mother. You have my hair, or the color it once was, but you have your mother's eyes and easy smile."

"Thanks," she said. taking in all aspects of this man, her father, who sat across from her. He was tall, athletic for his age. His eyes were direct and clear and he had an easy grace about him. His navy sports jacket, cream shirt and blue patterned tie showed good taste in clothes. She liked him, she suddenly realized. She liked him a lot. "You're the reason why I love sports, right? I mean, Mom wouldn't go to any sporting events. That was always my dad and me. He loved baseball the most," she said, remembering all the good times with him.

"Tell me about your dad," Bill said.

"He was a petroleum engineer. Because of his job, we lived all over the place. I have been to every major country in the world but Australia and Russia. My mom was devoted to him. They were inseparable. Sometimes I felt like an outsider around them."

"Wish I could have been there for you," he said, his tone sincere.

"I wish you could have been, too." Curious about him, she asked, "Do I have uncles and aunts?"

"You did have once. My sister passed away a few years ago. She had a daughter, Martha Singer."

"Martha Singer? Does she live here?"

"Out along the coast highway, between here and Camden."

She clutched her cup of coffee, realizing what it meant to have family living near her. "We should hold a family get together sometime. Maybe at Christmas? I'd like to get to know my relatives. What about my grandparents?"

He shifted in the seat, "Your mother's parents are both deceased. Buried in the cemetery by the Episcopalian church."

"And your parents?

"My dad still lives here. He's at the nursing home out on Cranberry Point."

Her dad's father was still alive, her only chance to connect with her birth father's past, her family. After moving all over the world, having a chance to find her father's family would be exciting. "I'd like to meet him."

"You will."

She felt strange, as if she'd entered someone else's life. "There's so much I want to ask you."

"I'll tell you anything you want to know. I'm a bit of a genealogy buff. If I start rambling on about your ancestors, feel free to stop me."

She glanced around, aware of the curious looks, wondering what people were thinking about seeing the local coach with her. Considering the speed at which news traveled in Spencer Island, she was pretty sure people had already heard something. "Did you tell anyone about me being your daughter?"

He looked a little sheepish. "I suspect my cleaning lady overheard my call to your mother...at least part of it. Hopefully not the part where I raised my voice."

"Why didn't you go after my mom, make her explain why she left?"

He rubbed his hands together, "When she hadn't bothered to tell me she was leaving, I was sure she'd fallen in love with another man. I figured that if she couldn't wait around long enough to tell me what was going on, there was no reason for me to try to chase her down for the answers." He scrubbed his face and looked at the wall. "I let my pride stand in the way of finding your mother."

He reached for her hand, holding it gently. "If I had known she was expecting you, I would have followed her anywhere. I'm so sorry that I behaved the way I did. My behavior caused me to miss out on you, being part of your life."

She met his sad gaze, her heart beating hard in her chest. "We've both lost out. But you need to know that I had a great dad. I loved Marcus very much."

"He was a lucky man," he said, his tone wistful.

She squeezed his fingers. "You and I can enjoy getting to know each other. I need a dad."

"Catching up with each other, getting to know each other. Those words are music to my ears." A look of contrition crossed his face, "There's something else I need to say to you. And I'm not very comfortable saying this."

"Go ahead," she said, seeing his expression change. Was he ill? Did he have something in his past that had stopped him from following her mother when she left Spencer Island?

"I'm the one who cleaned your tack room."

She gasped in surprise. "Why would you do that?"

"I didn't really mean to worry you. I know how dumb this sounds, but when the private investigator told me that my suspicions were true, I had to go out to your place. I needed to meet you. I guess I wasn't thinking very clearly." He smiled. "It's not every day you discover a daughter you've never known lives just minutes from you. I arrived at your place. You weren't home. I got out of my car and went to look around. The horses were there, and I thought maybe you had treats for them, When I went into the tack room and saw that it needed a good cleaning, I forgot that you hadn't given me permission to do it." He leaned back and looked at the ceiling: "You can tell me I'm weird and I creeped you out."

"You are weird and you did creep me out. Why would you do that and not at least leave me a note to say you'd been there?"

"I should have."

"I've asked Ted Langley to look into it."

"Yeah, I know. He came to see me." He shook his head. "I promise I'll call you before I visit. And if you need me to do anything, anything at all, you'll call me, right?"

"That's very kind of you."

He studied his hands resting on the table before glancing at her. "I wasn't only trying to being kind. It was also about wanting to be your father."

"You forget that I had a father that I loved." She saw the hurt and regret in his eyes and was immediately sorry. "I didn't mean that to be hurtful, really."

"It's okay. We have a lot to learn about each other. If you'd rather I didn't become involved in your life..."

She looked into his face, felt his love, his caring. Tears dampened her eyes. "We've already lived with enough lies, spent too much time not knowing each other. Let's start fresh from today."

He took a deep breath, stared up at the ceiling. When his glance returned to her, his eyes were red. "I'd like that very much."

They talked a little longer about their lives. A little while later he got up from the booth, his movements hesitant. She rose and stood beside him. There was an awkward moment when she was certain he wanted to hug her, but was hanging back, waiting for her to make the first move. She eased toward him, and his arms went out to her. Ever so gently he folded her into his embrace. She clung to him, wanting the connection with such a powerful force it frightened her.

While she waited for him to pay the bill, a new feeling came over her. She been alone in Spencer Island, but now she wasn't. She had moved here looking to start over. What she'd found was a family connection that filled the empty parts of her life.

CHAPTER THIRTEEN

*T*he week Nicole met her father, she felt so different. Everything seemed so new, so hopeful to her. She couldn't explain it except that she had her dad, who loved her, here in Spencer Island, A family she could count on.

She and her dad had met for coffee twice in the past week. She couldn't get over how different he was from Marcus. Her dad loved to read. Bill only read the sports section. Marcus loved going to the movies with her mom. Bill didn't have a favorite movie. Marcus loved the PBS channel. Bill liked the crime shows.

Today she wasn't going to think any more about her two dads. Matt and Gemma had invited Justin and her over to a barbecue. She had been too distracted to wonder why they'd been invited together, but she was so pleased to be going.

In all the confusion of the past week, she hadn't heard from Justin. She assumed they'd get a chance to catch up this evening. Seeing Justin would be great. She looked forward to a chance to talk with Gemma, another part of her life that she hadn't paid as much attention to as she usually did.

When she drove in her friend's driveway and got out of the car, she could hear laughter in the backyard. Justin's truck was parked at the curb, which meant that she was late. She glanced at her watch—six o'clock. No. She was on time. She gathered her purse, a bottle of wine, her freshly made samosas and headed to where she could hear voices. All three of them turned to greet her, but it was the guarded look on Justin's face that made her cautious.

"Hi, everyone."

Matt said, coming toward her, his barbecue apron snugged around his hips and a huge red chef hat perched on his head. He touched his hand to his head. "This is Gemma's idea. She thinks that if I'm going to have a career as a barbecue chef, I should look the part. What do you think?" he asked, hugging her before taking the bottle of wine she offered.

"I think you look quite..."

"Cute. He looks cute, doesn't he?" Gemma asked coming across the deck from the back door and folding Nicole in a hug. "Angie and Ted were invited as well, but they're in Boston."

"I'm so glad to be here," Nicole said. She had told Gemma a little bit about her first meeting with Bill and what had happened. She was looking forward to a few minutes alone with Gemma this evening when they cleaned up the kitchen after dinner.

"What did you bring?" Gemma asked, taking the wrapped plate from Nicole.

"I made my father's recipe for samosas, something he learned to make when we lived in Indonesia. You don't need to heat them up. They're great the way they are. I also brought the sauce for them," she said, aware that she was chattering like a schoolgirl. She couldn't seem to stop herself as she sought Justin's eyes.

He wasn't looking at her. He was flipping through the pages of a woodworking magazine, "Did I interrupt an interesting conversation?" she asked, directing her gaze to Justin.

"We were talking about older homes and house styles, and wood finishing. You own the old Henderson farm, don't you?" Matt asked.

"I do."

"Did you realize that it's the only Craftsman house left in or around Spencer Island?"

"No, I didn't. I fell in love with it the minute I saw it. The wood paneling and wainscoting in my house is truly spectacular. And so many nice windows."

"That's part of why I liked this house," Matt said, gazing up at the gingerbread work around the eaves and the tall stately windows. "We have a widow's walk at the top of the house, but we never go up there. Someday I'll fix it up and make a really exciting place for our children to play," he said, smiling at his Gemma.

"Matt and I want two more children. When we told Morgan, she was so excited, chatting away. You know what she's like when she's excited about something," Gemma said, her smile sweeping from Nicole to Justin and coming to rest on her husband's face.

Gemma moved into her husband's outstretched arm. Pulling her close, he kissed her. Justin's gaze was suddenly on Nicole, his expression a smiling question mark. She smiled back, happy to be here, to be with her friends and to see Justin,

Matt and Gemma stepped apart with a nervous laugh. "Sorry about that," Matt said, "but we can't seem to keep our hands off each other these days."

Gemma grinned up at him. "Why don't you open the wine Nicole brought and start the barbecue? Nicole and I will go in and get the other food ready."

Nicole put the plate she carried on the table, took the foil off and opened the dipping sauce, "Something for you to enjoy while you barbecue," she said, feeling Justin's eyes on her. She'd had one phone call from him this week. Nothing more. Yet he'd been so sweet and caring the last time she saw him. Justin seemed to blow hot and cold where she was concerned.

Nicole and Gemma went in the back door and walked along a short hall into the kitchen. Everything gleamed in the large open space. Gemma caught her looking around in amazement. "I decided the kitchen needed a good cleaning."

"It looks great."

Gemma began taking the salad makings out of the fridge. "Why don't you do this while I get the string beans and garlic potatoes started?"

"Sure." Nicole began chopping. "I didn't know you and Matt wore starting a family. I assume you have to be very careful with your health and your diabetes."

"I am." Gemma began to cut the ends of the beans. "Nicole, can I tell you something?"

She glanced at her friend. She was beautiful with her streaked blond hair and athletic build. The pale blue pants and matching top she wore fit her perfectly. She remembered the first day she'd met Gemma. She'd been nervous, wanting to make a good first impression with the clinic staff, especially Gemma. She needn't have worried. Their friendship started the day they met. "You can tell me anything."

"I took the home test and I'm quite sure I'm pregnant."

Nicole gawked in surprise. She went around the kitchen island and hugged her friend. "This is so exciting! I'm so happy for you."

"I am, too. It's what we've been waiting for."

"What did Matt say?"

"Please don't tell anyone about it, Matt and I haven't told

anyone yet. My mom will be so excited when I tell her. I need to see an obstetrician because of being a high-risk mother. He'll be able to confirm how many weeks along I am."

"1 won't tell anyone. Does Angie know?"

"Not yet. Mostly because she won't be able to keep it from Ted, and he won't be able to stop himself from worrying about me."

"That's what cousins are for, aren't they?" Nicole said, wanting to laugh and cry at the same time.

"You won't tell Justin, will you?"

"I'd have to be seeing Justin on a regular basis to have that kind of conversation," she said ruefully.

"Things not going well there?"

"I don't know. He's so sweet when I see him. The other day he encouraged me to talk to Bill Cassidy, to learn what I could about him. It really helped. Yet I've barely heard from him since then."

"Funny guy, really. Wonder what he's not telling you?" Gemma mused as she put the green beans on to steam and the potatoes in the microwave.

"I have no idea." Nicole mixed the salad greens together, placed them in a cut-glass bowl before drizzling dressing over them.

The women filled the other tray with glasses and napkins before joining the men out on the deck. Nicole was pleased to see that all the samosas she'd made had disappeared. Matt had just about finished the marinated chicken breasts, and Justin was setting the table with orange and turquoise plates and matching cutlery from a cart placed along the side of the deck. The image of him doing domestic chores pleased her. She liked a man who helped out in the kitchen.

They ate together, laughing and talking about Spencer Island, about the upcoming fall fair plans and how successful the fund-raiser for the fire station had been. Nicole really enjoyed this time together with her friends and Justin. He was a good conversationalist and listened intently while Matt told the story about his return to Spencer Island and laughed as Gemma playfully interjected her version of the story.

When they finished, the women cleaned up the kitchen and the men put the barbecue things away. All so perfectly natural and normal, Nicole wished her life could be like this someday.

After about an hour out on the deck, Justin leaned forward in his Adirondack chair and said, "Sorry to be a party spoiler, but have to be at a job outside of town for seven thirty in the morning, and I'm not sure how to get there. My truck doesn't have GPS, but one of the workmen is going with me and he says he knows the way."

"Oh. Wish you could stay longer," Gemma said, glancing at Nicole.

Nicole held her gaze for a second. "I'm on the early shift tomorrow." She gathered up the plate and plastic container she'd brought and rose. "I'll see you at work," she said, giving Gemma a very gentle hug.

Matt came to her, wrapping an arm around Nicole's shoulders. "It's been great. Thanks for the delicious appetizers. Sorry that Justin and I motored through them without thought to you girls."

"We'll live," she said, aware that Justin was standing on the other side of her.

Matt grinned. "If I'm not mistaken," he nodded in Justin's direction, "there's a man here who would like to spend a little time with you."

Nicole felt her cheeks flush.

Justin followed her out to the street. "Can we go out tomorrow evening? I'd like to see you, talk a little bit about what's been going on in your life and mine."

Was he about to open up to her? Did she want him to? Her life was already pretty complicated. She gazed up into his face, seeing the intensity of his gaze under the streetlight. There was something so sincere about Justin, and at other times he could be so...removed. There were moments when she wished they could start over again, recapture the excitement of the night at the Wayfarer Inn. "I'd like that."

"My apartment tomorrow evening around eight? I'll cook dinner." He smiled that special smile, the one that made her feel warm all over. "I don't cook dinner for just anyone."

"I'm among the lucky ones?" she asked, wishing he'd kiss her.

He didn't. Instead, he took her keys, unlocked her car door and held it open for her. "I promise you a great dinner."

She slid into the seat and looked up at him. "See you tomorrow. Can I bring anything?"

"Only yourself."

"I didn't know you could cook. Guess I'm about to learn a whole lot of things about you."

"You are," he said, kissing her lightly, before striding back to his truck.

The next day Justin stopped work early. He had to get into town and pick up all the things he needed to make Nicole a special dinner. He wanted to impress her. He had his mother's recipe for lobster thermidor, and he needed to assemble the ingredients. When he reached his apartment, he'd forgotten that he hadn't tidied up at all before going to work. There were dirty, socks, shirts, newspapers, dishes scattered everywhere; the accumulation of stuff dropped wherever during the past days due to the long hours he'd been working.

He tackled the kitchen counters and filled the dishwasher. Heading for the living room, he scooped up the dirty clothes and stuffed them in the clothes hamper. He gave the bathroom a quick scrub. On the shelf beside the sofa, he arranged his collection of wooden figurines he'd carved over the years.

He'd taken a quick shower and was just cleaning the lobster shells after putting the lobster meat and other ingredients into a bowl when the doorbell rang. "Coming," he called out, wiping his hands on the large white towel around his waist that doubled as an apron.

When he opened the door, his heart literally skipped a beat. Nicole was standing there, her face alight, her hair shining, but it was the red body-hugging top that riveted his attention. "You look...perfect."

"Thank you. Am I on time?" she asked with a tilt of her chin and a smile.

"Yes! Absolutely. Of course." he said, moving aside to let her come in.

He watched her walk into his Pullman-styled kitchen...those pants cupping her bottom. Heat rose through him.

Steady. Take a deep breath.

"I've never been in one of these apartments," she said, glancing around. "The wooden figures. My father collected wood carvings." He was pleased she'd noticed them. Her gaze swept the floor. "And a blanket on the carpet. Huge pillows. What are we doing tonight?"

"I'll fill you in on my plan for this evening once I've gotten this dish together." He pointed at the counter and the ingredients spread all ever. He put the saucepan on the stove, adding ingredients as he mentally ran through all the steps to making the lobster dish.

"We're eating lobster out of the shell?" she asked.

"We are. He noted that she'd climbed up on one of the

stools beyond the raised counter. "I'm filling the shells with the meat mixed into this sauce," he said as he beat eggs and stirred them into the pan on the stove. "You're not allergic to shellfish, are you?" he asked, mortified that he hadn't thought to ask her earlier. He grimaced and glanced at the fridge door, noting that business card of his favorite pizza place.

"No. I love shellfish: I'm just not very good at preparing it," She came around the counter and stood next to him, her fragrance waffling around him, distracting him to the point where he nearly burned the sauce.

"Did you know that lobster thermidor is a French recipe from the famous Café de Paris?" he asked, to ease the drum-roll beat his heart was doing.

"Seriously?"

He saw her smile out of the corner of his eye. "My mother was a huge fan of Julia Child."

He turned the heat off under the dish. "We're just about ready to eat. All we need is the salad from the fridge and the loaf of French bread I bought today at the market."

"Let me help," she offered.

He watched as she sliced the bread while he put the finishing touches on the salad.

"So, when are you going to tell me what the pillows are for?" She looked at him, a smile edging up the corners of her lips.

"It's something I got into when I lived in Haiti. At night after we'd finished our day, we often sit around talking."

"On the floor?" She looked at the wall next to the sofa. "Is that a real jukebox?"

"I bought it from a contractor in Bangor. He was demolishing a '50s diner and was getting rid of this beauty. I couldn't give up the chance to own something like this," he said, running his hands over the glossy top and the glass front of the cabinet.

"Does it really play?"

"Yes, I had to buy some replacement forty-fives to fit into the slots. It took me a while to get it all organized the way I wanted it. Pick a song," he said, stepping aside.

Her fingers played over the keys as she read the music choices from the front of the machine, "I think this one." She picked Roy Orbison's "Only the Lonely." After a short click and whirring sound, the singer's voice filled the air.

"Good choice," he said as she turned to him. Suddenly the music and the look on her face made every sane thought race from his mind. "Would you like to dance? I don't have to introduce you to my dancing style," he said, trying for humor to quell his apprehension.

She smiled. "I would love to dance with you."

He took her in his arms, his hand resting on her back as he held her. They moved slowly to the music, at first a little distant and anxious. Then gradually, without thinking, he cupped the back of her head, lowering his lips to hers. He felt her fingers climb his chest as she reached for him, pulling him closer. Breathing in her scent, he deepened the kiss, taking great pleasure in the way her body moved against his, the way she opened her lips to his.

The music stopped. He eased away from her. "That's a beautiful song."

"It is." Her words were whispered, her eyes intense.

"My mother had a huge collection of vinyl records."

A buzzer went off in the kitchen, interrupting him. "Sorry, I need to get back to work."

"Can I help?" she asked, following him to the kitchen.

"No, but I'd like your company." He tucked the towel around his hips. "Wish I had an apron for you to tie around me."

She laughed. "You remember?"

"Of course. It's not every day a man has a beautiful woman put an apron on him."

I'll remember to bring you an apron the next time you're making dinner. Something flowery and pink, what about that?"

"It would be covered with stains and smudges long before anyone noticed. Take a stool and then tell me all about your visit with your father."

"You mean with Bill Cassidy. I need a little time to get used to calling him 'Dad'."

"Sure. But for purposes of this interview, may we refer to him as Dad?" he asked, giving her a teasing smile.

"That's part of why this is so weird for me. To be my age and find myself referring to a man I've never met before as my father seems so..." She rubbed her forehead with her hand. "Seems somehow not right."

"But after talking to him you came to realize that he didn't have a choice."

"She pressed her fingers together on the raised counter in front of her "Maybe. What don't get is why he didn't go after her. Why didn't he follow her to Virginia? And then of course there's my mom, who made sure he had no role in my life."

"Speaking of your mother, aren't you glad that this whole thing is out in the open?"

"I guess so." She frowned. "What I'll never get is why Mom wouldn't tell me about Bill when I found out that Marcus wasn't my birth dad."

She gave him a quick glance before continuing. "What's worse is that when she realized I was moving to Spencer Island, she could have told me about my father and that he lived here. She didn't. Can you believe that?"

"People do a lot of strange things. Maybe your mom's

grief over losing Marcus had an impact on how she dealt with your questions around your birth father."

"It's possible,"

"But what's important here is that you can move on with your life. Your worries about who your dad is are now over."

Nicole's looked up at him, a tentative smile on her face. "Bill and I have a lot to learn about each other."

Justin was careful not to burn his fingers as he took the rice from the microwave. "So are you and Bill seeing each other?"

"We are. I have to admit I feel pretty strange when I'm around him. Yet each time I see him I feel a stronger connection."

Justin turned his attention to the dish he was making. He couldn't watch the uncertainty on her face, the anxious way she smoothed her hair and touched her neck.

Being needed and trusted by Nicole would mean he'd feel committed to her. It would expose his need for her, something he wasn't ready for. In his heart he hadn't resolved his commitment to Haiti and what the coming months would mean for him and to the life he left behind there.

He was so preoccupied with his thoughts he forgot what he was doing. "Whoops! Dinner's ready." He opened the fridge, took out a bottle of wine and started taking things to the table. "Good food waits for no man. Let's talk and eat. The table is set, and this is your chair," he said, pulling out the solid wooden chair and flicking her napkin open before placing it in her lap.

"A cook and a waiter," she said, inhaling deeply. "This smells delicious."

He was pleased by her praise and took his seat opposite her, thankful the moment had passed before he said something he might regret. "You and I have another thing in common."

"And that would be?"

"Neither of us has family in Spencer Island. I mean none that we knew, or in your case none that you knew of until a few days ago." He took a bite of the creamy dish and looked at her over his fork.

"Bill tells me I have a cousin and a grandfather living handy."

There was a lonesome smile on her face. He wanted to reach out to her but held back. He loved this woman, but he'd made so many missteps in getting to know her. "After my mom died, my sister wanted me to move to Texas. But, as far as I'm concerned, the people I worked with in Haiti became my family. Grant Williams, my team leader, is like a brother to me. We all worked long hours, but it felt good that we were doing something for people who really needed it. People who without our help would have been in even worse circumstances."

"Is Grant Williams back home here?"

"No. He's in Haiti with the rest of the team."

"Why didn't you stay with them? What brought you home when you loved what you were doing down there?"

"I saw some pretty awful things that left me feeling that I couldn't make any difference whatsoever to those people until I straightened a few things out in my life."

"Can I ask what they are?"

He looked at his hands to prevent her seeing the shame in his eyes. How could he tell her about the worst moments of his life? If he did, would she understand? He hadn't been able to open up to anyone, not even the psychologist he'd seen for a few weeks when he first got home. Talking about Haiti meant more sleepless nights. More nightmares. Since he'd moved to Spencer Island he'd been steeping better. But maybe it was safe to open up, at least a little bit.

"I left Bangor after my mother died. I finished up her

169

affairs, rented the house, gave the renters my sister's number in Texas, packed a duffel bag of clothing and a box of tools and joined Grant Williams's team. He was against me going with him because I was still grieving for my mother, but 1 convinced him.

"When we got to Haiti, I worked every day until I literally fell asleep. My group was made up of dedicated professionals, who demanded more from themselves than from me, but I soon proved to them that I could handle anything. Or so I thought. I'd been there a little over two years when one day we got an urgent call to go to a house where the roof had collapsed. I thought I was used to seeing poorly built houses that were a stiff breeze away from falling down. But nothing prepared me for what happened next."

Nicole leaned forward her attention riveted on him. "What happened?"

"There was a young woman, Anna Hilario, trapped in the debris of the destroyed roof, screaming for help. The only help available was her husband, Nene, and me. He was already trying to claw a path into where she lay trapped when I got there. All the while, he talked to her so calmly and lovingly. I'll never forget his voice and the risk he took in climbing into the debris. I realized we needed a bulldozer or at least people to shovel, someone to help us shore up the structure before the mass of rubble crushed her. People were gathering, but no one had a bulldozer, and there were three garden shovels. We worked frantically, but suddenly the roof part that had been shielding her came crashing down. She and her husband died that day, leaving two small children. They were now orphans in a country overwhelmed by children who had lost their parents."

Her eyes were dark with shock. She reached out and took his hand, her fingers warm and comforting. "What did you do?"

He breathed in slowly to ease the memory of that day, the hopelessness and anger he felt. "I lost it. I threw things. I screamed and yelled at no one in particular. The rest of it is a blur. Grant arrived and took me back to where we were staying. I flew home two days later. When I got to Bangor, my grief overwhelmed me, grief for my mother, for the husband and wife who died needlessly in Haiti, for the children, for every sad thing that ever happened to me."

"When we first met, you told me you wanted to return to Haiti someday. Why would you go back if that's what it's like there?"

"Because volunteers from Western countries are all Haiti has to rebuild their country. It's taking longer than anyone expected. Meanwhile, the community where the roof fell is short one teacher, and two little kids will grow up without their parents. If we don't go there and help out, there will be more tragedy," he said, feeling the old familiar passion burn through him. "There is something absolutely soul-cleansing to offer hope to those in need. Being a carpenter in Haiti meant I could bring hope to others."

"You really care, don't you?"

"Yes. That's what so strange. I grew up with lots of love and attention. I never really gave a thought to what other people were going through. Then I landed in Haiti and everything changed. So much needed to be done, so many children living in poverty. Grief and pain were part of everyday life, I was overwhelmed."

She looked away then back at him, "I've never done anything like that. Although Dad's job meant we lived in a lot of places, we often were in areas where it felt just like home; very American in the schools and shopping areas."

"No real risk involved, right?"

She picked up her glass, sipped her wine slowly, her eyes fixed on him. She put the glass down very carefully. "Yes, I can't imagine going to live in a country that had so few of the things we take for granted,"

"You're talking about Starbucks coffee, supermarkets, restaurants," he said, having heard this response from others he'd talked to since he returned home.

"That, too. For me it would mean giving up my home and my farm."

"And you wouldn't be willing to do that." He had to admit he'd felt that way before Haiti.

"I don't believe I could ever do what you did."

"Are you sure?"

"Why would I want to go to Haiti?"

She would not understand his need to return. And talking about it had made him realize how strong his need was to go back. "You wouldn't even consider visiting the country?"

"Why all the questions about Haiti and whether I'd go? Leaving here is the last thing I want to do."

He was suddenly faced with nothing to say to Nicole, and it saddened him. What he needed was a little perspective on what had just happened. She wasn't a bad person, and she hadn't had his experience, one he was sure would change her if she had.

"On a different subject, I'm going to hire you to do a little work on the stone on the front. The mortar is starting to give way," she said.

"How did we get from Haiti to your house?" he asked, genuinely surprised that opening up to her seemed to mean so little.

She fidgeted with her napkin. "I'm not very comfortable talking about being in Haiti."

"Not even for the chance to meet charming six-year-olds who are eager to learn anything you can tell them about? Children who are only different because they were born in a different country, a different culture. In every other way they are just like children here without the advantages of our society."

She sighed. "You really love Haiti, don't you?"

"I do. It changed my life in every way that matters."

"With Dad's work, travelling was a part of my life. Yet, I never really involved myself in anything other than going to school, taking the occasional trip through the wild areas of whatever country we lived in."

"In other words, you can't relate to what I'm talking about," he said.

"Not really."

There seemed to be nothing more to say on the subject, and Justin was too disappointed in her response to come up with a new topic. He listened as Nicole talked about her work, about how nice the dinner had been at Matt and Gemma's house the other night.

Feeling let down, he picked up the plates and took them to the kitchen counter. What had he expected from her, from this evening? She'd made it clear she couldn't relate to his experience. Her words created a distance between them, a moment for him to reflect om his feelings. He was suddenly lonesome for his friends in Haiti, the people who had welcomed him as if he were family. In that instant he realized that they were still a very real part of his life. He wanted to share that with her but knew it would be pointless, at least for now.

He brought the peach cobbler he'd purchased to the table, noting that Nicole had suddenly gone very quiet. "Are you okay?" he asked, placing the bowls in front of them and returning to his chair.

"Justin, I'm sorry. I know that I must seem very insensitive to you. I didn't mean to. It's just that I've had a rough few weeks." She glanced at him. "But when I hear you describe how life was in Haiti, I feel guilty. My concerns are nothing compared to theirs. Quite frankly, I don't know how you did it. I couldn't have faced what you did."

"You'd be surprised what you can do when you have to or feel a need to. Don't feel guilty about it. Your life is different from theirs, as is mine. When I got back to Bangor I was so glad to be home, and yet I felt guilty, as well. I had everything while they had nothing. I left them to fend for themselves because I couldn't handle something that for them has been a regular occurrence,"

"We are the lucky ones, aren't we?"

"Absolutely." He smiled to force back the memories. "But enough of that. Let's have our dessert before we get down on the floor."

"I've never dated anyone who wanted to sit on the floor," she said ruefully.

"A new experience," he said, taking a bite of the peach cobbler.

Once the dessert was finished, they took their coffees to the table near the jukebox. "Do you want to pick the next three songs?" he asked.

"No. You choose."

"Well, since you chose Mr. Orbison, let's continue on with him." Justin read down the offerings. "How does 'Oh, Pretty Woman,' followed by 'In Dreams' and "Blue Velvet' sound to you?"

She grinned up at him from her perch on a large pillow. "I'm ready when you are, I wish I had been around when he was a star. Imagine going to a concert of his."

The first bars of "Oh, Pretty Woman" rose from the jukebox as Justin settled on the cushion beside her. They both leaned back against the front of the sofa for support. He slipped his arms around her shoulders very slowly. She edged closer to him and smiled up into his eyes as the sensual music swirled around them.

He breathed in her scent as he whispered in her ear, "The next song is ours. We're going to dance to it."

They snuggled together, singing along to the words and laughing when they hit a high note. "We might make it yet. The dynamic duo," he said, leaning in and kissing her lips.

Her sudden intake of breath, her hands reaching for him, her lips kissing him back, all of it made him want more...way more. The song ended.

"Okay," he stood up and reached for her hand. "May I have this dance?"

"You may," she said, grasping his hand while he pulled her up and into his arms. As the first notes of "In Dreams" flowed through the room, he held her gently in his arms, imagining what it would be like to hold her whenever he wanted to.

"I love this song," she said, taking the hand he offered as he held her.

The heat of her body next to his, the flowery scent of her hair... He closed his eyes, holding her close, swaying to the music, his fingers entwined in hers. It was all so perfect, exactly what he wanted, his feelings from earlier slipping away. He'd been wrong to believe that making love to her would only be having sex. He wanted this woman, needed her in his life.

As he held her, the words of the song, about a dream where a man walks with a woman he loves, Justin was overcome with the urge to tell Nicole how he felt. When the song ended, he reached over and turned off the music.

He looked down into her brown eyes, touched her forehead and ran his fingers along her cheek. "Nicole, I love you. I've loved you since the first day I met you. The day you took my blood."

. . .

Nicole's breath caught in her throat. No man had ever said those words to her before. She was so overcome by the love in his eyes, the anxious way he rubbed her back as he continued to hold her. He meant those words. Justin Hadley loved her.

She loved him too, despite their rocky beginning and her insecurities where men were concerned. She loved him, wanted him and missed him when he wasn't around.

Yet, love had to be real, forever, like her parents' love. Justin had only been in Spencer Island a matter of weeks. He was clearly unsettled. He had issues around his time in Haiti, really difficult ones. His future seemed uncertain to her.

She'd been searching for a man like Justin, someone who was fun and exciting. She also had to feel safe, protected and be assured that he'd be around for the difficult times.

She remembered how kind and sweet her father had been when her mother was diagnosed with breast cancer. He'd taken her to her appointments, cheered her up when she was sad or not feeling very well. After each treatment, he went out and bought her a little gift. She remembered the Santa figurine he'd given her after her fast treatment, just a week before Christmas. Would Justin be that kind of man?

Yet there was one thing she knew for certain. She loved him. She wasn't sure how it happened or when. It didn't really matter. What mattered was that she couldn't tell him, not just yet. She was not good at sharing her feelings. Feelings were risky.

What if she told him she loved him, and tomorrow or next week he decided he had to go back to Haiti? It would break her heart, and she'd be left trying to figure out how to live without him. He had no family connection here. No reason to stay unless his love for her was strong enough to keep him from wanting to leave. And if that happened, would a part of him always be wanting to go to Haiti?

She looked up at him, at the kind, caring expression on his face and knew she couldn't say the three words he wanted to hear. "I don't know what to say. This is so sudden. I've had a really difficult time these past weeks. Finding my birth father, learning that he was the one who came on my property without permission really affected me. Then my mother, my biopsy. It's all been very difficult."

She heard his sudden intake of breath followed by a long sigh. Standing so close suddenly felt awkward. Justin moved aside, picked up his coffee cup and took a sip, his back to her.

Why had he turned away? Did he not want her to see what was in his eyes? Why hadn't he shown concern for all she'd been through these past few weeks? If he loved her, where was his compassion?

"Why don't we focus on us for a little while? Live in the moment?" he asked, his tone light.

She felt exposed, vulnerable, unable to figure out what to do next. She'd never been involved in something like this before. She'd never loved a man who loved her. "You're upset with me."

"No. I'm not. I shouldn't have said what I said, that's all. It's too soon."

So he hadn't really meant those words? They'd simply slipped out in the heat of the moment? She had once again accepted what a man told her because she cared about him, not because she knew him well enough to know he was telling the truth.

It was all strange and frightening to her. She'd been thrilled to come to Justin's apartment for dinner, and now it was going to end badly. Glancing around at the space, at his personal things, she felt removed from him. "I'd better go," she said.

He turned to her, his eyes kind but distant. "We both have to go to work tomorrow," he said, his voice low.

. . .

As if sleep walking through a dark dream, Justin managed to walk Nicole down to her car, his thoughts frozen, his legs wooden. He'd had so many plans for this evening. all of them involving Nicole, none of them remotely possible now that she'd rejected his love. He knew beyond a shadow of doubt he'd spoken too soon. Yet in the face of her rejection, he was certain of one thing. He loved her. Sure, he was hurt that she didn't share his passion for Haiti, but he hadn't really given her a chance to understand what it was like, how much volunteers were needed. He opened her car door.

She stood beside him, her hands clutching her purse. "I... I really enjoyed this evening. Thank you." She raised her eyes to his.

He couldn't look at her, not knowing how she felt about him.

She slid into the car seat, and he eased the door closed behind her. He stepped back as she started the engine. He turned as he watched her taillights flash red before she pulled out onto the street.

He stared up at the cloudless sky, at a full moon that no amount of street lighting could hide, wondering why and how things had gone so wrong. He thought he did everything right this evening. They'd had a beautiful meal, lots of warmth and sharing. Yet the one thing she wouldn't share was her feelings for him. He'd blurted out his feelings, clearly a mistake, yet she had barely acknowledged his words.

All this time he thought they were learning about each other, making mistakes along the way; like any couple. Yet where it mattered, where feelings were involved, Nicole held back.

What if she wasn't capable of committing to him, of wanting a real relationship? She'd been the one to suggest that he wasn't ready for commitment because of his impulsive behavior, his willingness to jump into a situation and damn the consequences. She'd made him feel on the defensive about his way of deciding things. Yet, tonight he'd made it utterly clear how he felt about her, and she'd remained silent.

What was going on? He didn't want a relationship where he spent his time second-guessing how she felt about him. Life was too short. His mother had taught him that after his father died. He had so much more he wanted to experience, to enjoy and explore, He had so much to offer someone who loved him as much as he loved her.

He unlocked the door to his apartment and went into the empty space. Glancing around at the counters piled with dirty dishes and a sink full of pots, he sighed in resignation.

"Weil, Hadley, the joke's on you," he said, cleaning the plates and putting them in the dishwasher.

CHAPTER FOURTEEN

*N*icole managed to get through the next day, despite the memory of Justin's arms around her, his confession of love. Followed by his statement that he shouldn't have said those words.

They'd been having such a good time: Enjoying each other's company. She'd assumed by the way he was behaving that they'd end up making love before the night was out. She'd assumed so many things. All of them wrong.

She'd been waiting for a man to say he loved her, to be kind, sweet and caring like Justin. She loved him, yet she'd said nothing about her feelings for him. He'd opened his heart to her, and she'd rebuffed him by her silence.

Why had she done that? Why couldn't she share her feelings? She didn't have to say she loved him, but she could have told him how much she cared, how difficult it was for her to open up about her feelings.

When she got home from work, her house felt empty. Lonely. When she went out to look after Zeus and Suzie, they seemed sad. When she saddled up Zeus and went out for a ride, his slow, almost lumbering gait was in stark contrast to his usual spirited behavior.

Back at the house she tried to concentrate on washing down the wainscoting in the dining-room, her latest house project. She'd begun cleaning the wood in the dining room while she searched the internet for the perfect vintage wall-paper. She'd already cleaned the beveled glass in the three windows at the end of the room. Normally, doing this sort of work was relaxing and fulfilling. But after an hour she gave up, put her cleaning things away, and turned on the TV. Anything to stop the remorse she felt over what had happened. Yet she couldn't concentrate on any program long enough to get the story in her head.

All the while, she didn't want to face the truth. She and Justin hadn't been able to communicate, and it was mostly her fault. She let her own misgivings get in the way of facing reality. Despite her concerns about his impetuousness, she loved Justin. Thanks to her behavior last evening, she'd prob-ably never see him again.

Why hadn't she told Justin the truth about her feelings? Why was she so sure that he would say he loved her on a whim? Was she afraid his words were said too easily, before she had a chance to sort out her own feelings? Had her mother's lack of honesty made her distrustful of everyone's motives?

She tossed the TV remote on the sofa in frustration. What should she do? She couldn't just go to Justin and confess her love for him. It was too risky. What if he made light of her confession the way he did about her biopsy and her fear of cancer?

A flash of headlights across the room where she sat made her jump. Had Justin decided to come and see her? Was it her father? But he'd promised to call first...

She recognized Gemma's car when she went to the door,

When Gemma and Angie got out of the car and crossed the gravel drive, she ran to greet them. "I didn't know you were coming, but I'm sure glad you're here."

Gemma and Angie hugged her. "We came to see how you're doing and to offer some unsolicited advice," Gemma said.

Angie held up a bag from the local bakery, "First we need a cup of coffee to go with these cinnamon rolls."

"I think I can manage that," Nicole said leading the way into the house and out to the kitchen. "I've been trying to get some housework done, but I guess I'm not in the mood."

"Would that have anything to do with your date last night?" Gemma asked.

Nicole nodded. "A whole lot to do with it, actually. Sorry I didn't tell you about the date."

"Yeah, we waited for you at coffee this morning. When you didn't show, we figured that something had happened last night," Angie said.

"By the look on your face something went really wrong. So, let's have it," Gemma said.

"Justin loves me."

"What!" Angie yelled out, nearly spilling her cup of coffee.

Gemma clapped her hands, "That's great. The other night at dinner I knew there was something big going on. The looks you were giving each other were way too hot for just friends." Gemma gave Nicole a quick hug, making her feel even guiltier. "Matt says he's a real nice guy.

"The evening didn't end up all that great. And it's mostly my fault," she confessed. "When he told me he loved me, I didn't say anything. I couldn't say anything. He took it the wrong way."

"Of course, he would. When a man tells a woman he loves her, he expects an answer."

"I didn't give him the answer he was looking for."

"Do you love him?" Gemma asked.

"Yes, I've waited all this time for the right man. He comes along and I blow it."

Gemma's eyes were damp, "Everyone gets it wrong at least part of the time. Look at Matt and me back a few months ago."

"Yeah, but this was really bad. I spent my time mentally going over all the reasons I shouldn't love him, while he waited for me to say something."

Angie's eyebrows shot up behind her mass of dark curls. "Are you serious?"

Gemma wagged her finger at Nicole, a triumphant smile on her face. "Do you still think he's hiding something big, something from his past?"

"No. He told me something last night that explains at least partly why he's been distant at times."

"So?" Angie asked.

Nicole knew that Justin had told her his story in confidence, and she would respect that. It was the least she could do. "His work in Haiti was very difficult."

"But you got a chance to understand him a little better?" Gemma asked.

"Yes, but it may not matter. I don't know if I'll be seeing him again."

"Why not?" Angie asked.

"Because he told me he loved me. He was expecting me to say something in return, I didn't. I couldn't."

Gemma pushed her plate with the cinnamon roll on it to one side. "It's time you told us everything about last night. You care about this guy, and we're here to get your love affair back on track."

Nicole couldn't help but smile. She turned to Angie. "You said she was a notorious matchmaker. Now I understand what you're saying."

Angie gripped her coffee cup with both hands, "Don't try to change the subject. I'm with Gemma on this. Confession time."

Nicole took her time telling them about the date, about how much she'd enjoyed being with Justin. She told them about the meal he made, his '60s music. The slow dancing together she had hoped would lead to his bedroom. She told them everything but the details of the incident in Haiti.

When she was finished, Angie's eyes were moist. "It sounds like the perfect date."

"It was until I completely messed it up," Nicole lamented.

"Why didn't you say anything about your feelings? I mean, you might feel you couldn't say you love him. I understand that. But why didn't you tell him that you really care about him? Heavens! Everyone at work knows. Why not tell Justin?"

Nicole sighed. Her first thought was to come up with an excuse. But that wouldn't work with these two women. "He took me by surprise. I thought we were on a date. I never expected him to say he loved me when we'd only been out a couple of times. Who confesses their love for someone so quickly?" Nicole closed her eyes remembering the look on his face. "I'm afraid he might have said he loved the way most people would say they liked me. It felt too soon for me. It felt flippant and off-the-cuff, just like the day I told him about my biopsy." She raised her head, looked from Angie to Gemma.

Gemma touched her arm. "You don't trust him. You think he has ulterior motives for telling you he loved you. Oh, Nicole, honey, I'm so sorry that you could even think that way." She put up her hand to ward off Nicole's protest. "I suppose it's possible that he did it for other reasons. But I don't believe so. The man doesn't seem the type."

"Nicole, have you been looking for reasons not to become seriously involved with Justin?" Angie asked.

"What?" Nicole demanded. "I... No! Of course not. I want someone in my life. Someone who wants what I want."

"Meaning a man who wants to marry you, have a permanent relationship?" Gemma asked.

Angie's eyebrows arched in question. "Don't you see, Nicole? Justin might be that man. Sure, you feel his confession of love is too soon, and you say it felt flippant. What if it isn't? What if he really loves you?"

Three days later Justin nearly hit his thumb when he hammered the last nail into the flower boxes, the last item on the list of carpentry tasks he'd been hired to do for his latest client.

Slow down. You're going to get hurt if you don't watch it.

He gathered up his tools, gave his invoice to the business owner and got into his truck. He was lucky he hadn't caught his fingers in the door. Sitting alone in the cab, he couldn't hide from the fact that he was still hurting over Nicole. How could he have been so wrong? He was sure she cared about him. Maybe even loved him. He'd been shocked when she blew him off, acted as if his confession of love was inappropriate. He'd been hurt and mortified.

He started his truck and pulled out onto the street. He had to figure out what to do. He loved Nicole, and he was sure she cared about him. He tapped the steering wheel in frustration. But if she did, why hadn't she said something? Was she afraid? Come to think of it, she looked a little anxious. Worried, maybe?

Was she still fixated on what had happened with Bill Cassidy? He'd been a little harsh with her on the end, all because his feelings were hurt. It wasn't often that a man confessed his love and got silence in return.

The more he thought about it, the more convinced he was that Nicole didn't mean to leave him hanging like that. She wasn't the kind of woman who would be that cruel. He was on the highway, on the outskirts of Spencer Island, when he spotted the turnoff to her place. Abruptly, he slammed on the brakes and swung the wheel. The blast of horn and squeal of tires from the car behind startled him. "Careful!" he said to the inside of the cab.

Once on Nicole's road, he drove more carefully. When he passed Ned Tompkins's place, he waved, and Ned waved back. He was relieved to see Nicole's car in her driveway. He suddenly realized he hadn't thought about whether or not she'd be home. But, damn it, he had to find out what happened the other night. Either that or lose a finger on the next job. He slowed to make the turn into her driveway.

Nicole was walking toward her house from the paddock, where Zeus stood next to the fence. She walked toward him unaware of how beautiful she was with her easy grace and gorgeous body tucked into a red plaid shirt and black jeans. She must have been out for ride. He pulled to a stop and got out of the truck. "I was hoping I'd find you home," he said, coming toward her, aching to put his arms around her and kiss her.

"It's good to see you," Nicole said, stopping a few feet from him, a wary look in her eyes.

"You, too."

She stood perfectly still for a few minutes. Justin held his breath waiting.

"Would you like to come in?" she asked, her tone a little anxious to his ears.

"Is this a bad time?"

"Not at all." She led the way into her house, moving

quickly into the kitchen. Reaching the counter, she turned to face him. "Did you need to see me about something?" she asked, her voice so soft he was forced to lean closer.

His thoughts raced. Why hadn't he come up with an excuse for seeing her on the way over? "I... I thought I should check. The night we had dinner at Neil's house you said you needed me to do some work for you, something about the mortar on the stone out front." He felt painfully awkward as he waited for her response.

"Yes, that's true, I do," she said, her words rushed.

Was she feeling a little awkward, as well? "Do you want me to take a look at it, price the work out for you?"

"Yes... Not right now."

She looked up into his eyes, and he saw her anxiety. "What is it?" he asked.

"I wanted to talk to you about the other night at your apartment. I behaved very badly."

He smiled in relief, his arms aching for her. "I got it all wrong. I didn't mean to scare you off."

She tucked her fingers into the belt loops on her jeans "You're not the only one who can't seem to get it right. Maybe we should..." She met his gaze, her eyes dark with feeling. He opened his arms. She stepped into his embrace. He drank in her scent, her warmth and felt his heart lift in his chest. "We need to talk," he whispered into her hair.

She lifted her face to his, her eyes searching his. "Yeah, we do."

He wanted to yell with pleasure. He settled for cupping her face in his hands and kissing her. She'd never tasted so good. His body hummed.

"Let's go into the living room, where we can be comfortable." She hugged him close as she walked with him into the next room.

"I'm so glad I turned off the highway and headed here to

see you. I made my decision so fast I earned a good blast of horn from the driver behind me," he said, settling in beside her, forcing his arms to his sides. He wouldn't hold her, his first urge. He needed a clear head for the next little while until they straightened out everything between them.

"Running on impulse again, are you?" she said, a smile in her eyes as she hitched her legs up under her and hugged a pillow.

"But it paid off," he said, her smile giving him the first moments of happiness he'd had since he'd told her he loved her.

"Where should we start?" she asked.

Nicole was overjoyed at the sight of Justin sitting on her sofa, so close she could smell his very male scent. He'd come straight from work to see her. "I'm sorry about the way I behaved when you said you loved me."

"No one has to behave a certain way. It should simply be a natural expression of feelings. You don't love me. I get it."

She ached to say the words. To tell him how she really felt, but something held her back. "I care deeply about you. But I worry that it's all too fast. We've only known each other for a few weeks. We have so much to learn about each other."

His eyes held hers. The way he looked at her made her heart pound with happiness. "Nicole, for me, love isn't something you work on. It's something your heart does to you. Have you never been in love before?"

"Love doesn't come that easily for me," she said, acutely aware that her words weren't true. She loved this man. The problem was she feared risking everything should he not feel the same two weeks or two months from now.

"Have you ever loved a man?" he insisted.

She hugged the pillow tighter. "Most of the men I've dated weren't really the kind I'd want to marry."

He reached for her hand, his fingers playing with hers. "That's not what I asked."

If she tossed the pillow on the floor and moved only a few inches toward him, she could be nestled in his arms. She squeezed the pillow, torn between staying where she was and reaching out to him. His eyes told her he'd welcome any move she made toward him. Her pride held her back. "No. I've never loved a man."

"Other than your father, I assume."

"My father was a very special man. And, yes, I loved him very much."

"So much that no other man ever measured up?"

"No! I'm just not very lucky when it comes to finding a man with the right qualities."

He toyed with her hand, massaging the skin on the inside of her wrist, driving her crazy with need for him. Her heart pounded against her ribcage.

"And what are these right qualities?" he asked. "Are they all traits you saw in your father?"

"Mostly," she said, wishing he would stop, or make love to her.

"The same father that didn't tell you that you weren't his biological child. The same father who didn't insist that your mother tell you about your biological father. The man who put his career first, ahead of any consideration of offering you a stable life in a community where you could form real attachments to real people."

"That's not fair!" she cried. *What was he doing?* "I thought we were going to talk about us. I'm not going to sit here and listen to you attack my dad."

"I'm not. I'm right here waiting for you to see that I may not measure up to what you had in mind, but I want you."

She took a deep breath to calm the anxiety racing through her. "My dad loved my mom. He'd do anything for her. He'd do anything for me."

"Including not telling you the truth about his relationship to you."

Nicole was so upset she could hardly breathe. "What right have you got to come in here and say these things to me?" she demanded, pulling her hand from his and getting up from the sofa.

Quickly he grabbed her hand, pulling her down beside him. Taking both her hands in his, he smiled a sad smile. "The right of a man who loves you, who wants a chance to prove it to you. But first, you have to face up to the fact that your dad wasn't perfect. That he had flaws like every other man on the planet. That searching for a perfect man that meets all your criteria isn't what life and being part of a relationship is about. Love simply is. Love is about needing another person more than you need anyone else in the world." His voice softened. "That's how I feel about you. I need you. I need you every day, in every part of my life."

Nicole met his heated gaze, her heart thudding against her throat. She wanted to be angry with him, to tell him to leave and never come back. She wanted to scream at him, to defend her father. "My dad was the best, I miss him."

"Of course, you miss him. You always will. This isn't about your dad. It's about us and where we go from here."

As she gazed into his eyes and saw the love there, she realized that Justin was right. Her father should have put her need to know who her birth father was first. He should have convinced her mother to do the right thing and tell her all about Bill Cassidy. "He was a good man," she insisted.

"But he and your mother made a mistake in not telling you who your father was."

"Yes, they did. I needed to know about my birth father

and his family. They kept it from me," she conceded. "But I don't believe Dad did it to hurt me. He did it because he thought it was the right thing to do."

"Regardless of his reasons, his actions meant you didn't have a chance to know your birth father," he said, moving her into the crook of his arm and pulling her gently back against the sofa. "Your parents may have believed they were doing the right thing by keeping their secret to themselves. But now you know, and you have to accept what they did if you want to get on with your life."

"I have a life."

"Can you honestly say you've accepted things if you're still angry at your mother? Forgiveness works both ways." He smiled at her, intimacy and awareness making his eyes dark pools. "Maybe you should think about forgiving your mother."

She wanted to tell him to mind his own business. But the look in his eyes told her he really cared, wanted to help her and was waiting for her to consider what he said. "My mom hurt me, you're right. As for my father, he didn't mean to hurt me." She felt tears well up in her eyes. "I loved him. I'll always love him."

"And you should," he said, his fingers massaging her shoulder, his breath gentle on her cheek, "You've had a lot to deal with lately. I simply want you to know I'm here, that I'd like to have a chance to have a future with you."

"What does that mean? You seem to think this is easy for me. It's not. We can't look forward to a future without knowing each other. I really can't speak from experience about relationships. But I do know that a long term, loving relationship is based on sharing things, getting to understand each other. My mom and dad shared everything. That's why moving around with my dad's work didn't feel like a sacrifice. My parents were happy simply to be together. That's the kind of marriage I want."

He smiled, kissed her cheeks, sending tingling sensation along her jaw. "We're talking marriage now, are we?"

"Don't play with my words," she said, turning in his arms to face him.

"That's not all I want to play with," he said.

He was so close. So touchable. She wanted to forget all her concerns, to simply let things unfold and see what happened next. She wanted to, but she couldn't. "We have a lot of stuff to work out between us."

He snugged her body closer to his. "I'm not worried."

"And that would be because?" she asked.

"You and I are meant to be together. You may not be able to tell me you love me right yet. But I promise you there will come a day when you will. And I'll be there."

His eyes were deep pools of blue, the kind of eyes she could lose herself in... If only she dared. She kissed him, slowly at first, holding tight to him, feeling a connection to this impulsive, openhearted man she'd never felt before in her life.

"Does this mean I'm staying the night?" he asked, running his hands down her body, lighting her desire for him.

She wanted him. He wanted her. Yet something held her back. Aware of her need for him, for everything he offered, she reached up and touched his chin. "Justin, I'm not ready to do that just yet. For me, making love means commitment. When we make love, if has to be something we're both committed to, not simply enjoyable sex."

He kissed her, slow and easy, with tenderness. "I guessed right the first time," he said against her lips.

"What do you mean?"

"The minute I met you, I knew you weren't the kind of woman who would settle for casual sex. You need commitment. I'm ready to offer you all the commitment you want. Wait and see. Your life's about to change."

He got up and pulled her up beside him. "Walk me out to my truck, where I will give you a chaste kiss, and we will agree to meet on the morrow," he said.

She couldn't help but laugh at him. "What am I going to do with you?" she asked, cuddling close to him as they walked together out to his truck.

"You could make all my dreams come true," he said, his smile irresistible.

"You're a wonderful dreamer," she said, as she kissed him.

As she watched him drive away, she knew one thing for certain. She wanted him to stay. She wanted him to make love to her. She wanted everything he offered, and she'd been a fool not to see that sooner.

CHAPTER FIFTEEN

*J*ustin had never been happier in his entire life. He and Nicole talked the next morning before they went to work and agreed that he would go to her place that evening for dinner. He offered to drop by the local fish market and bring fresh fish.

He worked like someone possessed, completing the steps Sam Paulson, a senior who lived alone in his own home since his wife passed away, had asked him to replace. As he put away his tools, Justin could hardly contain his excitement over seeing Nicole.

Sam had been watching Justin work while he talked about his life as long-distance truck driver. "You got to have the fastest hammer in town." the older gentleman joked as he paid him in cash. "Would you like to come in and have a glass of Scotch?"

"Another time, for sure. Right now, I need to get back home. I've got something I need to do, and it can't wait."

"You're certainly in a hurry today. Saw you hammering as if the devil were chasing you," Sam said, inspecting the new steps.

Justin chuckled. "Got a lot on my mind."

"Something to do with a woman is my bet," Sam said, eyeing him.

"Not much gets past you."

"Women have been a constant preoccupation of mine. Had three wives just to prove the point."

"You did? Which one did you like the best?"

"Can't say just yet. Might marry again, you never know," Sam replied, looking off toward downtown. "Life is filled with possibilities."

"Couldn't agree more," Justin said, putting the money in his wallet, gathering up his tools and heading for his truck. "Talk to you later," he said, waving at Sam as he got into his truck.

When he got back to his apartment, his cell phone began to ring. Hoping it was Nicole, he checked the caller ID. Grant Williams.

"Hi, Grant. Great to hear from you. How's it going?"

"Not bad. I'm back stateside and was wondering if you and I might get a chance to talk."

Happy to have his friend home, he said, "Whenever you'd like. Where are you?"

"I'm in Boston. Just got in, actually. I thought I'd drive up to see you tomorrow if that's okay."

He knew his friend well enough to know that if he was heading his way, it must have to do with Haiti. "What's going on?"

Grant's sigh echoed through the phone. "Juan Marquez left. His mother is very ill in North Carolina. He's gone back to care for her, probably for a couple of months. Maybe longer. All to say we really need you back in Haiti. I promised that I wouldn't bother you after you left. I'm well aware that you had a difficult time, but you're the best carpenter I've ever had working with me. You're also good at organization."

Juan Marquez was terrific worker and a friend. They had shared the same sleeping quarters.

"I'm sorry to hear about Juan's mother. You're looking for someone to take Juan's place?"

"Is more urgent than that. One of the orphanages was destroyed by fire."

"Which one?"

"The one just outside Jacmel."

"I know that orphanage." He remembered it as if it was yesterday. After the collapse of his friend Nene Hilario's house and the deaths of Nene and Anna, Justin had gone back to the rubble of what had been their home, found the children crying without their parents and took them to the orphanage. He hadn't known what else to do. Grant had promised to check on the children when he could. "Were the Hilario children still there when the fire happened?" Justin asked, fearful that the two young boys hadn't made it to safety.

"They're safe, and they've been moved to a temporary site until we can manage to rebuild the orphanage. I left a crew cleaning up the site, getting the debris from the fire moved. I'm back here to make a personal plea to my donors for the money to ship mobile home units down to the building site until we can arrange to build a new facility. I've got a plan drawn up to present at the meeting this Friday. The one thing I need to be able to tell them is that I have a carpenter to help in setting up the units and seeing that they are properly placed with stairs, skirting and all the other things. You know what I mean. Our donors are good. They insist on things being done right."

Justin's heart pounded in his chest. As a way to keep in touch with the Hilario children, he'd volunteered to fix an outside wall of the orphanage that had been damaged by rain, and had been surrounded while he worked by children asking questions, talking playfully. "Grant, I don't know. Are you sure I'm the right person to do the job?"

"The last thing I wanted to do was call on you. I respect your need for time to get your head together. I tried everyone I could think of, but each of them either had other commitments or didn't have the necessary paperwork or vaccinations to leave the country and go to Haiti right away."

Suddenly, the demolished house appeared in his mind, the pain, the fear, the sense of loss, leaving the children behind. He shouldn't go. He needed more time here, but faced with Grant's request his heart was moved.

These children, who'd already lost their parents, had been traumatized by a fire that took their home, and would now be scattered around to whoever could care for them. The children would lose their connection to each other and be set adrift by circumstances beyond their control. "How long will it take?"

"Once the units are delivered, probably months. I'm not sure."

Finding the units and purchasing them, assuming they were even available, would take a few weeks, if not months. Enough time for him to close his apartment and put his things in storage. "You don't have to make the trip up here to convince me. You can count on me."

"Thanks, Justin. I owe you one."

They talked for a while longer, organizing what had to be done, Justin feeling the pull of friendship, of shared experience together in a world most of his friends and acquaintances couldn't imagine. Yet it was his world, the place where he'd learned the true meaning of caring, of relying on each other for support and backup. The place where he truly belonged.

Once he'd hung up from his call with Grant, he looked around his apartment at the life he'd made for himself, and for a few minutes he was sorry he had to leave it. But the surge of excitement roaring through him convinced him he'd done the right thing for himself and for the children in Haiti.

He couldn't wait to tell Nicole, to share his plan with her.

What would she think? He needed to know she was with him on this. Would she understand his need to help those children? Nicole loved children. Her skills would be a perfect fit. And he needed her with him: with every fibre of his being, he needed her.

Suddenly aware that he was supposed to pick up fish and go to Nicole's house, he made for the shower, got cleaned up and drove to the fish market. He put a quick call in to Nicole, but it went to voice mail. He left her a message saying that he was running a few minutes late, but he'd have the fish with him and something really exciting to tell her.

Nicole was looking forward to dinner with Justin this evening. She was glad they'd had a chance to talk, to find a way back to each other. Being together didn't mean there wouldn't be issues, but in her heart, she knew they were meant to be together. A thought that made her really and truly happy.

Added to that they were going to talk about her house and what repairs were required to maintain it. She was thrilled to think that they shared a love of woodworking, of Craftsman house. Something they would always share. Having Justin care about her house meant a great deal. It meant that they had a place to start, a place to build from.

She smiled to herself as she organized the dinner. She planned to have twice-baked potatoes with broccoli and cheese to go with whatever fish Justin picked up at the market. She'd picked up gelato for dessert, along with pale yellow tapered candles for the dining room table. She decided to set the table using dishes her father had bought her for Christmas the year before he flew to Chile. They'd been shopping for a Christmas gift for her mother at Macy's when she'd spotted the set that reminded her of the four years they'd lived in Thailand. On Christmas morning they were under the tree for her.

She'd just finished setting the table when the phone rang. She didn't recognize the number... "Hello?" she said.

"Hi, Nicole."

"Mom? Why are you calling me?"

There was a long silence, which Nicole knew meant that she had hurt her mother's feelings. "I'm sorry, Mom, but I thought we'd agreed that you'd give me a little time to sort things out. How did you get my number?"

"I was talking to Bill. He gave it to me. Before you start blaming him for doing that, I told him I needed to talk to you."

"Mom. I wouldn't have blamed Bill, my father. I know how persuasive you can be. You haven't answered my question. Why are you calling me? Is something wrong?" she asked, annoyed that her mother had not respected her wishes. She glanced at her watch, Justin would be here in a few minutes, and she didn't intend to let her mother's needs interfere with the evening she had planned.

"Nicole, I've talked it over with Bill, and he's invited me to visit him. But I'd prefer not to stay at his house. I'm not ready—"

"What!" The last time she'd spoken to Bill, he hadn't expressed any interest in talking to her mom. Like her, he was still trying to adjust to what her behavior had done to their lives. What was going on? The last thing she wanted right now was for her mother to show up in Spencer Island.

"Mom. Why are you doing this? What do you want from me?"

"I would like to stay with you," she said, reproach evident in her voice.

From long experience, she knew that her mother had never let someone else's wishes stand in the way of what she wanted. "Mom. You can't come here. You can't stay with me. If you feel you have to come to Spencer Island to see Bill, you'll have to stay somewhere else. You must have relatives in the area. You grew up here."

"No, I don't." Her mother's tone held regret. "My parents passed away when we lived in Indonesia."

Nicole didn't want to feel responsible for her mother or her happiness. Those last months before she moved from Seattle had been among the worst of her life. Taking a deep breath, she tried to explain as calmly as she could how she felt. "Mom, you don't seem to understand how much you've hurt me. I didn't leave Seattle to have you come here, expecting to be part of my life. You can't be here...with me." She felt her throat tighten. How she wished her relationship with her mother was different. "Mom, I have to go."

"Wait! Look, I'm sorry for all the mistakes I've made. I can't go on like this. I love you. I want to make amends. Bill has offered to help me. He's a good man. I made some awful mistakes where he was concerned. Mistakes I can't fix. I'm so sorry."

"Mom, I don't want to talk about this right now. I'm busy—"

"My life is a mess. I have no one to blame but myself. I realize you're still angry at me, but I'm coming to Spencer Island very soon. I hope to see you when I do."

"Mom, I have finally found a man I love. Please understand that I can't deal with your issues. I want to enjoy my time with him. I want to get to know my father. I want to put together a life with the two men who offer me a chance at happiness. Can you understand that?"

"Yes. I can, Nicole. I'm sorry for upsetting you. I won't come to Spencer Island until you're ready to see me. If Bill wants to meet me somewhere so we can talk, somewhere away from Spencer Island. I'll do that and I want you to know I'm happy you've found someone. There's nothing quite like loving someone, knowing you have the capacity to love and to be loved in return. I'll wait to hear from you when you're ready." With that, the line went dead.

The truck engine roared as Justin sped around the turn onto Nicole's road, spitting up a plume of gravel. In the gathering darkness, the lights on her house were like a beacon. He'd picked up the fish and had stopped for a bottle of white wine, paying more than he'd ever had for one bottle. It was going to be a big celebration tonight.

He was going to the woman he loved to share his happiness over Grant's phone call. His mind hadn't stopped going over everything he'd have to organize and work on between now and when he had to leave. He and Grant were doing a conference call with the construction group providing the modular units early tomorrow morning.

He pulled into Nicole's driveway, braked hard and got out of the truck. He took the back steps two at a time and knocked on the door. No answer. He tried again. Still no answer. Had Nicole gone somewhere? He went back down the steps and strode out to the horse barn. The horses gave him a welcoming whinny, tossing their heads in greeting.

He backed away, checked the tack room as he took out his phone. Still no answer. What was going on? He returned to the back door and knocked again.

Nicole appeared, her face stained with tears. "Nicole!

What's the matter?" he asked, stepping inside, putting the fish and the wine on the bench beside the door and gathering her in his arms in one easy motion.

She sobbed into his chest, her body shaking. He patted her back, soothing her as best he could, waiting for the tears to subside. "What's going on?" he asked, smoothing the hair from her cheeks when she looked up at him.

The pain he saw in her eyes had him pulling her closer. "Whatever it is, I'm here for you. You can tell me."

She sniffed and wiped her cheeks. "My mother."

"What about her?"

"She called a little while ago. She wanted to come and see me. I told her no. That I didn't want to see her," she sobbed.

"Okay. Let's sit down," he said soothingly.

They settled on the sofa in the living room, Nicole snugged up against him. "Start at the beginning," he said.

He listened as Nicole described her call with her mother in between bouts of tears. Nicole clearly missed her mother but couldn't seem to resolve the issues between them. He could understand her feelings. A mother who let her daughter come to Spencer Island without telling her that her birth father lived here had some pretty serious issues. He really didn't understand, but then again he wasn't a parent. All he knew was that Nicole was upset, and he wanted to help her feel better.

"What am I going to do? I shouldn't have been so rude with Mom, but she hurt me so much." Nicole pushed her hair away from her face.

"I'm not trying to defend your mom here. But do you suppose that part of the reason she didn't tell you about your dad years ago was because she didn't want to put any strain on her happy family life? She felt safe und loved. Could your mother simply have been protecting those she loved from facing something she'd done a long time ago? Something she wasn't proud of?"

"Who knows? My mother is...so hurtful." Nicole got up and walked back and forth in front of the sofa, narrowly missing the end of the heavy wooden coffee table on one of her circuits. "I wish I could turn back the clock sometimes. Back to before Dad died. Everything had been perfect then."

"Back before you found out about your birth father."

"I had a right to know," she cried.

"You did."

"That's what hurts so much. Mom and I were really close until...until I confronted her with the fact that Marcus wasn't my birth father. Why wouldn't she tell me the truth?" She wiped her face with her hands.

Justin went to her, took her hands in his. "I can't imagine how that must have felt. Mom and Dad's life was an open book. They went to the same school, were high school sweethearts. Dad went to technical school. Mom became a teacher's assistant. They got married and had my sister and me. Perfectly happy until Dad passed away and Mom had to cope on her own.

He tipped her chin up and looked into her beautiful eyes. "But you know what? Everyone has things in their lives that cause them pain. And you've had your fair share. Why don't you let it go for now? I brought fresh fish..." He looked around, forgetting what he did with it. "Maybe it's still out in the truck." He smiled. "See, just the thought of seeing you rattles my senses."

"What a lovely thing to say." She sniffed, smoothed her hands over her waist and sighed. "Thanks for listening. Why don't you retrieve the fish from wherever it is, and I'll finish organizing dinner? Before my mom called, I was perfectly happy getting ready for this evening."

"Well, then, dial back to that moment, and let's enjoy

ourselves," he said, kissing her lips, feeling her body move toward his. He planned to stay the night, to share his excitement about their life together. They would be with each other, together in every way that mattered. He couldn't wait for them to start new with only each other, to feel how wonderful and gratifying life could be. His family, his mom and dad and sister, had lived a wonderful life together. He wanted the same. He'd tell Nicole all about his plans while they prepared their meal.

Nicole was so relieved to have Justin here with her. He'd been so helpful and understanding about her issues with her mother. She really appreciated his sweetness, his caring. When he returned with the fish she was humming to herself as she worked in the kitchen. With a new sense of ease between them they began making dinner. "Would you like an apron?" she asked, unable to hold back a grin.

"If you're tying, I'm buying," he said, turning to her as she pulled an apron off the hook beside the fridge.

"Thanks for being here," she said as she put the apron on him.

As she turned back to him, she saw the love in his eyes. Her breath halted in her chest.

He leaned down, his lips brushing hers, taking her breath away with his touch. "You're welcome. There isn't anything we can't do if we put our hearts and minds into it," he said, steadying the salad bowl between them as his gaze held hers.

This was a moment she would remember forever. The beginning of lots of moments they would have together. The idea made her smile, her whole body warming to his closeness. "I'm glad you arrived when you did," she said.

"Me, too."

This evening would be special, especially for her. The old

doubts about his caring had been put to rest when he held her and let her cry. For her, something had shifted between them.

Lots of men would have offered comfort, but Justin had made her feel safe, protected. She felt his concern in his touch, the way he held her. She loved him and had begun to believe, that although they were different in many ways, they had a lot in common. She'd tell him tonight how she felt. Once dinner was over and they were settled on the sofa, she would share all her feelings, and her love for him. If she had her way, he wouldn't be leaving tonight. For the first time ever, she was going to be very clear about her feelings for a man. There would be no reason for her to hide from him.

Justin brought the plates of baked haddock, broccoli and potatoes to the table. "We're going to celebrate tonight. I have great news."

Nicole placed her napkin on her lap and gave Justin her undivided attention. "I can't wait to hear."

"First we'll eat. Wouldn't want to have our food get cold." He settled into the chair across from her, his eyes on her, the air between them sizzling with awareness.

She watched as he poured wine into their glasses and put the bottle back carefully while his gaze kept searching her face, his eyes meeting hers as if she was the only woman on the face of the earth. She loved it. This feeling of being the focus of his caring attention, the way he made her feel special.

He held his glass up to her. "I'd like to propose a toast to you and me."

"A toast," she said, a smile hugging her lips.

He took a sip. "So often we forget how fortunate we are." He put his glass down. "I want you to know I'm the luckiest man alive, and it's all because of you."

She picked up her glass again, excitement dancing through her. "To happiness."

"And to us," he said. "Nicole Simpson, you and I are going to be very happy."

"You can see the future?" she asked, trying for a teasing tone while his words filled her heart with joy.

"Very clearly. You and me together. It's inevitable, you know."

"What is?" she asked, knowing the answer but needing to hear the words.

"Me and you," he said. With his voice filled with love, he got up and came around the table, knelt beside her, turned her toward him and kissed her with so much gentleness she melted in his arms.

He touched her cheek. "I love you."

His words took her breath away. It was as if they had been together for years, not a few weeks. She needed him with her, wanted his attention, his caring and love. For the first time she experienced some of what her parents must have felt for each other. They always seemed to be in a world all their own. Now she understood why. When two people loved each other nothing mattered us much as being together.

Her body tingled at his touch, the look in his eyes. She returned his kiss, stroking his face, feeling her body reach for his. She was in new territory. Her feelings for Justin were real, her need for him overpowering. With her heart thudding in her chest, she looked into his eyes. She wanted to tell him she loved him. That she'd never felt like this before and never would again. He was waiting for her...

She ran her fingers along his jaw, soaking in the feel of his skin, the scent of him. Was he about to pick her up and carry her to her bedroom and make love to her? Her heart rose in her throat, and a happy kind of anxiety and excitement made her feel as if she could take on the world.

"Ah... I think it's best that we move on," he said, a little sheepishly, his gaze wavering. "Hate to admit it, but this floor is a little hard on the knees."

'I love you' had been on her lips.

They both gave a weak laugh to cover their predicament.

Feeling that she once again missed the chance to tell him her true feelings, she ate slowly, listening to the '60s music, her attention centered on the man sitting across from her, his hair tousled and so touchable.

"Like the view?" he asked, a teasing, sexy tone back in his voice.

"Yeah, you could say that," she murmured, taking one final bite of her fish. Justin placed his fork on the plate, picked up his wine and leaned back in the chair. "I have something special to talk to you about. About our future," he said, the old excitement back in his eyes.

Oh! Was he going to propose? No! Too soon for that. Was he going to suggest they move in together? Maybe... "Come on. Don't keep me in suspense."

"Where should I start?" he said, looking into the distance.

She held her breath, anxious and excited and so much in love with this man.

"Don't do this to me. Tell me!"

"You remember me talking about my team leader in Haiti, Grant Williams?"

"Yes..." What did Grant Williams have to do with them?

"He called today. He's in Boston on business." Justin leaned forward, reaching for her hand.

A little surprised but still wanting to know what he was talking about, she slid her hand across the table to meet his. "I hope it's not bad news."

"Yes and no..." Justin stroked her fingers. "One of the

orphanages our organization did the maintenance on burned down. The children are safe. They are going to be placed wherever there is room for them. Some will end up in other communities, all of them will lose what they'd come to consider their family. These children who have lost so much already are losing again."

Nicole could only imagine the loneliness and fear these children must be feeling. "I'm so sorry to hear that. Grant must be really upset, and the other aid workers..."

Justin leaned closer, his expression filled with compassion. "These children need our organization's help. Grant is home to make arrangements to provide that assistance, and he called me for advice."

"Do you need to go to Boston? Or is he coming here to see you? I'd love the chance to meet your friend."

Justin clasped her hand in his. "Grant has asked me to go back to Haiti to reconstruct an orphanage with modular units, to reunite these children as quickly as possible."

"But you told me you needed time to recover from everything you'd seen and experienced in Haiti. Surely, he can't expect you to return to the place, at least not yet."

Justin didn't speak, but his gaze never left her face.

What did he want her to say? Where was he going with this? "Are you seriously considering this?"

"Those children need me."

"I need you. We need each other, don't we? I mean, we've just started to get to know each other. You said you loved me." She could feel something shift inside her. She suddenly felt left out of his life, alone. "I thought you wanted a relationship with me."

His blue eyes focused on her, he whispered, "I do, We're perfect together."

How could he look at her that way? Make her feel what she was feeling, and then talk about Haiti? "Then...you're not going back to Haiti, are you? You'll help Grant coordinate things from here?"

"I told him I'd go back with him. We're going to work out the details later this week."

Shock rifled through her. She loved him. He loved her. Just when she believed they had a chance together, just when she was sure she'd never felt this way before about any man.

How could he do this to her? To them? She had never felt this horrible, stomach-twisting feeling of loss, of loneliness. All because she let herself believe that a man loved her. A man who, after one phone call from a friend, had made plans to leave her.

She pulled her hand away from his, drawing in a deep breath, betrayal settling around her like a cloak. He said he loved her. She was about to tell him she loved him. She believed in them, in the happiness she felt when he was around.

And he had shattered it all with his words. What a fool she'd been to trust Justin, when all he could think about was what he wanted. It had been that way since the first time they'd met, when he was supposed to meet her for coffee and forgot. She'd been too blinded by the possibilities of what he offered her to see him for what he really was: a totally self-absorbed man. "Then I guess that's it."

"What do you mean? It's only the beginning."

"For you, obviously."

"No! Nicole, I love you, I want you to come with me to Haiti. You have so much to offer these children. You could work in the local clinic drawing blood like you do here. You could help the families you meet in the clinic. You could do so much. You would make such a difference in these children's lives."

"Why did you do this to me? To us?" she asked, betrayal tightening her throat.

"What? I thought you'd understand how much we're needed." Disbelief stood out on his face.

"You made the decision you wanted to make. Not the one *we* wanted. When you arrived here so full of caring for me, I thought we were..." She scrubbed her face to keep from crying. Was this how her mother felt when her father made it clear he couldn't leave Spencer Island? That the decision was his to make, not hers? "I thought you loved me."

"I do, Nicole, I do."

"There's no relationship if you make the decisions without talking to me first. If we are a couple, if we have a future together, you would have wanted me to be part of your decision."

"Nicole, I'm sorry. I didn't think—"

"No, Justin, you didn't." Her heart was a hard ball in her chest. Her tears were about to flood down her checks. She stood up, nearly knocking her chair over. "It's best if you leave."

For a few minutes he hesitated as if he wanted to say more, but she couldn't bear to hear another word. "Please."

He got up, moved toward the door, looked back at her, his face dark, his expression glum. "I'm sorry."

CHAPTER SIXTEEN

$\mathcal{N}$icole watched him leave, fierce tears of betrayal coursing down her cheeks. She loved him. She'd trusted him. This was supposed to be one of the happiest nights of her life, the fulfillment of her dream of finding a man who loved her and whom she loved in return. Yet here she stood, watching his truck go down her driveway, feeling like the biggest loser on the planet.

What had she done? Why hadn't she tried to reason with him? What if she'd told him she loved him? Would it have made a difference?

She glanced around her empty kitchen at the leftovers of dinner, the untouched dessert, and knew she couldn't be alone right now. Grabbing the phone, she called Angie, who picked up on the first ring.

"Hey, thought you were getting together with Justin tonight," Angie said.

"We did," she said, struggling to hold back the sobs.

"What's wrong?"

"Can you come over?"

"I'll be there in a few minutes."

Nicole heard Angie's voice us she called out to her son, Troy, just before she hung up the phone. Hearing her friend's quick response made her feel a little better. What would she have done if Angie hadn't been home? She could have called Gemma, but Gemma was expecting a baby. She didn't need to be called out so late.

Relieved not to be facing the rest of the evening alone, she hurried around, putting the dishes in the dishwasher and cleaning off the dining room table. She had to keep busy or cry. Those were the choices. She was just blowing out the candles on the table when she saw a car pull in her driveway. Hurrying to the door, she opened it and went out to greet her friend.

"Tell me what happened," Angie said, as she wrapped Nicole in a tight hug.

"Let's go inside. I've got coffee ready. I hope I didn't bring you away from anything...Ted?"

"Ted has gone to a basketball game with Daniel Reeves, one of the teenagers he's working with. Troy wanted to go but he has a test tomorrow. He's doing so much better in school these days. I can't believe the difference in him."

"Does he ever hear from his father now that he's out of prison?" Nicole asked, thankful to have a subject of conversation that wouldn't make her want to cry.

"No. Thank heavens. To think how much I worried over that disastrous situation, the mess I nearly made of my life by not telling the truth about Harry. Thankfully, it all turned out right in the end."

Angie had been married to Harry Young, Troy's father, when Troy was born. When Harry went to prison for nearly killing a police officer, Angie divorced him and moved to Spencer Island to escape her life in California. It was only a few months ago that Harry had been reunited with his son after being released on parole from prison. "Is Troy's father still involved with fellow convicts?"

"Don't know. Since he hasn't stayed in touch with Troy on a regular basis, I have no idea what he's doing. Troy doesn't seem to mind that he's not around; not surprising since he never knew his father. Troy and Ted are getting along really well with each other. Ted is so good to him. "Angie sighed. "But I didn't come all the way out here to talk about Harry." She slid into the chair behind the kitchen table and shrugged her coat off. "Now tell me what's going on."

Nicole took the gelato out of the freezer and brought it to the table. "Justin was here. We were having a beautiful dinner together. I was so sure that we were going to be able to work things out. He seemed so caring, attentive and made me feel wonderful."

Angie sighed. "Sounds perfect."

"Not quite. He told me he's going back to Haiti. I'm pretty sure he never intended to stay here in Spencer Island. Being here was simply a chance for him to rest up for a while. He let me think he wanted a relationship with me, when the truth was he didn't plan to stay. All this time... I had so much hope that this time was different. I was so wrong." Tears stung Nicole's eyes.

Angie gave her a stunned look. "Back to Haiti? I didn't know he was even considering such a move."

Nicole poured two cups of coffee and got the milk out of the fridge. "Neither did I. He didn't ask me what I thought. Nothing about us or our relationship. I feel so stupid for believing that we were beginning a loving, caring relationship, while he was off agreeing to return to the work he did in Haiti. I know he loves children, and I do too. He talked about going back to Haiti someday, but I thought that was out there somewhere in the future. I believed we would talk about it when the time came. I never expected him to do something like this." She pressed her lips together to keep from crying, "He's made another impetuous decision. It's how he likes to live his life, how he behaves. When I first met him, he warned me that this is how he operates, I should have listened. I can't be around someone like that."

"Nicole, I'm so sorry."

"I am, too. Justin said he loved me. I want someone to love, who loves me, but I can't do this. I can't be with someone who doesn't share things, especially something this big."

Angie touched her shoulder, reassuring her. "This probably not a good time to bring this up, and I will understand if you feel I'm not being very kind here."

Nicole sat down across from Angie and poured milk into her coffee. "You're always kind to me."

"Then here goes. I think it's time you looked at your life from a different perspective."

What did Angie mean? "Go on."

"You can't change your mother. She hurt you terribly, and you've had to deal with it the best way you knew how. You moved here. You're happy here. I think you should take stock of your situation and decide where you want to focus your energy."

Nicole frowned. "I don't understand."

"You've let your mother's behavior influence how you see your life for as long as I've known you."

"I moved here because of her," she said, trying to figure out what her friend was getting at.

"And it must have been a difficult decision."

"It was. And I'm still trying to figure out how to deal with her."

"Exactly. She has forced you to react to her decisions, a very difficult and painful thing to do to you. She didn't take your feelings into consideration, which has been hurtful for you. But you're not responsible for your mother or her behavior. It's time you stepped out of her shadow. She's not you. You wouldn't do what she did. You are kind and caring. Focus your time and energy on what you have right here."

"What I did have, you mean? Or thought I had?"

"Justin made a mistake in not telling you. I'm sure that he left here wishing he could apologize and try to make it right. I'm sure he'll be back to try to convince you that he's sincere in his feelings for you." Angie stirred her coffee slowly. "In the meantime, you have to do a little soul-searching. If you want this to be about you, if you want Justin to put you first, you need to tell him how you feel. You love this man. Don't give up on him."

"I don't think I have a choice. He did something without telling me, something that changes our relationship."

Angie shook her head slowly. "You didn't tell your mom how you really felt about what she did to you; how much you needed to know the truth from her. You got angry and said things I'm sure you both regret. You carried that distrust from Seattle to Spencer Island and let those negative feelings hold sway over your life rather than letting go."

"Yes, I did that. But I felt I didn't have a choice," Nicole said.

"But you do with Justin. You love him. Why don't you tell him how you really feel? Don't hold back. Trust him with how you feel."

Nicole heard the truth in her friend's words, a truth that frightened her. She'd never trusted anyone in her life the way she'd have to trust Justin if they were going to work this out.

Angie took a sip of her coffee. "Remember what I was like when I let what happened in Anaheim spill over into my life here?"

"Yeah, I remember."

"Then trust me. If you want to be happy, you must accept

your mother for who she is, not who you want her to be. Once you do that, you'll be able to work through your feelings where Justin is concerned and decide what's best for you."

"Maybe so..."

"Not just maybe. It's for real. You have to tell him how you feel, what you need from him. To do that you have to trust him with who you really are."

"I don't know…"

"Look, Nicole, you felt betrayed by your mom, and rightfully so. But what Justin did wasn't a betrayal as much as it was a mistake in judgment."

Angie's eyes were sad. "Please don't judge Justin through the lens of your experience with your mother."

Nicole felt Angie's words in her heart. "I hear what you're saying, But what kind of relationship would we have if Justin doesn't take my interests into consideration?"

"Probably not a good one. But if you care about him, tell him exactly how you feel. Don't let there be any doubt in his mind. If you want this relationship, fight for it. Make him understand what his actions did to you."

Did she have the courage to do that? Sure, she'd gotten angry before, which meant that she couldn't talk things out in a meaningful way, but she wasn't good at confrontation. "What if this is a pattern with Justin? What if he can't change how he does things? I can't be with someone who doesn't share what's going in his life. He should have told me about Grant's request before he made his decision, not after."

Angie nodded. "That's true. It's also true that you love this man. Are you willing to let go of him, of the happiness you might find with him in your life, without setting the record straight?"

Nicole couldn't answer.

Meeting Justin had changed her. His love had changed

her. Yet she hadn't been honest with him about her feelings. "If I'd told Justin I loved him, do you think he would have talked to me first about Haiti before he made his decision?"

"You'll never know. But don't go back over what happened. Look ahead to what you want. If Justin's what you want, tell him."

"I may not see him anytime soon."

"I'm betting you will."

Angie's cell phone rang and she answered it. When she finished, she turned to Nicole. "I'm needed at home. Troy needs me."

"So glad you two are close again," Nicole said.

"Me, too. Being the parent of a teenage boy can be challenging." Angie gave Nicole a quick hug. "Gotta go. See you at work tomorrow."

Nicole spent a restless night mulling over what Angie had said. She finally got up and went into work early. Being in before the phlebotomy clinic opened meant she could go to the cafeteria for breakfast, but all she managed to have was a coffee.

She worked her shift, her heart pounding every time any man who even slightly resembled Justin came near her desk. She had to really focus on labeling the blood specimens so as not to make a mistake. She didn't know that love could be this painful. She'd never felt this sort of hollow feeling whenever she thought about him, whenever she remembered his smile, the way he made her laugh.

All she really wanted to do was talk to him, to see if, as Angie said, he felt sorry for what he'd done. He said he was sorry when he left her last evening. But she didn't know if he meant it. Feeling this uncertainty was worse than anything she could have ever imagined.

When her day was finished, she made her way out to her car. The drive home seemed so dreary and hopeless under the dark sky of an impending rainstorm. She stopped at her mailbox before pulling up her driveway. Thankfully, she'd been inside when the rain started. She'd wait until the rain shower passed and change her clothes before going to the barn.

An hour later her phone was ringing when she got in the door. She scooped it up. "Hello." she said, shrugging off her jacket.

"Hi, it's me," Justin said, his voice a soft caress in her ear. "I wondered if I might come over this evening to talk with you. I have something I need to say."

"I don't..."

"Please. I need to explain."

The urgency in his voice, the sincerity in his words left her wanting him with all her heart. "That would be good. We need to talk."

"I'm on my way home from a job, and I'm not far from your place. I'll be there in a few minutes."

"I'll be here." Her heart was beating hard as she hung up. She glanced around, uncertain what to do. Feelings of excitement chased the panic rushing through her. She should comb her hair and brush her teeth. All the while, her mind wrestled with what would happen when Justin got here. She wanted to understand him, to have him convince her that he had made a mistake, that he was sorry. Most of all she wanted him to change his mind about going to Haiti.

He had to see things her way. She couldn't go with him. Her life and her career were here.

The doorbell rang. She finger-combed her hair. She grabbed a lip balm out of the wire basket on the kitchen counter, rubbing the color into her lips on her way to the door. When she opened it, Justin stood there with a contrite expression on his face. "Come in," she said as she stood back, her hand shaking on the doorknob, her heart racing.

CHAPTER SEVENTEEN

*J*ustin couldn't believe what a screwed-up mess he'd made of things. As he stood looking down into Nicole's beautiful brown eyes, he wished that he could change his decision. He wanted Nicole in his life. But he needed to go to Haiti. There didn't seem to be any way to manage both. He put his hands gently on her shoulders. "I came to apologize."

Her gaze met his; uncertainty clouded her expression. "I'm glad you're here. There's a lot we need to talk about."

He followed her into the living room, choosing to sit on the sofa, hoping she'd join him. She sat in the armchair next to the sofa, crossing her legs as she watched him. Her sleek gold top and tight jeans made his body sizzle. He'd never wanted any woman the way he wanted Nicole.

"I'm not sure where to start, how to explain." He rubbed his hands together. "I... When Grant called asking for my help, all I could think about were the children. There are no facilities...I could make a difference, a very real difference. He glanced at her to find her watching him. It made him feel exposed and uneasy. He cleared his throat to force back the anxiety messing with his concentration. "You can understand that, can't you?"

"Yes. I can. What I don't understand is why you didn't explain to Grant that you had to talk to me before you made your decision."

He would regret that dumb move for a very long time. His decisions had always been his to take, and he never doubted his ability to make sound choices. Yet being near Nicole, seeing the hurt in her eyes, he recognized his mistake. "You're right. I should have. I didn't do it, and I'm sorry. I'm not very good at this. What I mean is there's never been anyone I've loved like I love you. My life before you was all about me. About what I needed."

She drew in a deep breath and pressed her hands into the arms of the chair. "I find it really difficult when people don't consider my feelings." Her eyes met his. The air stilled between them.

What was he going to say next? How could he convince her to see that he needed her in is life; that he never meant to exclude her? "I won't make that mistake again. From now on we'll talk things out between us."

"From now on? You're talking about future decisions, not this one? That means you're leaving for Haiti soon. What about me? Where do I fit in?"

"I want to marry you. If had my way, we'd be going to Haiti together."

"But we're not married. You haven't proposed. I haven't accepted. We don't even have a real relationship, and this whole thing about Haiti is proof that we have a long way to go before we can really be a couple."

Why hadn't he used his head and told Grant he'd get back to him about going to Haiti? That he needed to include Nicole in the decision? "You're right."

She shifted in her chair, her hand going to her throat, her voice thick. "I don't want to be 'right'."

He scrubbed his hands together, feeling the callouses, trying to work out how to answer her. He had to start over with Nicole, make her see how much he loved her. He needed to take things slow, to include her. How could he have been so self-centered? "You mean the world to me. I've hurt you by moving too fast. What can I do to fix this?" he asked, feeling in way over his head.

She folded her hands in her lap and looked into his eyes. "You could call Grant back and tell him that you've got to rethink your decision. That you acted quickly without considering my feelings."

He may have rushed his decision, moved too fast. Yet deep in his heart he knew whether he waited, talked to her before giving Grant his answer, he wouldn't change his mind. "Can we come to some sort of compromise?"

"What do you mean?""

"Would you consider coming with me?"

"Just like that? I'm to give up my life here, the life I love, to go with you? Is this your idea of a compromise?"

Hell! What was he going to do? "I gave Grant my word, I can't go back on that."

She slumped in her chair. Her eyes glistened with tears. "Then, we don't have anything more to say to each other."

"That's not true! I love you. I believe you love me. Are you willing to throw all that away because I made a mistake?"

"A mistake that can't be fixed if you won't consider my feelings."

Through her tears she could see the hurt look in Justin's eyes. How could things have gone so wrong? A few weeks ago she wouldn't have imagined that this could be possible. Now she realized that there was little chance that they could work out their differences.

Justin's gaze held hers. "Can we talk about this a little more?"

She didn't want to talk about any of it. She needed to be alone. Hurt blocked her throat, but she forced it back. "Justin, I really care about you." She couldn't say the word love when he'd thrown marriage around like a tennis ball.

She gazed at him, the eagerness of his expression, the ways his eyes searched hers. She felt exposed to him, an odd feeling of being contained by his love and caring. She couldn't feel this way, not when she had no hope of life with him. "Do you know the meaning of love?"

"Yes, I do. And I'm a very patient man when it comes to getting what I want," he said, his smile so engaging, so intimate she was forced to look away.

He reached for her.

She pulled back. She couldn't be drawn in by his charm. There was too much at stake. "Loving someone means commitment to that person, to their feelings, their plans and aspirations. I can't go to Haiti with you. I love my life here. I left Seattle and came here uncertain as to how it would all work out. I'd never taken such a crazy chance in my life before and was terrified. But I did it. I have friends here. A good job. My own horses."

She drew in a deep breath. "I found my father. Someone I didn't know existed until a short while ago. I want to get to know Bill Cassidy, spend time with him. There's so much I need to learn about him. To do that I need my life just as it is. This is important to me."

He pulled back away from her. "I see that."

"Then you can also see that I can't possibly go away to a totally new country."

"You've done it before. You did it with your father."

"That was different."

"Only because it was your father."

Why was he being so stubborn about this? If he knew anything about her at all, he'd know that going to Haiti was out of the question. "I had both my parents. We were a family."

"And in Haiti you'd have me. We'd be together, doing wonderful important work for those who truly need us."

"Important work for you, maybe. For me, it would be a strange country, unfamiliar customs, no friends..."

Justin reached once more for her hand, and she let him. Despite how she was feeling, she needed his touch, his closeness. But holding hands was as far as she could go. As far as her hurt would allow.

"Nicole, I came home completely stressed out by what I'd seen in Haiti. I couldn't take it any longer: I admit that. I'd been naïve when I first joined Grant's team, but I learned pretty quickly how difficult and heartbreaking the work was. Yet something kept me there. Kept me focused on helping. I came home, knowing I'd go back as soon as I could."

"Why didn't you tell me that when we met? Why didn't you say that you were heading back as soon as you felt rested and well enough to go?"

"I hadn't decided yet. But I should have been more up front about my struggle with how I was feeling since I came back home."

"Yes, you should have. I knew there was something you weren't telling me. When you first talked about Haiti, I thought the collapse of the house was what you were hiding. But that wasn't the whole story, was it?"

"No, Haiti is a part of my life. The Hilario children are... special to me. I didn't know when I left that I would fall in love with you. That you would come to mean so much to me, I had no idea I could fall so quickly and easily for you," he said, his voice hoarse with emotion.

His touch on her hand, the play of his skin over hers as he stroked the inner side of her wrist was almost more than she could bear. She wanted to pull away from him, but she couldn't. She needed this. "I don't know what to say."

"We have so much, you and I. We're good together. We could make a real difference in people's lives." His fingers continued to draw circles on the inside of her wrist, driving her crazy. "What do you want out of life?" he asked.

"I want to live my life as if every minute counts. I love people. Children. It feels so great to help them."

"Yes. That's it. That feeling that you've helped someone in a very real way. That's what Haiti does for me."

She looked into his eyes...his beautiful blue eyes. "Why can't you do that here?"

"But what you and I could accomplish in Haiti would be nothing short of a miracle. All you have to do is take a chance on me, on us."

"I'm not good at taking chances. I'm not a risk taker like you. I need to feel safe and secure. As for seeing another country, I've done that all my life. I'm finally settled here. I'm comfortable here."

His sad smile made her want to cry. Instead, she concentrated on his touch, on making him see that maybe there was another solution. "Would you consider staying here for a little while longer? Giving us time to be closer, to understand each other better?"

He didn't respond, and it was as if her life stopped.

Finally, still holding her hand, he stood and pulled her to her feet, wrapping his arms around her waist and leaning down to look directly into her eyes. "Nicole, I love you. Just this once, take a chance. Go with your heart. This is our big chance."

Justin held her close, breathing in the scent of her hair, her skin. All he wanted to do was make love to her, to show her how much he cared about her. Yet he'd never been more aware of the distance between them than at this moment. She wouldn't look at him, and her arms hadn't moved from her sides.

What if he had lost her? What if his impetuousness and lack of concern, as she saw it, put an end to their relationship? He struggled to remain calm as he looked back over the weeks since he met her. "I will never forget the day we met in the clinic. It was as if I'd been asleep until you smiled at me. I've never believed in love at first sight." He kissed her forehead, letting his lips linger on her soft skin, storing up the memory of her, of how she felt in his arms. "Until that day I was beginning to believe that love wasn't in the cards for me."

She drew in a quick breath. "Oh, Justin, what a lovely thing to say. But I don't believe that people fall in love that way. Love like that is really just heightened awareness and the excitement of meeting someone special for the first time."

"I'm proof that love at first sight can happen. When I saw you that day working with that child, it was as if nothing else existed. You were the focus of my universe." He gave a quick laugh of embarrassment. "I'm making a complete fool of myself, aren't I?"

"No. Not at all. But this has never happened to me before in my life. No one has loved me from the moment they met me. I feel a little lost, adrift with this. Love for me is something that develops over time, with shared experiences, getting to know how the other feels about…everything." Her smile entered his heart, making it rise in his chest.

"Oh, Nicole, I love you so much. But I can understand that this is way too fast for you. But sometimes we have to take a chance, to trust in ourselves. I would never hurt you." As he spoke he knew with certainty he couldn't leave this woman behind. She had to came with him. But how could he convince her? "I can't be without you. In my dream we're married when we go to Haiti."

She looked at him, her eyes searching his face. "Your dream is that we're married. Is that a proposal?"

"There I go again, right?"

She nodded, but she didn't pull away.

"Okay. I might as well tell you everything. I dream that I'll ask you to marry me and we'll go to Haiti together. Then we'll come home to your farm, if that's all right with you, and we'll start a family. There, that's my plan. Now, feel free to tell me I'm an impulsive, impossible person."

"You are an impulsive, impossible person," she said, with a hint of a smile on her face.

"And I don't want to go to Haiti without you. If you'll agree to go with me, and you don't like it and want to come back, we'll return home to Spencer Island."

He held his breath, anxious and fearful that she would turn him down for good. If she did, he didn't know what he'd do. He'd never felt this way, this feeling of indecision. His life, his decisions, had been easy until now.

Her eyes met his. "I'm not like you. At this moment I feel we're very different."

"I've noticed," he said, holding his breath.

"I need time to think this over."

Could he postpone going with Grant? He needed to get to Haiti as soon as possible, but he also couldn't leave Nicole. Why did everything have to happen at once? "That makes sense. It's a huge decision for you." He mentally crossed his fingers.

Leaning down, he kissed her lips, savoring the taste of her, drawing her into his arms, holding her close to shield himself from the real possibility that she might decide not to go with him, "I won't make the same mistake again. I want you to understand that no matter what decision you make, I love you. I will always love you."

With that, he kissed her. Maybe for the last time.

CHAPTER EIGHTEEN

The next morning Justin took the steps up to the entrance of the high school two at a time. It was only eight, but he was pretty certain Bill Cassidy would be there. He'd looked his address up on the internet and went by his house earlier and there was no vehicle in his driveway. When he got to the school receptionist's desk, he stopped and asked directions to Bill's office.

He got to the door and stopped. What was he going to say? What if Bill Cassidy called his daughter and told him Justin had been to see him? How would Nicole react when she learned that he'd gone to her father for his support?

He'd never done anything like this before. He'd never loved anyone enough to take a chance like this for somebody other than himself. Blocking all his anxious thoughts, he tapped on the classroom door.

"Come in," called a man's voice.

He opened the door and walked in. The man sitting at the desk had Nicole's deep brown eyes, and Justin had seen that same guarded, anticipatory expression on Nicole's face.

"Do you have a minute?" Justin asked.

"Have we met?" Bill Cassidy said.

"No, we haven't. I'm Justin Hadley."

A small frown formed on his rugged features. "Ah... Nicole's friend."

So Nicole had told her dad about him, which was a good thing. It made what he had to say so much easier. "May I sit down?"

"By all means, I'm glad to meet you, young man. My daughter speaks very highly of you." He motioned to the chair across the desk. "I've asked around a little, and everyone praises your carpentry skills."

Justin suddenly had a good feeling about this. If the man knew who he was and respected his abilities, it was a positive sign. "Did she tell you that I... That we are... That we care for each other?"

"Yes, she did. My daughter and I are just starting to get to know each other. I'm looking forward to every minute of it," Bill said, his pride showing.

Did this mean that he wouldn't help him because he wanted Nicole to stay in Spencer Island? He sighed. He wouldn't know until be asked him. "I've come to see you because I need your help."

Bill leaned forward, resting his elbows on his desk. "Is there a problem? Nicole seems happy...very happy."

"She is. I am, too." He rubbed the callouses on his hands. "I love Nicole. I want to marry her."

Bill's eyebrows shot up. "That fast? Are you sure?"

Justin faced the man's careful scrutiny. "I'm sure."

"Are you here to ask my permission?" he asked, a smile beginning at the corners of his lips, a smile reminiscent of Nicole's.

"No. Well, not right yet. I haven't proposed, not really, I plan to, but there's a bit of a complication."

"Meaning?"

"Before I came to live in Spencer Island, I worked in Haiti. I came home because I needed a little time off." He rubbed his sweaty palms together. "I was pretty stressed when I got home."

"Working in Haiti wouldn't be easy, I imagine."

"No. It wasn't. But I loved it. I want to go back there."

"When?"

"In a couple of weeks."

"What? You're seeing my daughter, but you're preparing to leave her?"

"Not exactly. I want her to come with me."

Bill Cassidy clasped his hands together, his lips tight. "What did she say?"

"She's going to decide. I'm waiting for her answer."

"And you want me to talk to her."

He felt his chest tighten. "Yes."

"What would I say? Nicole's an adult with a mind of her own. Besides, I can't interfere in her life"

"I realize that. She's very excited about getting to know you. You're one of the reasons she says she can't go."

It was Bill Cassidy's turn to sigh. "I want to get to know my daughter, as well. Nicole and I have a whole lifetime to catch up on. Finding her was a gift, the best gift I could ever have imagined."

Bill Cassidy had plans where his daughter was concerned. Justin couldn't blame him. If he was in the man's shoes, he wouldn't let his daughter out of his sight. Bill would probably tell Nicole about their conversation, and it would all be over. "I shouldn't have come here." He swallowed against the sudden pain in his throat. "It's just that I love your daughter. I've never loved anyone the way I love her. I wouldn't do anything to hurt her. But I made a commitment to go back to Haiti, and I want her with me."

The room was silent.

He glanced at the older man. "I understand. I shouldn't have asked you to help me. It's not fair to you or to her. I'm sorry."

"Wait a minute. No, you don't understand." Bill leaned forward, the look in his eyes one of compassion. "I know what it feels like to love someone, having them leave you just when you needed them most. Just when you thought your life was perfect, so much to look forward to, they disappear from your life. I don't want that to happen to Nicole. She deserves to be happy. But I won't get involved in making her decisions. That's up to her."

"I understand. If I had a daughter I'd feel the same way." He shouldn't have come here, putting this man he hardly knew on the spot about his daughter. He had to find a way to convince Nicole that they would be happy together. "Thanks for listening. It's been nice meeting you. I won't take up any more of your time."

Nicole didn't know how many more sleepless nights she could handle. When she got in to work the next morning, Gemma stopped by the phlebotomy clinic wanting to know about her evening with Justin. She told her all about what had gone on, and that she had a decision to make.

"Are you going to Haiti?" Gemma asked.

"How can 1?" Nicole replied. "My home is here, my friends, my horses, my life. How can I simply pack up and leave?"

"I couldn't do it," Gemma said. "You're brave to even consider it. Except for my time in college and a few years working in Bangor, I've always lived in Spencer Island. It's home to me. Besides, what do we know about Haiti?"

Nicole saw Gemma's anxious glance, adding to her concern about leaving Spencer Island. "Not much. But

Justin says there's lots to do, that my skills are really needed."

"With both of you working all the time, the long hours, how would you find time for each other?" Gemma asked.

"It would be tough," Nicole admitted.

Gemma smoothed her hair from her face. "Where would you live?"

"I forgot to ask that," Nicole said.

"What if you get there to discover that you don't feel the same way about him?" Gemma asked.

Gemma suddenly looked as if she'd faint. "I... I'll be right back." She got up and ran from the room.

Nicole followed Gemma to the restroom down the corridor. Once inside she leaned against the sink trying not to listen to the quiet retching going on in the stall across from her. "Gemma, are you okay?"

A few minutes later, Gemma appeared, her face shiny with perspiration, a huge smile on her face as she went to the sink, washed her hands and wiped her face, her gaze meeting Nicole's in the mirror. She turned to face her. "I planned to tell you at lunch today. We got the results back. It's official. Matt and I are expecting a baby."

Nicole hugged her friend. "This is great news! I'm so happy for you. When are you due?" Nicole asked.

"The first week of March."

"Is Matt excited?" Nicole asked.

"He's been so cute. He's constantly asking if I'm feeling okay. He is always fretting about my morning sickness. Found him standing outside the bathroom door the other morning."

"He's worried about your diabetes and how it will affect your pregnancy."

"For sure. I am, too. But we'll cope. We both want this baby."

"And what about Morgan?"

"She is unbelievable. I love her more every day. At first being a stepmother was difficult, but since the wedding Morgan has been so supportive. When we told her our news she cried, then she laughed and cried some more. We didn't realize how much she wants a brother or sister." Gemma smoothed her damp hair away from her face. "Matt and I are so lucky in so many ways."

Nicole had to agree with her. Even though she couldn't help worrying about Gemma's diabetes. Almost a year ago, Gemma had nearly died. The thought chilled her. Gemma had been so much a part of her life since she'd moved here to Spencer Island. "Have you told Angie?"

"Not yet, but I suspect she knows something's going on. She's been behaving like a mother hen."

"This is so exciting. Angie and I will get busy and plan a baby shower."

"I would rather wait for a few months just to be certain."

Nicole understood Gemma's caution. Being diabetic and expecting a baby was a lot to adjust to. "Do you have any names picked out?"

"Not yet. If it's a boy, I'd like to have Matt somewhere in the name. He'd like to have his father's name—William. He agreed that if it's a girl I can choose the name."

"Do you have one in mind?" Nicole asked.

"I'm working on that. I want it to be an old name—Elizabeth, or possibly Charlotte." She shrugged. "First we have to wait and see if it's a boy or a girl." She chuckled as she patted her tummy.

Caught up in the excitement of her friend's news, Nicole knew she couldn't leave Spencer Island. She wanted to be here for the birth of her friend's baby.

After they left the restroom and went back to work, Nicole knew her decision was clear. Yet if she insisted that

Justin stay here with her, would he regret it? Would he come to feel that he'd given up what he wanted for her sake? Would he come to resent her for her insistence that he stay here and give up his plans?

If he left and went to Haiti, would their relationship have a chance? She'd waited a long time for someone like Justin. Was she willing to wait longer? What if he went away, and she really didn't miss him that much? No. She would miss him. When her dad had to go away for a few weeks, her mom missed him terribly and was so glad to see him come back home.

But her parents were married, committed to each other and their relationship. She and Justin didn't know enough about each other, and getting married wouldn't change that. They'd still need time to adjust to each other, to learn about one another. It was all too soon, too sudden.

Despite her preoccupation with her situation, she managed to finish her shift. She hadn't called Justin because she didn't know what to say. Yet, being Justin he'd expect an answer, and she didn't have one. When she got home, changed her clothes and started out to the barn to see to Zeus and Suzie, she suddenly heard a vehicle coming down the road toward her house.

She didn't recognize the car. At the same time, she couldn't help but wish that it was Justin. Silly thought, given that she was well aware what she would say to him. She waited as the car came up the drive and was surprised to see Bill Cassidy behind the wheel.

What was he doing here?

He got out of the car and walked toward her. Suddenly, she wondered what her mother and her father had been like together—at fifty he was a handsome man. She tried to imagine them in a town her mother wanted to escape from. How had they been together in high school and for four years while he was in college, yet her father had no idea of her mother's feelings around living in Spencer Island?

If her parents couldn't communicate well, and they had love and years together to make it easier, how were she and Justin going to find a way to settle their differences? "Hi... Dad. I didn't know you were coming here this afternoon."

"I apologize. I should have called. I told you I would, but I needed to see you, to talk to you."

"If it's about Mom, I don't want to hear it."

"No. It's not about your mother. I had a visitor in my office this morning."

What did he mean? "Why don't we go inside where we can talk?"

"Sounds good."

"Would you like coffee?" she asked, leading the way into the kitchen.

"That would be great." He glanced around. "This is a nice house. The Henderson family owned it when I was growing up."

Nicole spooned coffee into the coffeemaker, filled the carafe with water and pressed the button. "Yes, I bought this house from the widow. It needs a little work, and I was hoping that Justin would be around to do it for me."

"And he's not going to be," her father said.

"How do you know?" she asked, placing the sugar bowl on the table and getting the milk out of the fridge.

"He came to see me this morning."

Nicole nearly dropped the milk carton. "What did he want?"

"He told me he's going to Haiti, well, actually, returning to Haiti. He told me he loves you."

Nicole felt her cheeks warm, her heart pound in her chest. "I know that, Dad."

"He wants you to go to Haiti with him."

"That's right."

"Are you planning to go?"

She slumped into the chair across from her father. "I don't know what to do. It's such short notice. We've hardly spent any time together. My life is good here. I don't want to leave Spencer Island." It felt good to be talking to her father this way. She hadn't had a family member to share her problems with for a long time.

"Do you love him?" he asked, reaching across the table and taking her hand in his.

His touch was warm. She let her hand rest in his and felt a bond with him that hadn't been there before. "Yes. I do. I've been waiting for someone just like Justin. But his determination to go back to Haiti before we have a chance to spend more time together, get to know each other a little better, has me worried. He's impulsive. I'm not prepared to give up my life here based on a rash decision he made without talking to me first."

"Have you told him you love him?"

"Not in so many words, but I'm sure he knows."

"When it comes to love, don't assume anything."

"I'm so confused by all this," she confessed. "If I go with him, give up what I have here and our relationship doesn't work out, I will have done all of it for a whole lot of heartache."

"And if you go, and the two of you fall deeper in love, what about that?"

"I've never been in love this way, this sense of not knowing... I have to be reasonable. I can't simply move away. I'm afraid it won't work. I'm afraid that Justin's decision to return to Haiti could end everything. I don't want that. I want a chance to see if we can make it. Haiti is not the place to do that."

He patted her hand. "Let me tell you a little bit about your mother and me. We were in love in high school. I went away to college while she waited here for me. I came home from college as often as I could afford. We started talking about what we'd do after I graduated. There has never been anyone I loved more than your mother, not before her and not after her. But I made a stupid mistake."

"What was that?"

"I assumed your mother wanted what I wanted. That living here in Spencer Island was best for both of us. To be honest, we really hadn't talked if out. I saw your mother's life being one where I worked at the high school while she owned a craft shop, or an art gallery. That was it—-my wishes, not hers. I couldn't get it through my thick head that your mother needed more. Even now I find it hard to believe that I could have been so blind. I loved her. I failed her."

"So why didn't she make it clear to you that she wanted that? Could she not have traveled to Portland to take courses in interior design, like she wanted?"

"Yes, but I encouraged her to take a job while she waited for me. The courses she wanted to take were during the daytime, and she wasn't off work until five o'clock. I only got the details of this from her recently." He smiled and shook his head as if in disbelief. "But here's the thing. What she wanted took a backseat to what I wanted. I should have talked to her more about what we would do together. I assumed we'd live in Spencer Island. She couldn't face staying here."

"And her answer to the problem was to run off without an explanation to you? Hardly the right way to solve a problem," Nicole said with a niggling sense that she'd done the same thing when she hadn't explained how she really felt.

"No. She should have talked to me, given me a chance to see if we could find a different solution." He leaned back and scrubbed his face, returning his gaze to her. "But here's the thing. I should have gone after her. I should have insisted that she tell me where she was, what she was doing. I shouldn't have accepted her explanation that she'd gone to Boston. I should have followed her there." He slouched in the chair. "I let my pride make my decision for me. I blamed her for running away, but I wouldn't let myself go after her. It was stupid of me. I loved her. I wanted her. I couldn't imagine my life without her, and yet I let her go."

Nicole saw the agony in her father's eyes and smiled at him in sympathy. "It must have been awful for you."

"Not just for me. I don't want you blaming your mother for what happened. It takes two to make the kind of mistake we made. I was as responsible for what happened as your mother was. The truth is, had I been willing to follow your mother and work out a solution, I wouldn't have missed being part of your life. Your mother and I have had a couple of really intense conversations about all this these past weeks. We've started working on what happened back then and whether or not we have a chance at a relationship."

"You and Mom?" Nicole asked, surprised.

"Yeah. I'm slowly getting over my anger, and she's beginning to understand why leaving Spencer Island was out of the question for me."

"That's nice, I guess..."

"It's more than nice, but that's not why I'm here. I don't want you to make the same kind of mistake I made. If you love Justin, tell him. Say the words. He needs to hear them. The two of you need to talk this out, find a way to reach out to each other. Love is too precious to pass up over something as simple as where you live. Look at your mother and Marcus. It didn't matter where they lived. They loved each other, and that love carried them through every move they made."

Nicole nodded. "That's true." She smiled at the memory

of her parents having a late-night dinner talking excitedly about their plans, kissing and laughing while she hid from sight, feeling just a little bit anxious about the next move, the next school she'd have to attend. The friends she'd have to make all over again.

"I don't have any idea what is best for you whatever decision you make. But if you do decide to go and need me to look after your place, I will. You don't have to worry about that. After everything I've missed, I want to be around to support you now."

"Thanks, Dad. I really appreciate that," She shrugged and smiled at him, so happy to have her dad with her, "I'm so glad you came here today. I feel better about everything."

"Does that include your mom?"

Did it? Clinging to the negative feelings she held where her mother was concerned wasn't doing her any good. Besides, her mother lived in Seattle and was unlikely to visit her here in Spencer Island anytime soon after their last conversation. "Yes, it does." She smiled at him. "Would you like to stay for dinner? I have to feed the horses and let them out into the paddock for a little exercise, but we could eat after that."

"Are you a good cook?"

"You'll only find out if you stay," she teased. She was so lucky to have found her father.

CHAPTER NINETEEN

They had dinner together, a wonderful evening, during which she learned a great deal about her father. He loved country music. He'd taken her mother out on their first date after a basketball game during which he'd scored the winning basket. He was a meat-and-potatoes kind of guy, and he loved trout fishing. He'd spent his summers in high school on a scallop dragger, following his dad's career choice. But he had decided that he didn't want to make a living fishing, and with dreams of being the coach at the local high school, he'd gone off to college.

They were enjoying a cup of coffee when her father brought up the subject of Ellen. "I never stopped loving your mother. After she left, everyone kept saying that I'd find someone else. I wanted to, believe me. It's lonely living on your own. I had always dreamed of having a family. I used to kid your mother about how we'd have a family big enough to start our own basketball team. But as the years passed, my students became my family. I put everything I had into being a good coach and a good instructor. My life settled into a very comfortable routine punctuated by the occasionally well-meaning friend or neighbor setting me up with a date. I seriously tried to find someone and went out with several different women, but it never felt right."

Nicole put her cup down on the coffee table. "You loved Mom that much."

"I did. In the early years I thought about going to find her, but when it came time I made an excuse. Eventually it was too late, I assumed a woman as attractive as your mother would have married. I didn't want to make a fool of myself by showing up on her doorstep. The one instance when I did attempt to find her, there was no record of her. Of course, by then she was married and had you and a whole other life of her own." His smile was sad as his gaze met Nicole's. He reached for his cup and took a slow sip, his eyes focused on her.

"I'm sorry, Dad."

"Don't be. We all make choices. The scary thought is, one small choice can alter your life forever." He got up from his chair. "I have to get home. Got a big day tomorrow and a championship game here this weekend."

"I'll walk out with you," she said, feeling so close to this man. She could hardly believe they hadn't known each other all these years.

When they got to his car, he turned and hugged her. "I want you to think seriously about what you want out of life. Finding someone to love is a precious gift not to be squandered on some misplaced sense of pride." He squeezed her shoulder. "Remember that."

"I will."

He opened the car door. "And you'll be at volleyball practice next week?"

She smiled, feeling connected and happy. "Wouldn't miss it."

Going back into the house, the familiar rooms held a

feeling of emptiness she'd never experienced before. Filling the sink with water to soak the pots, filling the dishwasher, cleaning the counters did little to case the turmoil in her mind.

She loved Justin. She wanted him. He loved her. Yet there didn't seem to be an answer to what held them apart from each other. She glanced at the phone. Should she return his call? She'd been putting it off all day. He had to be wondering what she was doing, how she was feeling. Or maybe he had been calling to tell her that he was on the way to the airport. Knowing him, he might be sitting in the Boston airport now. No, he wouldn't do that to her.

She snatched up the phone, anxiously dialing his number. He answered before the second ring. "I've been waiting for you to call," he said.

"Where are you?" she asked, fearing she might be right about the airport, as she could hear voices in the background.

"I'm sitting in my apartment waiting to hear from you. Hold on a minute while I turn the TV off." He came back to the phone. "There, that's done. How was your day?"

"It was okay. My dad had dinner with me. The first dinner we've had together. Seems so strange to be saying that, but it's true. He is my dad. I'm planning to invite him to dinner again soon,"

"And what about us? Have you come to any conclusions?" he asked, his voice oddly quiet.

"I... I know it's late. Would we be able to get together tomorrow?"

She heard something hit the floor. "Are you okay?"

"Yes, I'm fine... I'd like to come over right now. I can be there in half an hour. Would that be okay?"

What was she going to tell him? Her heart pounded in her chest at the thought that he would be expecting her to agree to go with him to Haiti. She had to make him understand that decision like that was very difficult for her. She wasn't good at decisions that involved change of any kind. Darn! She needed time to know her heart, to find her way through to what worked for her. Yet if she didn't sit down and talk it out with him now, she was almost certainly facing another sleepless night. "Yes."

She hung up, raced to the bathroom and brushed her teeth. Looked at herself in the mirror and realized she needed to put on a little makeup, that the jeans she was wearing she'd been wearing in the barn when she groomed her horses. She fumbled through her closet looking for a clean pair of yellow pants and an orange top before pulling earrings that matched the top out of her jewelry box. All the while, her hands were shaking so much she could hardly finish dressing.

Why had she agreed to his coming here when she didn't know what she was going to say? She was still trying to figure it out when she saw the lights of his truck coming along the driveway.

Meeting him at the door, she felt frantic about what she should do. They had so much to work out between them. She drew in a deep breath to ease the fluttering of her stomach.

Slowly, ever so slowly, she began to feel calmer. She could do this. She would listen to everything Justin had to say, then she would go with her feelings. She'd never done it before, but her feelings were what really mattered here. She was finally clear in her mind what she needed. Whatever she chose to do, it would involve loving someone more than she loved herself. She would not let her mother's influence inter- fere in her feelings for Justin.

She loved her mother, but Angie was right. In order to be happy, she had to be her own person.

Justin got out of the truck and came around toward the open door where she stood.

He walked up to her, his eyes intent on her face, his smile tentative. Ever so gently he took her hands in his, his warmth reaching out to her making her feel safe, the sheer maleness of him stopping the air in her lungs. "That didn't take long," she said, acutely aware of how trite her words sounded.

"In the past few hours I had considered parking at the end of the road where it turned off the highway and hope you might pass, that I'd get a chance to be with you." He gave her the smile, the one he smiled the day they met. She was mesmerized.

"Then I thought better of it, thought maybe you'd think I was stalking you. Or, equally as bad, an overzealous cop would pick me up for behaving like a pervert."

"All those thoughts all at once?" she asked, feeling her lips shake as she smiled up at him.

"That's me." He looked down at her, his gaze radiating a strange vulnerability she hadn't seen before.

She was torn between wrapping her arms around his neck and making some flimsy excuse about needing to go to do something...anything. "Come in."

They walked into the living room, each sitting down on either end of the sofa. "I'm not sure what to say," she said, folding her hands in her tap, "Where would you like to start?"

Justin felt her words like a dagger to the chest. If she was about to say she'd go with him to Haiti, she wouldn't have started off that way. He struggled to think of a smart come-back, something that would ease the tension rising through his body in a wave so strong it took his breath. He braced himself, waiting for her words of refusal. "You can say anything to me, anything at all. I love you."

A smile flickered across her face. "A few weeks ago, I was afraid that I had cancer. I don't, and that was such a relief."

He wanted to reach for her, to cradle her in his arms, but knew the futility of that. Nicole was her own person and obviously had something to tell him that he probably didn't want to hear. "A whole new chance, a new beginning in a way, don't you think?"

"Yes." She worked her fingers over the cotton fabric of her yellow pants. He wished it was his fingers touching her. He had to fight down the urge to reach for her.

She didn't meet his gaze, "I've always been reluctant to take risks. I believe I told you that moving here was the biggest risk I'd ever taken."

"Yet you did take the risk and you've been very happy with the outcome."

"Absolutely. But maybe it's time I took another risk."

"Like what?" he asked, holding his breath, terrified of what she'd say next.

"I've always wanted to make a difference in people's lives. It's probably why I enjoy tutoring children and working at the phlebotomy clinic. When you came here wanting me to give up my life and go to Haiti with you, I couldn't see myself doing such a scary thing." She turned to him, her hand reaching across the space between them.

He moved closer, breathing in her scent, his body tense with anticipation. "Yeah, I thought maybe I should have done that differently."

"I'm still not sure I could do such a thing. I mean going to Haiti." She shrugged. "I need to tell you that I should have done something differently, as well. I should have told you the truth."

Oh, no. You're finished, Hadley.

She worked her fingers into his, without meeting his eyes. "I'm sorry. I should have told you I loved you days ago."

The air whooshed from his lungs. He had waited to hear those words, had wanted to hear those words. Now he wasn't sure what he should do next. Taking her in his arms was his first thought, but Nicole hadn't met his glance since he'd sat down. "Yeah, it would have been good if you'd told me you loved me. Real good."

Finally, she looked into his eyes, her brown eyes filled with warmth and caring. "I love you, Justin Hadley. I want to see if we can work something out between us."

"I knew it." He gathered her in his arms, his heart flooding with happiness at her words. "The two of us together. Two people who love each other," he said, smoothing her hair from her face, feeling the softness of her skin beneath his fingers.

She took his hands in hers. "I don't know if I can go to Haiti with you. I can't leave my life right now. Gemma is expecting a baby. My father and I are really getting along well. I love you, but I also love my life. Can you understand all that?"

There was no way he could let Grant down in the middle of such a crucial project, but if he worked really hard and pushed to complete the project early, they could be back here in a matter of months. Maybe if he postponed going until the modular units were on-site, he could stay here a little longer with Nicole. "What would you think if I told you that I would be willing to go to Haiti only after the units are in place?"

Her smile brightened. "What would that mean for us?"

"I've been thinking that we might be able to make this work if once the modular units for the orphanage have been shipped to Haiti, which is a few weeks from now, you'd have more time to get used to the idea of living in Haiti."

"But I want to be here for Gemma's baby."

"We can be back here in time for that. If not, you could fly home to be with her." He took her face in his hands and turned her to look straight into his eyes. The moment hung between them. "We love each other. We'll make this work."

"Justin, are you sure about this? The only way we'll ever have the kind of relationship we need is for us to be honest with each other."

Looking into her eyes made his words so much easier. "I would like to commit for longer in Haiti, but I don't want to lose you," he said, feeling the sincerity of his words go straight to his heart. "I don't want to be without you. I've done my best in Haiti. Now I want to do my best for you."

"I want to be with you. But are you sure this could work? I don't want you to regret taking me along."

"Then what about this for a compromise? We go down to Haiti together. Hopefully, we can get your paperwork and immunizations completed sooner rather than later. Then we can go for as long as you feel comfortable."

"How will you complete this orphanage project if I get down there and want to come home?"

He could insist that Grant hire a second carpenter or someone willing to learn the basics and work alongside him. He'd prepare a list of what needed to be done, and with the support of the salesperson who sold Grant the units, they'd be able to finish the project. He'd teach the man Grant hired everything he needed to know to complete the work. If necessary, he could fly down to help finish up. It would be expensive for the organization Grant worked for, but if they needed him this urgently, they would have to accept his conditions.

The one thing he was certain of: he was not going to leave without Nicole. He pulled her into his arms. "You let me worry about the details. Grant and I will work something out."

She smiled up into his face, her dark eyes shining with happiness. "Are you sure about all this?"

"The more important question is are you sure?. What about your farm and your horses?"

"My dad says he'll look after everything for me." She tapped his chest. "But he can't do that forever, and, besides, I can't leave my horses for very long, either."

"You won't have to. I promise." He tipped up her chin and kissed her lips, happy in the sudden intake of her breath, the way her body melted into his. They clung to each other. He held her tight and kissed her, blood pounding in his ears, his hands following every curve of her body.

He wanted to make love to her, to claim her as his own. He wanted to be near her every minute of every hour. She felt so good in his arms, so right. Whatever it took he would not be away from her ever again.

When they finally moved apart. she smiled. "Would you like to stay the night?"

He had waited a long while to hear her say those words. As he touched her face, reveling in the smoothness of her skin, the vulnerability in her eyes, he hadn't felt like this in his life. "I'm here as long as you'll have me."

"Then what are you waiting for, Hadley?" She pulled his face to hers and kissed him, her mouth open, inviting and irresistible.

Nicole pressed body into his, her fingers curled around the back of his neck as she kissed him slowly, her lips moving over his, her heart, pounding. His musky scent excited her. He returned her kiss, his touch eager, as he lifted her off her feet and into his arms.

"I'm not going to let anyone interrupt us this time," he

said, holding her tight in his arms, a determined smile on his face as he started up the stairs.

She snuggled deeper into his embrace, feeling safe and loved and completely happy all at once. "First room on the right," she said as he turned at the top of the stairs.

He eased her onto the bed, tossing the pillows to the floor. He kissed her throat, his lips making their way to hers as he reached for her tank top and began peeling it off her heated body.

Her skin tingled at his touch, the cool air caressing against her skin. With one movement he tore off his shirt and tossed it to the floor beside her top. She reached for his belt, his sudden intake of breath spurring her on. She undid the belt, struggling to get at his zipper.

"No fair. Ladies first," he said, pulling her pants off, followed by her flimsy panties before yanking his own pants down over his feet where they joined the growing pile of clothing on the floor.

"You're fast." she said, teasingly, as need made her tremble.

"I'm just getting started," he whispered next to her ear as he stretched out beside her, his fingers playing over her body, easing toward the space between her legs.

His eyes were dark as he gazed into her face, watching her expression as his fingers moved against her heated flesh.

Her hands reaching for him, she touched his lips, his face, as if memorizing it.

He kissed her slowly. She writhed beneath his demanding touch, the tension building to an exploding point.

She looked at him, saw the lust and need in his eyes and pulled him closer.

"I love every part of you," he said, trailing his hand up her body to her lacy bra. "I'm going to take all evening to prove it."

"Please..." She wanted to touch him, feel him. With a low groan of pleasure, he moved on top of her, his breath hot against her cheek. He eased his body along hers, slowly at first, exploring her. She cupped his head in her hands, pulling his face to hers, pressing her lips into his in a frantic dance that seemed to have no end. She'd never felt such need for another man.

"Just a minute," his voice shaky as he scrambled to the edge of the bed and took a condom from the pocket of his jeans, slipping it on in a hurried movement.

Her body pulsed with his as he entered her. It was as if the world had stopped turning, that she no longer was separate and alone. She moved to his rhythm, her whole being attached to him as their bodies arched together. She clung to him, to his strength, responding to every nuance of his touch.

He made love to her that night, a love that claimed her body and soul. With the sheets twisted and sweaty, they fell asleep in each other's arms.

When she woke the next morning to the sound of Suzie and Zeus calling from the paddock, she knew that her life had been completely and irrevocably changed.

Her eyes sought his face, relaxed and trusting in sleep. She was right where she wanted to be, and that could be any place in the world that held Justin.

EPILOGUE

A month later:

"Can you believe this?" Justin called out to her over the noise of the crowd milling about them where they waited for the fundraiser to kick off.

"Where did all these people come from?" Nicole asked, recognizing faces she saw routinely at the phlebotomy clinic. She and Justin had moved in together ten days ago, the most wonderful, exciting ten days of her life.

With Shelly Webster's help they were holding an event to raise money for Haiti. It was amazing how easily she and Justin were with each other. He talked to her about everything he was doing, his excitement about raising money for the people of Haiti. She discovered that she had a knack for organizing an event like this, which made her feel part of his passion for his work.

Justin rested his hand lightly on her shoulder. "All these people are here because of you, I suspect," he said, his smile surrounding her, suspending all rational thought.

"More likely it's you they've come to see," she said.

"What's the saying? I only have eyes for you?"

"Lyrics to a song, possibly?" she chided, waving at Ned Thompkins. When he'd learned that she was leaving for six months he'd offered to do anything she needed done around the farm. He and her dad had offered to look after everything while she was away.

Grant Williams joined them at the podium. "You're not going to believe this. Spencer Island has raised ten thousand dollars for our Haiti relief fund. This will mean we can complete the orphanage. This is the most generous group of people I've ever met."

"That's fantastic," Justin said, hugging Nicole close.

She loved the feel of his arms around her, the soft flannel of his shirt against her cheek, the feeling of inclusion, the love they shared, all of it wrapped up in the moment.

As the three of them stood together, Matt Dixon came up to them. "Good news! Gemma had her ultrasound and everything looks great. She'll be here in a few minutes. She and Claire have been out shopping for things to put in the nursery."

"That's great. Congratulations, Matt," Justin said, shaking his hand vigorously.

"Thanks." He glanced over at Grant. "Guess we'd better run through what we're going to talk about this evening."

"Thanks for taking this on. Who better than a doctor to explain the needs of these children," Grant said, taking Matt aside to talk to him.

"Are you happy?" Justin whispered in Nicole's ear.

"I am. And I'm amazed at the response to our fund-raising efforts. We couldn't have done it without Shelly's help."

"And yours. You made all the difference. Not being from Spencer Island, I didn't have much to offer by way of contacts."

"I've never done anything like this before. All the reading I've done on Haiti has shown me how much is needed there. I couldn't help but talk about it at work. What's even more amazing is how different I feel now from a few weeks ago."

"Meaning?" he asked, his hand caressing her back down toward her waist.

"It feels good to share what I have, to be a part of something essential to needy children. Being involved like this is so rewarding, so meaningful. My life has changed completely and it's because of you."

"You've changed me. I didn't know I could love someone as much as I love you," he said, close to her ear, sending a shiver of need down her body.

"Good evening, ladies and gentlemen. Welcome to this evening's event on behalf of the children of Haiti," Matt said, his smile warm as he spotted Gemma and Claire coming to stand next to Nicole. "I'd like to thank Shelly Webster for her unflagging support."

There was a round of applause, as Shelly moved to stand next to Matt, touching the microphone as she spoke. "And I'd like to introduce Grant Williams, the man heading up this project. He'll give you the details of what it's all about, and how you can be part of the plan for these children. This will be followed by a silent auction and a local band, The Bay Boys, a group you're all familiar with I'm sure."

Happy and content, Nicole glanced around the room, searching for her father. He said he'd be here and she wanted him with her on this final night of planning this event. He'd been so supportive and caring. He and Justin had become close, and they were so much alike in many ways. They shared a love of sports and pizza.

She glanced around the room one more time to see her father coming in the door...with her mother. She gasped in surprise. She met her father's glance from across the room.

He was holding her mom's hand and they both looked completely happy. She shouldn't have been surprised as she knew they were in touch and spending time together.

As they drew closer, she could see tears shimmering in her mother's eyes, and an anxious look on her face. She waited for the familiar resentment seeing her mother caused, but it wasn't there. Instead she felt the closeness they'd once shared. She beckoned for them to join her and Justin, just as Grant stopped speaking.

"It's good to see you both," Justin said, nodding in welcome to Bill and her mother.

"We're so pleased to be here," her mother said, as she awkwardly hugged Nicole.

Nicole knew in that moment, that she needed to be close to her mother, to be part of her life again. She was starting a new life and wanted her mother to be part of it. "Love you, Mom," she whispered as she hugged her close.

"Oh, Nicole, darling..." her mother whispered clinging to her.

"We're on," Justin said, as he took Nicole's hand and led her to the podium. Nicole listened as Justin described his love of Haiti and its children, how his experience with them had changed his life. When he finished, people clapped and whistled. He pulled Nicole to him. "Isn't this great?" he asked as he reached to turn off the microphone.

"It is," she whispered close to his chest, watching the people who were smiling at them.

"I love you," he whispered.

She knew in that moment she had waited her entire life for this. And she wanted to spend her life with this man. "Justin, will you marry me?" she asked, suddenly hearing her voice echo around the room.

"Whoops! The microphone's still on," Justin said, laughing. "And to your question, I thought you'd never ask. Yes,

Nicole Simpson, I will marry you anytime, anywhere, any place."

"Kiss her," someone yelled from the crowd.

"Gladly," Justin said, pulling her into his arms.

The End

∽

Dear Reader,

I hope you enjoyed When First We Met. And thank you so much for being there, for reading the story I've created. It is such a blessing to have you in my life. I write my stories for you and no one else. Simple as that. The Spencer Island series is filled with characters I love, and hope you do too.

If you could, I would really appreciate you posting a review on AMAZON.COM or on AMAZON.CA

My next book in the Spencer Island series, **Anything for Anna**, is the story of one woman's love of her child, a love that transcends all else...almost.

Hardworking single mom Cathy Collins thinks she knows everything about her teenage daughter, Anna. Her daughter is the centre of her world. They share everything. When she learns Anna is being bullied, she wants to do what she can to put an end to it. But when the school offers Mark Wilson as the one person to help Anna, Cathy is dismayed. She has a history with the charming psychologist, a history she doesn't want to repeat.

Cathy has good reason to dislike Mark, but her daughter comes first. Grudgingly she agrees to accept his help. Mark has mixed feelings about working with Cathy, but Anna is a special young person who needs his support.

It's difficult at first, but as Cathy and Mark work together, she begins to see the man he really is. As tensions turn into undeniable attraction, Cathy finds herself in dangerously unfamiliar territory. Because now she doesn't just need Jake's help, she needs him.

Sign up for a pre-order of **Anything For Anna**

ABOUT THE AUTHOR

Stella MacLean is a story teller. Simple as that.

An author of books, both fiction and nonfiction, she has served as Writer in Residence at Vancouver Public Library in Vancouver, British Columbia. She loves to travel, spend time with family, along with her husband and her fur babies in her home near the Bay of Fundy in Atlantic Canada.

Stella relishes the hours she spends hiding out in her office making up stories about the lives of imaginary people. Having found love again in the third act of her life, Stella enjoys telling stories about people who find love elusive and complicated, but still try with all their hearts.

Stella's past includes being a registered nurse, from which she has drawn story ideas for several of her books. She went back to university when her children were older and was granted a Commerce Degree, majoring in Accounting, from Mount Allison University in Sackville, New Brunswick, Canada.

Visit Stella's website; www.stellamaclean.com

OTHER BOOKS BY STELLA MACLEAN

SPENCER ISLAND SERIES

You Have My Heart

Not Alone Anymore

When First We Met

THE RIGHT GUY SERIES

Finding Mr. Wrong

Finding Mr. Gorgeous

Finding Mr. Valentine

Finding Mr. Fixit

Finding Mr. Amazing

LOVE ALWAYS SERIES

Remembering You

The Good Daughter

LOVE IS ETERNAL

Young Love

Of Love and Life

WOMEN IN DANGER

Unimaginable

Desperate Memories

Desperate Acts

Falling Prey

HARLEQUIN BOOKS

The Christmas Inn

NON-FICTION

Living Successfully With Chronic Pain